HOPE LOST

By

David Johnson

HOPE LOST

Copyright © 2020 by David Johnson

All rights reserved.

No part of this book may be reproduced in any form or by any electronic or mechanical means, including information storage and retrieval systems, without written permission from the author, except for the use of brief quotations in a book review."

OTHER TITLES BY DAVID JOHNSON

Hope's Way

Ransom's Law

Ransom Lost

The Woodcutter's Wife

The Last Patient

Toby

The Tucker Series: Tucker's Way (vol. 1)

An Unexpected Frost (vol. 2)

April's Rain (vol. 3)

March On (vol. 4)

Who Will Hear Me When I Cry (vol. 5)"

Life never runs in a straight line.

CHAPTER ONE

Tension squeezes the muscles in Michael's neck and shoulders as he makes his way home. It is Friday afternoon and he still doesn't know what he's going to preach about this Sunday, which means he'll be back in the office tomorrow, continuing to pray God will give him a sign.

As if that's not enough weighing on him, Sarah hasn't responded to any of his texts this afternoon. It wouldn't be the first time she hasn't responded to him, as it's become a passive-aggressive game she plays, pretending she didn't get a text just so it will put him on edge. Ever since her veiled threat to hurt herself, he has continued to try and keep a watchful eye on her, even though there have been no outward signs she's about to do something.

Pulling into the driveway, he shuts the engine off and gets out of the car.

A light breeze, warmed by the lengthening days of late April, carries with it the scent of wisteria blooming in the top of the maple tree in their front yard. The smell takes him to childhood and images of his grandmother who used to wear a perfume that smelled of wisteria. He smiles at the memory.

Opening the backdoor of the house and stepping into the kitchen, it doesn't surprise him that there are no aromas of supper cooking. He's essentially taken over that chore since Sarah has gotten into this mood of hers in which she does hardly anything around the house except watch the Discovery ID channel. He makes his way to the den where the image of Detective Joe Kenda fills the TV screen as he relates the details of the murder case this particular episode will dramatize.

Michael tried joking with Sarah about her obsession with these kinds of show: 'Should I be sleeping with one eye open? Are you planning to do me in?' Sarah reacted to the questions with a stony expression, which did nothing to settle Michael's unease.

He continues toward the bedroom, assuming she's taking a nap—another daily ritual for her. The door is closed but is not latched. Not wanting to wake her, he slowly pushes the door open.

As he suspected, she is lying on her back in the middle of their bed in the dim room, but she's on top of the covers rather than under them, and there are no wrinkles that indicate she has tossed and turned. Another oddity is she's dressed like she's going to church, even wearing a pair of dress shoes.

He considers backing out of the room and going to start supper so she can finish her nap, but something draws him closer to the bed. Each step he takes feels heavier than the first, as if he's wearing shoes with lead soles. He frowns, and whispers, "Sarah?"

It's not until he stands beside the bed that he realizes her eyes are open. "Sarah?" he says clearly. When there is no reply or movement from her, he moans, "Oh, Sarah."

He crawls onto the bed beside her and lays his hand on her chest, hoping against hope he will feel her heart beating—but there is nothing. He puts two fingers on the side of her neck like he learned in a life-saving CPR class. It confirms what he already knows.

"Oh, Sarah, Sarah," he says to her, "why did you have to do this? We could have worked things out. I'm sorry I—" He stops in mid-sentence as he spies a piece of paper lying on the bed on the other side of her.

He switches on her bedside lamp, and reaching across her, picks up the paper. It is folded in half. As he unfolds it several odd-looking pills fall onto the bed. He picks one up. It is a small, purple rectangle that is segmented. *What in the world is this?*

When he turns his attention to the message on the paper he sees it is made up of letters cut from magazines, giving it an almost comical look. Then he reads the message: YOU'RE WELCOME.

Michael stares in disbelief and shock. He suddenly feels as if he's having an out-of-body experience and looking down at himself and Sarah. It is a quiet, unfeeling place. He floats there, waiting to see what the man will do. Then, just as quickly, he is thrown back into reality and every emotion imaginable rushes in from every region of his body with the force of a runaway train.

He tries to make his mind work but is unable to string any coherent thoughts together. He jumps off the bed, leaving the paper to find its own resting place, and begins pacing back and forth. *Think, think, think, Michael! What are you going to do?*

The pills? He cannot figure out where the pills came from, assuming that's what killed her, and he's certain it is. He's never seen any pills like them and not seen any pill bottles from a pharmacy recently.

He stops pacing and looks at Hope. When he does, a new thought hits him so strongly he staggers backward. *Brittany! Did Brittany do this and make it look like Sarah did it to herself?* He grabs his chest as a knifing pain shoots through him. Sweat covers his face, and he can't catch his breath. He drops to his knees, falls on his side and curls into a fetal position. The light in the room dims.

Please, Lord, please go ahead and take me, too. Let this be the end of my miserable life. My only hope is that your grace will cover me. He closes his eyes and waits for death to come.

Instead, the pain in his chest slowly subsides and his breathing returns to normal. At first, Michael interprets it as he has died, which brings tremendous relief to him. But when he opens his eyes and sees he is still in the bedroom, disappointment chases away relief. But disappointment barely makes an appearance before an avalanche of emotions tumble in: regret, sadness, guilt, confusion, suspicion, and fear.

He gets to his feet and spots the letter lying on the floor. Picking it up, he looks again at the message. *If the police see this and word gets out about it, everyone is going to think I'm somehow to blame, that I drove her to suicide. It will be the end of my ministry here. Or if they find Brittany's fingerprints, and that will open up an even messier situation.*

Taking the letter with him, he goes to the kitchen where he tears the letter into pieces and drops them into the trashcan.

CHAPTER TWO

Jed stares at the empty suitcase lying open on the bed and thinks what a perfect metaphor it is for his life. He looks at Liz standing with her arms crossed on the opposite side of their bedroom. "For the last time, Liz, please give me another chance."

"We've already been through this," she answers. "I need some space to figure things out, to decide if I can live with you or not."

"But how can we work things out if I leave?"

"That's just it, I don't know if I want to work it out. This way I'll experience what it might be like if we divorce and either I'll learn that it is exactly what I want, or I'll discover life without you is more painful than life with you."

He feels as if he's sliding down a mountainside and trying to grab hold of anything that will stop his fall. "How long will the separation last?"

"I don't know."

"Will I still be able to see you?"

"Only in the sense that we will undoubtedly bump into each other because we live in a small town. But, no, we won't be getting together to meet. I don't intend to talk or text you either, unless it involves something going on with Mark. I need to be completely away from you so I can clear my head."

Throughout this painful disintegration of his marriage Jed has held back one last card to play, hoping it will be the one to put a brake on things but fearful it will completely push her away. Now, though, he sees no reason not to play it. "Aren't you worried how this will affect your music ministry at church?"

But the question he intends to be an arrow bounces off her like she's wearing a suit of armor. Her expression does not change. "Of course I'm concerned about that, and I'm concerned how this will affect the members of the church. People look up to us, Jed, and see us as an example to follow. They will be shocked and hurt, and I will hate that the most. Whatever Pastor Michael and the church deacons decide to do about my role as music director will be up to them. If they remove me, I may seek another church I can serve in. I just don't know. I'll cross that bridge when I get there." She pauses, then asks, "Will you step down from your position as a deacon?"

Outwardly, his expression doesn't change, but inwardly he winces as if she has stepped on his instep with one of her high-heel shoes. He does't want to give up that position of power and prestige for fear it will hurt his business. "I feel like the other deacons will want me to stay. They recognize my value to our efforts to build our church."

The tiniest of smirks ripples across Liz's features, which irritates him. He's about to say something about it when his phone rings. He answers, "Hello, this is Jed."

As he listens to the caller his jaw drops open, and he presses the heel of his other hand against his forehead. "Oh ... my ... God," he finally says, but his voice sounds hollow. "I'll be right over."

Jed ends the phone call and stares blankly at Liz.

"Who was it?" she asks.

"Brother Michael."

"What's wrong?"

He swallows hard. "Sarah has committed suicide."

*****

"I appreciate you going with me," Jed says to Liz as they drive to the Michael's house. He hopes this event might somehow draw them closer and make her reconsider the separation.

"Of course" she replies. "I'm just in a state of shock. It's so unbelievable."

"Poor Michael."

"And what about poor Sarah? What a sad, dark place she must have been in to do something like this. Maybe if I'd tried harder to reach out to her ..."

"Don't start blaming yourself," Jed says. "We both know she had problems. You even got her hooked up with a therapist, but sometimes people just can't be helped."

"I'm not sure how committed she was to going to counseling. I didn't ask because it was none of my business, and of course I couldn't ask Dr. Elliot about it. Did Michael ever mention whether the two of them attended couples' counseling?"

"It never came up in our conversations."

They drive in silence for a bit, then Jed says, "I can't help but wonder how this is going to affect our church."

"I wondered how long it would take you before you brought up that topic. I know how your mind works. It's always about numbers, isn't it? Attendance starts dropping off, contributions fall off, and your dream of an even bigger sanctuary goes up in smoke."

It frustrates Jed how transparent he is to Liz. She sees through every smokescreen and spin, looks past his words all the way to his heart so that it's pointless to deny the truth. "I can't help it. There's a practical side to everything, and I always think in those terms. It doesn't mean I don't care about people." That Liz gives no reply bothers him more than if she'd argued with him.

As they reach the street Michael lives on, the blazing red lights of an ambulance approaching from the opposite direction catches their attention. At the same time, a police car with its blue lights flashing comes up behind them.

As Michael pulls over to give them room, he says, "I wish they'd turn those lights off. It just draws more attention to everything. There's no need for it."

"That's what they're supposed to do, Jed. At least they don't have their sirens blaring."

"That's true."

Once the two emergency vehicles turn down the street, Michael puts his car in drive and follows them.

Red and blue lights bounce off of the trees and the faces of the houses, creating a visual kaleidoscope of alarm.

"I've never known anyone who committed suicide, have you?" Jed asks.

"I had an uncle who killed himself when I was just a child, but I don't remember much about it. It was my mother's brother, and I remember her crying a lot, but that's about it."

"It's just weird that a person who you regularly see and you expect to continue to see makes a decision to kill themselves. It feels different than when someone dies in a car wreck or of natural causes."

"It scares me."

He glances at her and sees she is crying. Scared is not an emotion he's ever heard her confess to. She's the most fearless and strong-willed person he's ever known, and when he hears her speak of being scared his heart mirrors the emotion. "Why does it scare you?"

"Because I wonder who I know that will be the next person to do something like that? Could it be someone I work with? Or maybe go to church with? Or someone in my family? I've read that once multiple suicides occur within a short time in a small community, more suicides often follow."

"That's astonishing and doesn't make sense. I would think when people saw how many people are hurt by such an act they would think twice about doing it."

Liz nods. "That's what common sense says, but there's nothing common sense about suicide. What it does is it makes suicide seem normal, like a reasonable alternative."

Jed pulls to a stop in front of Michael's house and shuts off the car. They sit quietly for a moment, then he says, "Okay, let's do this."

CHAPTER THREE

For the third time in the last thirty minutes, Hope cranks her car and checks the time on the dashboard. She looks around at the dark, empty church parking lot and then at the unlit entrance to the church building. *I don't understand. He's never been late for one of our appointments; he's always here first.*

Worry stands up and starts dancing at the edges of her thoughts. *Maybe he's tired of meeting with me. Maybe we don't have the connection I thought we had.* Those two thoughts awaken depression, and it swoops in on clouds of darkness. *How could I be so stupid as to believe someone like Michael might be interested in me.*

She powers on her phone and waits to see if he has left her a message. She squeezes the phone as she waits. Finally, she has a notification that she has one voicemail. Relieved, she presses a button and listens.

HOPE, THIS IS JUSTIN. I NEED TO TALK TO YOU. I HAVE GOOD NEWS.

The message only creates frustration rather than curiosity, so she throws the phone onto the passenger-side floorboard.

It's pointless to try and call Michael again. I'll just get the church answering machine.

Ten minutes later, she says aloud, "He's not coming."

She toys with the idea of driving by his house to see if his car is there. A tiny twinge of guilt follows because she learned where he lives by doing some Googling and snooping. So far she has stopped herself from going by the house just to have a look, fearing he will see her and get the impression she is a psycho stalker or something. Now, though, she asks herself what will it hurt?

And so, fifteen minutes later she eases down his street and is immediately alarmed by what she sees—two or three police cars are among the two dozen or so cars that line both sides of the street and fill his driveway and yard. Her heart thunders in her chest. As she creeps closer she spies people crying in the dimly lit front yard. Their faces are masks of disbelief and horror.

Has something happened to Michael? The question short-circuits any ability her brain has to be logical, leaving her emotions in complete control. She stops in the middle of the street, puts her car in park and gets out. Like a zombie, she walks stiffly across the yard and passes by the other people without acknowledging them.

Later, she would not remember leaving her car nor walking to the house. But she will never forget the scene she walks into inside. There is Michael, sitting in the middle of a couch, flanked by Liz, Mark's mother, and a man Hope doesn't know. The man has his arm draped around Michael's shoulders, and Liz is holding Michael's hands.

Michael looks unlike anything she has ever seen from him—small, afraid, broken. His eyes are red and staring but unfocused.

Other people are standing or sitting in chairs, on the arms of chairs, or on the floor. A few are looking at Michael, but most are looking at the floor. And no one is saying anything.

Hope's emotions begin to ebb and thought returns. She is thankful Michael is okay, but clearly something devastating has happened. Perhaps one of his parents has died suddenly, orr maybe his wife's parents.

She looks around the room to see if she can figure out which of the women is his wife. She wonders why she isn't sitting with him on the couch and holding his hand instead of Liz. None of the women fit Michael's description of his wife, so she turns her focus back on him and wonders what she should do next—go to him? ask someone what has happened? quietly leave without a word? At that moment, Michael's head turns and their eyes connect.

She reads surprise in them and waits for them to turn into warm recognition. But that doesn't happen. What she sees is the tiniest shaking of his head as if he is telling her not to approach him, then he bends his head toward Liz and whispers something in her ear. The move upsets Hope because it has a sexual seductiveness about it, a move one makes with someone they are intimate with.

Liz's face registers no surprise or offense to the move, which bothers Hope even more. *Is he sleeping with her?* This question opens the door where jealousy lives, a feeling she has rarely if ever experienced because she's never had a man leave her for another woman. She's always been the one to leave. *So, why should I be jealous? We're not seeing each other, not in that way.*

As she watches the scene on the couch, Liz, Michael, and the other man stand and move through the throng of people toward a hallway. The man stops and turns around while Michael and Liz continue down the hallway, then the man says, "Michael wants everyone to know how much he appreciates you coming and expressing your condolences. Right now, he's going to lie down. As you can imagine, he's been through a lot the last few hours. Please pray for him, and pray that God will be merciful to Sarah's soul when she stands before our Maker."

Soft 'amens' are tossed into the air, but they fall flat and carry no buoyancy with them like they do when pronounced at church.

A man steps forward wearing a tired face and holding his arms at his sides. "What are we to tell people, Jed? This news will travel fast and people will be asking questions."

Liz returns and stands beside Jed. She says, "You tell them the truth. Tell them Michael's wife has died, and we are all grieving the loss with him."

The man who asked the question shuffles nervously, and says, "And if they ask us if it was suicide?"

"Then tell them, yes," Liz replies. "We cannot continue to let the subject of suicide live in the shadows and whisperings between people. We, everyone in Bardwell, needs to be educated as to what suicide is about, what are the signs, what can we do to help."

Liz is still speaking when Hope stumbles out of the house unable to catch her breath. The word 'suicide' blinks on and off like a red neon sign in her brain. She notices people looking at her as she staggers toward her car.

A man reaches for her. "Ma'am, are you okay?"

Hope shoves his hand away and continues her desperate quest to reach the safety of her car.

Finally, she jerks open the door and collapses into the front seat. *Please let this be a horrible nightmare. Let me wake up.* She slaps her face. Then slaps it again. But she is still sitting in the middle of the street, in front of Michael's house—where his wife has committed suicide.

She has a flashback of Lisa hanging on her closet door, and she wonders how Michael's wife, Sarah, took her life. *Hopefully it won't burn an image in his memory like Mama T or Lisa did mine.*

A policeman walks toward her car, so she cranks it and slowly drives off.

She pushes aside all the why questions regarding Sarah and immediately feels her heart go out to Michael. *I know what he is going through. I wish I could hold his hand like Liz was. I can help him like no one else can because I've lived it.*

Aloud, she says, "It's not fair, God, that you would let such a cruel thing happen to such a good and perfect man. I get why you let it happen to me, but to Michael? It's just not right."

CHAPTER FOUR

Hope drives around for an hour, trying to sort out her thoughts about Mike's wife committing suicide. When she finally leaves town to head home, she decides to turn on a gravel road that will take her to the river.

Once there, she shuts off her engine and steps outside. Now that the sun has been down for several hours, the tail end of winter chills the air, and she wishes she had a jacket to put on. She walks the thirty or so yards that take her to the bank of the river. Here it makes an oxbow, leaving a small island in its middle. Moonlight dances on the tips of the ripples. A loon sings its wistful song. The ground is warm enough that spring peepers have awakened from their winter-state of suspended animation and pushed their way through the mud to the surface and sing their syncopated song.

Hope looks up to see the stars, but the full moon's brightness seems to have put them to shame, and they have turned out their lights. Just then, a v-formation of geese passes between her and the moon high above. They are so high it takes a second or two before their honking reaches her ears.

It's a scene she would never have witnessed if she had lived her life in New York City, and its beauty is not lost on her. She used to be afraid of being alone in a setting like this, but now she relishes it.

The river begs her to throw a rock into it and so she does, enjoying the *ker-plunk* sound when it enters the water. She either heard or read somewhere that you can never step in the same river twice. She never understood the saying until she came to western Kentucky and spent time watching the area rivers' ever-moving journey toward the Mississippi and then to the ocean. The millions of drops of water that make up the river at any given point are only there for a split second before they are gone and replaced by a million more.

She spies a large piece of driftwood on the shore and sits down. *I need Michael's cellphone number so I can check on him when I want to, especially during the nights when he'll be unable to sleep because there will be lots of those.*

A new thought occurs to her that makes her more hopeful, even though she knows she shouldn't be. *What if he's glad she's dead? I know he wasn't happy with her and she didn't sound like she was a happy person either. Maybe he feels set free...maybe free enough to...*

"Stop!" she says aloud. "Don't even think it."

She hears a pack of coyotes yipping and howling further up the river, and it sends a chill down her back. Luther has told her coyotes are dangerous because they don't fear humans. Quickly, she gets up and heads to her vehicle.

When she pulls in her driveway, her headlights reflect off the taillights of another vehicle. It's not Luther's because he's back on the river. The driver of the vehicle steps out, hitches up his pants and looks toward her while shielding his eyes.

"Justin?!" She dims her lights and pulls to a stop alongside him. Ever since she told him she wasn't interested in him until he moved out of his mother's house they've rarely spoken to each other.

She gets out, and they meet in front of her vehicle. "What in the world are you doing here?"

Beaming with a smile, Justin says, "I've done it, did what you told me to."

"What is that supposed to mean? I haven't talked to you in weeks."

"Yeah, but the last thing you told me to do was move out of my mother's house. And I done it!" He hooks his thumbs in the pockets of his jeans and puffs out his chest, but the effect is minimal because of his expansive midsection.

Hope rummages through her memories, looking for the conversation he alludes to. "Oh yeah, I remember. So, you came all the way out here, in the middle of the night, to tell me? Why?"

Like a punctured tire, Justin's confident air measurably deflates. "Well...I thought...I thought I'd come over and help you get your stuff together so you could...you know..."

Suddenly, she realizes his intent. "Move in with you?"

Her question re-inflates his ego, and he smiles. "Yes."

"Oh my gosh, Justin, you are so dense. All I told you was I wasn't interested in being with you as long as you lived with your mother. I didn't tell you I would move in with you the instant you got your own place." But yet, she holds his offer in her mouth and savors it a bit longer than her words would suggest. His timing is perfect because she's grown more and more tired of Luther, in spite of her efforts to ignore his irritating ways.

The pinging sound of her engine cooling fills in the gap in their conversation.

Justin twists the toe of his boot on the ground and keeps his head down. "It's a real nice place, Hope. I think you'd like it. It's not out in the middle of nowhere like Luther's. It's in Bardwell."

An idea dawns on her. *Being in town will put me closer to Michael and make it easier to check on him.* "Where is it exactly?"

He sees a glimmer of hope in her question. "It's in Hutchinson's Trailer Park. And before you say anything about it being in a trailer park, this one is really nice. My buddy, Nick's, parents own it, and they don't put up with no crap from the people living there. And this is just a first step for me. I'm not going to live there permanent or nothing, just until I can afford to buy a house. You want to come look at it?"

The sweet taste of his offer suddenly turns sour. "I don't know, Justin. I've lived in some sketchy places before, but a trailer park? Everybody knows what that sounds like. I would hate to tell Whitney and Carol Anne I'm living with you in a trailer park. They would think I'm crazy." Still, though, the offer hangs in front of her by a spider's thread. *That trailer park is just a few blocks from where Michael lives. I could walk there, if I wanted to.*

"Since when do you care what people think?" Justin asks her. "People are always going to talk."

It's a fair question because she long ago quit worrying about what others thought. But since she's become close with Whitney and Carol Anne, what they say matters to her, *whether it should or not.*

Fatigue from the emotional roller coaster she's been on this evening begins to settle on her shoulders. She sighs, "Okay, why not?"

Justin claps his hands together. "Yes!"

"Let me get a few things together just for tonight, so I'll have something to wear to work tomorrow. Luther is on the boat so there's no hurry to get everything else. We can do it this weekend."

He throws his burly arms around her, lifts her off the ground like a rag doll and spins around. "You won't regret this, I promise."

I hope not.

CHAPTER FIVE

The longer Michael lies in the darkened bedroom, the guiltier he feels about Sarah. Whether she took her own life or Brittany had a role in it, the finger of blame points directly at him. *I never treated her like I should have. I should have done more to get her the help she needed for her depression. But mostly, if I wasn't a self-absorbed sex addict, her life would have been so different.*

It has only been in the last few weeks that he's wrestled with the possibility he's a sex addict. An article he saw on Facebook that listed the symptoms shook him to his core. To have the label 'addict' applied to him felt like the biggest disgrace possible, therefore he chose to throw up a wall of denial. *I'm a servant of God and a successful leader of his people. I can't be all that and an addict, too.*

Getting out of bed, he walks to the window and peaks through the curtains to see if everyone has gone. He's relieved to see the street has emptied itself of cars. Jed and Liz's car is still in the driveway and so is a police car, which causes him to wonder.

Liz. When she had walked him down the hallway to the spare bedroom, he imagined what it might be like if she climbed in bed with him. A chill of pleasure runs through him as he revisits the memory.

All of a sudden, a light tap on the door douses the memory with cold water. "Yes?" he replies.

"It's Liz. May I come in?"

Can you come in? Oh my, can you ever. He quickly lies back down on the covers of the bed. "Sure," he answers her.

A shaft of light enters when she opens the door. Standing there, backlit by the light, she says, "Everyone's gone except me and Jed. Can you come to the living room?"

He answers affirmatively and follows her into the living room.

Jed is standing there with a policeman, who Michael knows as Jessie Pinkston. He's met him at some of the breakfasts he's gone to with Jed.

"I'm sorry we had to bother you, brother Michael," Jed says, "but Jessie here says he needs to ask you some questions." He looks at the officer, and adds, "I don't see why. It's obvious what has happened. But he says it's his job."

Michael's body tenses.

Jessie returns Jed's look, and says, "At least I was willing to wait until everyone had left."

Liz cuts in, "Would you like for Jed and I to go to another room, Jessie?"

"That's up to the pastor here."

Michael weighs the option. *If I ask Jed and Liz to leave, will they think I'm trying to hide something? Might their presence influence the officer to be less antagonistic? If I have to lie, will Jed or Liz see through it?* All these thoughts pass through his mind in a nanosecond. He turns to the officer. "I don't mind them staying."

Jessie reaches in the pocket of his shirt and pulls out a small pad and pen. "Let's go in the room where we found Sarah."

"Now look, Jessie..." Jed begins.

But Liz cuts him off. "Let him do his job."

Michael wonders how he should act, how the officer expects someone in his position to behave. The truth is, he doesn't want to go in the room because behind that door lies a mountainous volume of regret.

Not waiting for Michael to agree or disagree with the request, Jessie walks past him toward the bedroom, and the rest of them follow.

Michael's mouth goes dry when they arrive at the closed door, and Jessie says, "I'll let you go in first."

Even though he knows it's impossible, gripping the doorknob sends a shot of electricity up his arm, and he wants to jerk his hand away. But he forces himself to turn it and open the door.

His reaction to looking at the bed where Sarah's body lay catches him completely off guard. A wave of sadness like he's never experienced washes over him, and he immediately begins to cry. Visions of the happy, energetic Sarah he met in seminary, the Sarah few people got to know after she became his wife, pass before him. *How much different her life would have been if she'd never met me!*

He tries to stem the tide of tears but his grief will not be denied this avenue of expression. Falling on his knees beside the bed, he grabs the edge of the covers, presses his face into them and cries, "Oh, Sarah!"

After several moments, Jed kneels down beside him and puts his arm around his shoulders. "I'm so sorry, but we're going to help you get through this." He presses a handkerchief into Michael's hand. "Here, use this."

Michael draws strength from the warmth and kindness of the gesture and is able to compose himself. Jed helps him to his feet. "I'm sorry," he says to the three of them, "I didn't expect that to happen."

Liz reaches over and gives his index finger a quick squeeze. "It's okay."

Officer Pinkston appears unfazed by it all. "Normally we would have done all this when we first arrived, but in deference to you and your position I was willing to wait. If you would, take me through what happened when you came home this evening."

Michael gives him as detailed a description as he can, except, of course, leaving out about the note he found.

"Did you touch or move the body after you found her?"

"I...I don't remember if I kissed her or not."

"Do you know of anyone who would want to hurt your wife?"

Michael immediately thinks of Brittany, but says, "No, no one."

"Why ask that question?" Jed interjects. "She wasn't murdered. She committed suicide."

Jessie keeps his eyes on Michael as he answers Jed. "We won't know that until the coroner gives us his report."

Does he suspect it was murder? Are there clues I didn't see? Will this lead to Brittany and then to me? In spite of his rising panic, Michael is able to keep a calm exterior.

"Had your wife been having any problems?"

"Problems?"

"Yes, like was she depressed? How were you and she getting along?"

This is the question he expects everyone in Bardwell is going to be discussing around their dinner tables, at the beauty shops, and restaurants. It's the question he fears will tarnish his image and perhaps call into question his ministry.

He chooses his words carefully, uncertain if Liz knows anything more than Sarah's history of depression. Furrowing his brow, he says, "Sarah has battled depression for quite some time, I'm afraid. I did everything I could to help, but..." He lets his voice trail off and shrugs his shoulders.

Out of the corner of his eye, he notices Liz folding her arms across her chest and her eyes narrowing. *Please don't say anything. Please don't say anything.*

Jessie makes some notes, then asks, "Was she seeing a counselor or psychiatrist?"

"She did, but not consistently. I encouraged her to stick with it, but she didn't think it was helping."

"I see. Was she taking any medication for the depression?"

"She was supposed to be, but, again, she didn't think it was helping and had quit taking it."

"Did the doctor give her any benzodiazepines?"

"What's that?"

"Medicines like valium, Klonopin, and Xanax."

"Not that I know of. It was an antidepressant that was prescribed for her, Effexor, I think. Why do you ask?"

"We strongly believe the pills she took, if they were the same ones we found beside her, were Xanax, which can easily kill a person if taken in large doses. Do you have any idea where she would have gotten something like that?"

The floor berneath Michael seems to buckle as if the house has been hit by an earthquake, and uncertainty squeezes his chest. *Brittany, that crazy bitch!* He stares mutely at the officer, not remembering if the last thing he said was a statement or a question to be answered.

Jessie cocks his head. "Well, do you?"

"I'm sorry," Michael says, "I'm having difficulty keeping my thoughts on track."

"I asked if you had any idea where she would have gotten Xanax."

"I have no idea."

"We'll check her medical records and see if there's something there. You didn't answer my other question."

"What was that?"

"Were you and Mrs. Trent having marital problems?"

Michael's face grows warm. He turns slightly so he can't see Liz's face, and answers, "Of course no marriage is perfect, and neither was ours. But we were happy." The lie feels bitter on the tip of his tongue, and he wishes he had a drink of water.

"You told me when I first arrived there was no note. Is that true?"

Michael feigns indignation. "Are you accusing me of lying?"

The demeanor of the officer remains unchanged. "When people are upset it's easy to get confused and misremember things. That's what I'm asking you."

"I apologize, I shouldn't have snapped like that. No, there was not a note."

Jessie makes a note. "After you found her, where did you go next?"

"Let me think ... I believe I was in the kitchen when I called Jed."

"And that was the first call you made?"

"Yes."

"Why was that? Why not an ambulance to see if they could save her?"

The question stops Michael like a brick wall. He'd never even considered doing that. *Probably because I wanted her to be dead.* Now, though, he has to explain himself. "I'm embarrassed to tell you I don't know why. I checked her pulse, and her skin was already cooler, so I knew she was dead. I guess I figured there was no point in calling an ambulance. I see now that was stupid of me." He works to gather up some tears. "She might still be with us if I had." He blows his nose into the handkerchief Jed had given him.

"You say you took her pulse. Where did you check it?"

"I checked her carotid artery like I'd been taught in a CPR class I took."

"I see. And did you attempt CPR on Mrs. Trent?"

The questions squeeze him like a vise. For a second, he almost vomits the truth onto the floor. Instead, though, he forces himself to swallow it back down. *If I tell him I did, he'll know I'm lying because Sarah's clothes were completely unwrinkled, and there'll be no raw or bruised skin on her chest.* The truth, though, is a damning witness against him. He turns his hands outward in a gesture of helplessness. "I don't know what to say. It sounds horrible, but I did not try to do CPR on Sarah. I guess the shock of finding her drove any logical thoughts from my mind." He shakes his head. "What kind of man am I?"

Jed speaks up. "You're a good man, brother Michael, a godly man, faced with an ungodly situation. No one knows how they'll react when faced with something like that. Don't blame yourself."

Jessie studies Michael's face for a moment, then says, "Let's move to the kitchen."

Liz leads the party there. Michael cannot read her and wonders what is going on in her mind.

Jessie asks, "You mind if I have a drink of water?"

"Sure," Michael says, and walks to the cabinet, gets out a glass and moves to the sink. When he looks in it, what he sees frightens him more than if there was a coiled snake lying in wait. There are two pieces of the note from the bedroom lying on the floor just under the edge of the cabinet. He loses his grip on the glass, and it crashes against the floor, sending glass shards in every direction.

Liz cries out, and for a second, no one moves. "Where's your broom and dustpan? I'll clean this up," she says.

Her question draws Michael out of his daze. "It's between the refrigerator and the cabinet."

Liz steps carefully around the broken glass, grabs the broom and hands the dustpan to Jed. "You hold this."

The sound of the straw bristles against the floor does a poor job of drowning out the sound of Michael's heart beating in his ears. He glances around to see if anyone else can hear it and wouldn't have been surprised to see them staring at him. But everyone is focused on the glass and pointing out tiny pieces for Liz to sweep up.

Once she has it in a pile, she points at Jed. "Put the dustpan here."

Just as she sweeps the initial pile into the dustpan, Jessie says, "Hold it a minute."

Everyone freezes as he steps forward and squats down beside the pile of glass. Using his ink pen, he sifts through the pieces, then stops. Reaching inside his pocket, he pulls out a small cloth container and unzips it. He removes a pair of tweezers and gently picks something out of the shattered glass.

"What's that?" Jed asks.

"Looks like a tiny piece of paper."

CHAPTER SIX

Carol Anne sits at the bar in her kitchen, drinking her before-leaving-for-work cup of coffee and watching the early morning news on TV. This has become her routine since filing her lawsuit against Lloyd Biddle because reporters sometimes learn things before her lawyer knows or tells her.

So far, three women have pulled out of the class action lawsuit, citing the stress a protracted court case would place on their families. The source of that stress? The public that still idolizes 'the coach' who brought glory to their school or town, 'the coach' that taught them life lessons and inspired them to be the best they could be.

A tragically funny Freudian slip occurred with one of them when she was interviewed live outside her home. When asked why she withdrew, she replied, "Coach Biddle helped me find my breast." It took a beat before she realized what she said, and she quickly corrected herself, "I mean my best, he helped me find my best." But Carol Anne believes what the woman said first was probably an accurate statement.

Carol Anne has been accosted in public so many times she has resorted to avoiding restaurants completely and shopping for groceries late at night.

She turns off the TV. *No news is good news,* except that she was dismayed to hear about the pastor's wife who committed suicide. Grabbing her keys, she heads to the driveway to get in her car, but she gets no farther than just outside her door when she stops abruptly. On the side of her white Toyota Prius are bold, red, spray-painted letters spelling the word SLUT. She looks every-which-way in hopes of seeing the perpetrator, even though she knows they wouldn't be brave enough to let her see them.

She walks to her car, touches the paint and finds it sticky, which means it was done in early dawn with enough light outside that one of her neighbors could easily have seen them. But she has no confidence any of them will come forward, just as no one did about her mailbox being stuffed with horse manure.

Stepping to the other side of the car to see if there is damage there, she is dismayed to find the word BITCH keyed across the doors. *Nothing's going to fix that except a new paint job. Does my insurance even cover things like this?*

She gets inside the car, but hesitates before starting it. *Surely no one would plant a bomb in my car.* The longer she sits there the greater the possibility grows in her mind. Her palms are sweating and her eyes are closed when she pushes the start button. Relief floods her when the quiet motor purrs to life.

On the drive to work she again mulls over her parents offer for her to move in with them until everything is settled. "I've got a gun, and I know how to use it," was her dad's reasoning, a not-so-subtle threat Carol Anne did not doubt for an instant he would carry out. But she's grown accustomed to living alone and does not want the added stress of readjusting to life with her parents.

On her drive to work several people gawk at the word emblazoned on her car. She avoids making eye contact with any of them, and when she gets to work she parks between two vehicles so that the graffiti will be less noticeable.

As she makes her way to her office, she meets Justin, who has a wide smile across his face.

"Good morning," he beams. "Ain't this a great morning?"

She's never known him to be this jovial, and it grates against her sour mood. "Well, I'm glad it's good for you, but I'm not so lucky."

The effect of her words on Justin's face couldn't be more dramatic if they were an eraser on a white board because all the animation in his face disappears. He looks at the floor and walks past her with sagging shoulders.

In her office, Hope is logging on to her computer. "Morning, Hope." "Hey" is all she gets back from her friend, but that isn't uncommon as she isn't a morning person. Normally Carol Anne tries to draw her out and engage her, but this morning she's fine with not talking. She has too much going on in her head.

Therefore, it surprises her when Hope turns her chair around and says, "Are you okay?"

"Yes...no, no I'm not. I'm pissed off, frustrated and scared," the words pour out of her. "My car was ruined last night by vandals and no one's going to do anything about it. Another woman has dropped out of the Biddle lawsuit, probably because things are being done to her like me, but she's afraid to say anything. I have no idea what to do or how I should feel about all of it. Maybe I should drop the lawsuit."

"Hold on right there," the voice of Whitney entering the room draws their attention. "I don't know what else you've said, but I heard those last words. What's happened that's got you so shaken?"

Carol Anne retells what she's shared with Hope.

"Where's your car right now?" Whitney asks.

"In the parking lot."

"Good." She picks up the phone receiver on her desk. "I'm calling WPSD-TV and making them bring a reporter and camera over here. This is how you fight back; you plaster this all over the media and shame all those cowards out there. I'll take pics and post them on Facebook and Twitter and tell all my friends to share it on their pages."

"But is it really worth it?" Carol Anne asks.

"Is what worth it?"

"The lawsuit."

Whitney studies her face. "Okay, let's think about that. What will happen if you drop the lawsuit?"

"All this firestorm will go away," Carol Anne answers.

Nodding, Whitney says, "Yes, and Biddle will go on abusing young girls because he thinks he's untouchable and can't be held accountable. Is that what you want?"

"Wait a minute," Hope interjects, "you're putting all this on Carol Anne's shoulders. Don't you think that's unfair?"

"Sure it is," Whitney answers. "But life's not fair. The only thing that produces change is when one person stands up and says, 'I'm not going to take this anymore,' just like Rosa Parks did. Carol Anne's the right person for this, she has the power to expose evil for what it is, to drag it into the light for the world to see." She looks at Carol Anne. "And she has me and you, Hope, two strong women," she pauses to flex her biceps, "to have her back one hundred percent."

Carol Anne swallows Whitney's words and passion. She straightens her back and squares her shoulders. "You're right, I can do this. I just got a little shaky. I'm going to stare Biddle down in court and watch him squirm like the worm he is."

"That's the spirit," Whitney says.

"You can do this," Hope agrees.

Whitney takes a seat at her desk and turns on her computer. "Hey, Hope, I heard what happened to your preacher man's wife last night. I'm real sorry."

"That was his wife?" Carol Anne exclaims. "I didn't make the connection. I'm so sorry, Hope. Do you know how he's doing?"

"Most likely a state of disbelief, like I was with Lisa. I went by the house last night, but it was full of church people, so I didn't get to talk to him. I think I can help him, since I've been through a similar experience."

"Better be careful, girl," Whitney cautions. "When a drowning person thinks they can save another drowning person, the both of them are likely to drown."

"What's the church going to do about it?" Carol Anne asks Hope.

"About what?"

"About Michael now that his wife has committed suicide."

Hope furrows her brow. "I don't know what you're asking."

"What she's asking," Whitney explains, "is if the church will fire your preacher man and hire someone else."

"Why would they do that?"

"You either forget or don't know how people are around here," Carol Anne goes on. "Suicide scares people, like they are afraid the survivors are somehow infected by the same 'germ' that caused the suicide and they're more likely to do it too. So the church might replace him before he does it to himself and causes another black eye on the church."

Astonishment rearranges Hope's features. "You're serious, aren't you? That's the stupidest thing I've ever heard of. His wife commits suicide, a devastating blow, and then the church fires him? Could that really happen to Michael? What kind of Christ-like attitude is that?"

"A pretty sorry one," Whitney answers. "But what churches teach and what they practice don't always look the same."

CHAPTER SEVEN

Jed looks at the faces of the men gathered round the table in the conference room of the church. "We'll begin, per usual, with the roll call of the deacons. Lester Wade, Price Jenkins, Bobby Lancaster, Jonathan Williams, Ron Winters, Mike Rankin." After each man's name there is a 'Present' announced by them. "So, everyone is here. Thank you for responding to this emergency-called meeting. I assume you all know why we are here."

"I do, and I don't like it," Bobby Lancaster speaks up. His bald head shines with sweat. "Our pastor's wife is not even in her grave and here we are discussing whether we're going to keep him or not."

"I've barely even come to grips with fact she committed suicide," Price Jenkins says. "What a sad thing."

Ron Winters speaks up, "But we've got to protect the reputation of our church. We've just recently overcome the bad feelings generated by our last pastor. We can't afford another black eye. I think it's best to let brother Michael go and begin searching for another."

"You call him 'brother,' Lester Wade intones, "is that how we are to treat our brother when he is hurting? Is that what our Lord would have done?"

Jonathan William says, "I'm sort of on the same line as Ron. How is the town going to react to this news, and will it affect how they view our church? The good of the church is more important that the good of one man, brother Lester."

Jed listens intently to each man, realizing that these same men could be meeting soon to decide whether to take away Liz's role as Music Minister and remove him from his position as a deacon. "What I think about," he says, "is how would I like to be treated if I was in pastor Michael's position?"

"Yes," Bobby joins with him. "Shouldn't we be merciful in order that we will receive mercy?"

Price Jenkins clears his throat audibly and everyone's attention shifts to him. "I am the eldest member of this group and have seen much more of life than you men. That is not to say I am in any way more important, because I most certainly am not. There is both a practical side and a spiritual side to this situation involving our pastor. The practical side involves us acting in our own best interests, selfishly if you will. The spiritual side, though, has us asking God's guidance and following that guidance. I can see and argue either side, but I suppose I've already said more than I should have, so I'll shut up."

There are no rejoinders to Price's brief soliloquy. Instead, each man seems to be peculiarly interested in their hands or an invisible piece of lint on their pants that needs removed.

Jed notices Mike Rankin looking at him. "Is there something you'd like to say, Mike?"

"I've been thinking. I wonder how Sarah's suicide is going to affect pastor Michael. It might change him. I know it would me if something like that happened. How could it not?"

"What's your point?" Lester asks.

"I'm just saying he may no longer be the same man who has drawn so many people to our church. It could change both the content and the delivery of his messages. That's all I'm saying."

I hadn't thought about that. Jed suddenly realizes he's been idealistic in thinking nothing will change about Michael. *But how is that even possible?* He had entered this meeting prepared to defend Michael all the way. *If I convince them to let Michael stay and then people start leaving the church because he's changed, the deacons will point the finger of blame at me. That is, if I'm still a deacon.*

"Mike brings up a good point," Bobby says. "What will we do if that happens?"

"We'll have to let him go, I guess," Lester answers.

"Exactly," Mike agrees. "So, wouldn't we be better off going ahead and doing it now rather than risk him bringing harm to the church members?"

Price speaks up, "And what will people think of us if we let this man go during the darkest hour of his life?"

Jonathan chimes in, "We can talk to brother Michael and tell him we believe it would be best if he made the decision to leave on his own rather than getting fired and that we will give him a good letter of reference. That way the onus for him leaving won't be on us."

Several of them nod in agreement.

Jed decides to offer his idea. "One thing you have to think about is the sympathy factor. I think there is going to be a wave of sympathy for brother Michael from everyone around here, and that will cause even more people to visit the church and perhaps join it. I would hate for us to not see that silver lining in this tragedy. Maybe all of this is God's way of blessing our church. I propose waiting until we see how all this plays out, that we give God room and time to work out His will. Then, if brother Michael's messages lack the fervor he's become known for, we'll do as Jonathan suggests."

Price says, "I take Jed's statement and present it in the form of a motion."

"I second it," Jonathan says.

Jed takes the reins. "We now have a motion and a second. Is there any more discussion before we vote?"

No hands are raised.

"Alright then. All those in favor of waiting to see how things play out with Michael, signify yes by raising your hand."

To his relief, every hand goes up.

*****

When Jed arrives home, Liz asks, "Well, how did it go?"

"It was touch and go for a bit. I thought they we going to sack brother Michael. Thank goodness, though, they did not. We're going to let things play out and see how they go."

"Did you tell them we're getting a divorce?"

Jed feels as if she's punched him in the stomach. "Divorce?! I thought we were just going to separate for a while and try to work things out between us. You can't mean you're divorcing me. Please don't throw away all the years we've been together. I'll change. Tell me what you want from me, and I'll do it." Tears sting his eyes as he reaches toward her.

"I'm sorry, Jed, I truly am, but Sarah's suicide is a wakeup call for me. Life is too short to spend it being unhappy. I don't know why, but she wasn't happy being married to Michael. Something was off between them, and I can't help but believe she would never have taken her life if she wasn't married to him."

Jed's mouth drops open. "Are you so miserable with me that you're thinking of killing yourself?"

"No, that's not what I'm saying. I just don't want to become like Sarah. In hindsight I probably should have divorced you after you cheated on me because nothing's been the same since then. And I'll take responsibility for that. Maybe a better woman would be able to let that go."

"But I thought you forgave me for that?"

"I have forgiven you, but I can't forget the hurt. And that's just part of the reason I have to divorce you. We've just evolved into different places in life, have different priorities and want different things."

Jed feels as if he's hanging off the edge of a cliff and his fingers are slipping. "What about Mark? Think about how this will affect him. Don't you care about him?"

Liz gives him an icy stare. "I can't believe you would say such a thing." Shaking her head, she says, "You're a real piece of work, Jed. For your information, I've already talked to Mark about this. He says he's happy for me, and he thinks he'll be happier, too."

This blow is too much. He loses his grip on the cliff and free-falls toward an abyss of uncertainty.

CHAPTER EIGHT

The day after Sarah's funeral, Michael pulls to a stop in the church parking lot, gets out of his car and squints at the bright mid-day sun. His feet are sore and his back hurts from standing so much during the past two days. He was both shocked and humbled by the outpouring of support from the church and the community. It seemed like everybody in town came to speak to him, which is what he hoped for but wasn't sure if that hope was realistic. *The auditorium may be overflowing this Sunday.*

Walking to the door of the building, he presses the security button and waits for Helen's voice. She has yet to let him in without putting him through her version of an inquisition, and even though he's certain it's just her way of playful banter, he's grown weary of it. This time though there's no response to the buzzer, so he presses it again. Still no response, and his agitation rises.

He's about to press the button and hold it there when the lock to the door turns. So focused was he in getting through to Helen he didn't see her coming to the door minus her walker.

Holding the door open, she says, "What in the world are you doing here? You should be home resting. I can see you're exhausted."

"I couldn't stand being in the house by myself. It's funny how different it feels from the times I've been home alone before because I knew Sarah would be coming back. But now..." He steps inside, and they walk to the office area. "Where is your walker?"

She gives a dismissive wave of her hand. "The physical therapist finally turned me loose, thank goodness." Turning to face him, she says, "Listen to me, brother Michael, I know a thing or two about grief; I've buried two husbands and my only child. Grief is a place you live for a while after experiencing loss. You think you can decide how long you'll live there, but you can't. You might think you're walking out of the front door only to discover you're walking in through the back door. Sometimes it's a maze of twists and turns, hills and valleys, and dead ends, and you'll feel lost—but you're not. Wherever you are is where you're supposed to be. You just have to do it your way, in your own time. Don't let anybody tell you how to do your grief."

Michael's eyes blur. "Thank you for sharing that with me. I'm going to try and remember what you said."

She turns and walks to her desk. "People think I have a heart of stone because I'm so plain spoken. But my heart beats like everyone else's. Maybe when I get old I'll soften up." The tiniest of smiles squeezes the corners of her eyes as she sits down.

He finds his way to his office and closes the door behind him. Sitting at his desk, he writes on a legal pad:

HOW DO I REALLY FEEL ABOUT SARAH BEING GONE?

WILL THAT PIECE OF PAPER THE OFFICER FOUND LEAD ANYWHERE?

DID SARAH TAKE HER OWN LIFE OR DID BRITTANY DO IT?

He stares at the three questions that have been plaguing him, keeping him awake at night. *The answer to the first one? 'Guilty' because, ultimately, it's my fault she's dead. If I was a different person, it wouldn't have happened. I would have made her happy rather than miserable. But I also feel relieved she is gone; being married to her wasn't easy. I won't have that knot in my stomach every time I come home, wondering what I will face when I walk in the door. I do feel some sadness, but not like everyone thinks. It's just sad that someone so young lost their life before they found it.*

The answers to the other two questions, the two questions that scare him the most, are impossible to know. He's played out in his mind every 'what if?' scenario he can imagine.

He looks down at the bottom right-hand drawer of his desk. *Dare I look to see if Brittany's texted me?* There's something about knowing a thing but pretending you don't know it that makes a person feel safe even in a dangerous situation. It's almost like the child's game of if-I-can't-see-you-then-you-can't-see-me. So, Michael chooses not to look at the secret phone.

Ripping the sheet of paper out of the pad, he wads it up and throws it in the trashcan.

Just then, there's a tap on his door and Jed walks in. There are bags under his eyes, his hair is uncombed and he's unshaven. "Helen said it would be okay for me to come in. I hope you don't mind." Absent is his confident air, and uncertainty colors his tone of voice.

Standing up and walking to him, Michael says, "Of course it's fine. But clearly something's wrong. What's happened?"

Jed walks to the loveseat and collapses onto it. "It's Liz."

Michael's heart jumps, and he quickly sits in one of the armchairs. "Oh my god, don't tell me she's...one suicide in a small community can trigger others, but I never would have dreamed Liz would —" Jed's look of surprise stops him.

"No, no," Jed says, "it's nothing like that, although I'm not sure that would hurt any worse that what has happened."

Michael gives an exhale of relief. "Then what is it?"

"She's going to divorce me."

"You've got to be kidding me. Divorce? You two? I don't believe you. You have the perfect marriage and family. Everybody envies you guys."

"Yeah? Well, I thought we did, too, but apparently it was just a facade." He leans forward, puts his elbows on his knees and hangs his head. "I just can't believe it." Looking up at Michael with bloodshot eyes, he says, "I need your help."

Michael starts to tell him the truth, that is, how can I help you when my own marriage was a wreck? But he hears his father's words of caution and advice, "When you counsel someone, the last thing they want to hear is how troubled your own life is. You must take on the mantel of a pastor and adviser and at least give the appearance you know what you're doing. Sometimes it's simply the trust people put in you that makes them feel better, not necessarily anything you say."

"Do you think Liz would do couples counseling?"

"We did that in the past, and I think it helped. At least it kept us from divorcing. But something's different this time with her. She's not angry and lashing out at me. It's more matter-of-fact, a dispassionate statement of facts. She seems more sad about it than anything."

Michael clears his throat. "Is there someone else, another man or another woman?"

"Not on my part. I learned my lesson there. The grass is not greener on the other side of the fence no matter how good it may look."

Michael's not so sure he agrees with Jed on that, but he keeps his opinion to himself. "Do you suspect Liz of seeing someone?"

Jed shakes his head. "Not really. She's not that kind of person."

Michael's mind veers off, and he wonders if he and Liz could end up getting together. *That would be a fantasy come true!* He suddenly notices Jed staring at him with an inquisitive look. "I'm sorry, I was trying to think of how best to deal with this. Did you ask me something?"

"I want to know your view on a divorced man serving as a deacon. Do you think I should resign?"

That hadn't crossed Michael's mind. He would hate for that to happen because he sees Jed as a very important ally and somewhat of a friend. *But yet, the Scriptures are pretty clear about the qualifications of a deacon.* "Has this church ever been faced with a situation like this?"

"No. The closest thing would be when we let the last pastor go."

"And when you all appointed deacons when the church formed, were there certain qualifications the men had to have?"

"The majority of the church back then came from a Baptist tradition, so we followed that path and used those passages in the Bible that talk about deacons, and of course they specifically say the man must be married."

Michael is very familiar with the passage he's referring to, and it was the very one he was thinking about. He realizes this is the first major decision he's going to have to make with this church that will risk disturbing the tremendous growth and harmony the church is experiencing. *Those who disagree with my decision may very well leave the church*, which is the last thing he wants.

He searches his mind for a way out of the dilemma. "You know," he begins, "we are a non-denominational church and as such don't have to follow any creeds or dogmas and risk being ostracized. We need to be known as a church that seeks to do God's Will as we see fit. Many churches today have women pastors, elders and deacons." *Not that I agree with that.* "Perhaps it's time for us to pray about what kind of men can serve in the office of a deacon. Maybe the requirement to be married is not as significant as it used to be."

Jed's sad eyes brighten a bit. "Really? Do you think so? I would hate to give it up. I love this church so much. But I'll do whatever you think is the right thing to do."

"I'm not saying what my decision is. I'm not sure. We just need everyone to be praying about it and asking God to direct us."

"You know," Jed says, "I feel like a real jerk coming in here and leaning on you when you just buried your wife, but I honestly didn't know who else to turn to. I don't have those kinds of friends."

Patting him on the shoulder, Michael says, "That's okay. I'm glad you came by. It helped take my mind off my own sorrows, and that's a good thing."

CHAPTER NINE

Hope enters Justin's trailer, *excuse me, 'mobile home'*, and smells food. *Spaghetti and bread?* It's not the first time he's had supper waiting since her 'just-for-the-weekend stay' that has yet to end, and she appreciates the effort. It's just that food is not her thing, never has been. Of course, none of the food goes to waste because Justin is a machine when it comes to eating.

It's comical to watch him cooking while he keeps having to hitch his pants up. She keeps expecting them to fall to his ankles any moment, but he is quick on the draw and grabs the waistband just in time.

As she walks into the kitchen, he is bending over to take something out of the oven, exposing a significant portion of his butt-crack.

"I'll have it ready in just a minute," he says, as he straightens up and turns around. His face glows pink and sweat beads cover it.

"You know," Hope says, "you ought to consider wearing suspenders. Lots of guys do."

"I'm afraid they'll make me look fat," he says with a frown.

Hope barely stops herself from burting out laughing. She walks up to him and pats the sides of his stomach. "This is part of who you are. If you're ashamed of it, do something about it. If you're not, then don't worry about what other people say. You do realize, don't you, that if we go out together that you're going to make me look horribly skinny and I'm going to make you look like an elephant."

He smiles. "You mean, we're going to be going out together? It's going to be you and me now?"

"I'm here, aren't I?"

"Yeah, but you made it sound like it might just be a temporary thing."

"That's because it always is with me, Justin. I don't stay with anybody for very long. My advice to you is take it one day at a time, because if you want me to make some huge long-term commitment, I'll pack my stuff now and move back out. Take it or leave it."

Suddenly, he drops the hot pan of bread and slings the pot holder to the floor. "Yeow, that's hot!" He bounds over to the sink, turns on the water and holds his hand underneath.

Hope calmly retrieves the pot holder, picks up the pan, places the bread back on it and sets it on the counter. "You got any aloe vera?"

Justin looks at her with raised eyebrows. "Aloe what?"

"Aloe vera. Everybody has aloe vera in their kitchen to treat burns. It's the best thing and works every time."

"I'll buy some tomorrow," he answers. Turning the water off, he shakes his hand. "Man, that burns. I thought pot holders kept you from getting burned."

"They do, but not if you hold the hot pan forever. So, do you have any kind of burn ointment I can put on your hand?"

"Mama always took care of that stuff. I'll go to the Walmarts tomorrow and stock up on stuff."

"It's Walmart."

"Yeah, that's what I said."

"No, you said Walmarts, with an 's'. It makes me want to poke people in the eye with a sharp pencil when they say that. Walmart doesn't have an 's'. Never has and never will."

He cocks his head to one side. "You're serious, aren't you?"

She closes her eyes and shakes her head. "Let's sit down and eat." *What am I doing here? I haven't been here a week and I'm already ready to leave.* She takes a breath and exhales. *Slow down, Hope, give it a chance. He means well and will probably do anything you tell him to.*

As she takes a seat at the table, he sets in front of her the largest plate of spaghetti she has ever seen. It is so full, noodles are lolling over the rim of the plate. Some of the sauce follows the pasta's lead and drips onto the table. *It's enough spaghetti to last me for a week!* She sticks her fork in, twists it and lifts a mouthful. As soon as she puts it in her mouth, her eyes grow wide.

With his arms folded across his chest, he sits and watches her. "It's good, isn't it?"

When she finally chews and swallows the bite, she says, "It is delicious, Justin. I mean, really, really delicious."

"I knew you'd like it. Everybody says my mama makes the best spaghetti sauce in these parts."

"Well, they need to taste yours. I had no idea you could cook like this."

His eyebrows knit together. "What do you mean? I didn't make it. Mama come over and put it on this afternoon."

"Has she fixed all the meals we've had since I moved in?"

Justin hesitates. "Would that be a bad thing if she did?"

"Oh my lord, Justin. The whole point of you moving out of your mama's house was for you to be on your own and take care of yourself. I didn't move in with you so I could be your mama." She sighs, "I think I moved in too quickly. I don't think this is going to work."

He pushes his plate away. "Don't say that, Hope. I'm crazy about you, and I'll do anything I have to do to make you stay. I'll tell mama to quit coming over here and cleaning up and cooking supper."

"She does the cleaning, too?! I thought you were doing that. Gee, Justin." She puts her elbow on the table and rests her forehead in her palm.

"I'm sorry, Hope. I can tell you're disappointed, but just give me a chance. This is all new to me. I know it shouldn't be, but it is. I'll get it right. You may just have to give me a little direction at times."

She closes her eyes. *A little? I hope he knows how to wipe his butt.*

The reason she moved here in the first place comes to her—*Michael*. She's been longing to see him. It hurt that she couldn't go to his wife's funeral because she's missed so many days at work.

Looking at Justin, she says, "Let's eat supper, although I'll never eat this much, and make a list of things you need to buy at Walmart."

"Walmart," he says with a smile.

*****

After supper is finished and the list is made, Hope says, "I'm going to let you wash up everything while I go for a walk."

"You're going for a walk, now? After dark? You want me to come with you?"

"Yes, I'm going for a walk after dark. And no, I don't need you to come with me to protect me. We live in Bardwell, not Louisville or St. Louis. I'll be fine."

"I'll be glad to do with you."

She gives him a stony stare.

"Okay, okay," he says, "I'll clean things up here and see you when you get back."

Grabbing a light jacket, Hope walks outside. She hasn't walked from Justin's to Michael's house, but she's driven it a few times and then moved slowly past Michael's house.

She starts out at a brisk pace, going from one puddle of light to another given off by the few muted street lights.

It takes her a bit longer than expected before she turns down the street Michael lives on. As she gets closer to his house, anxiety begins to build. *What am I going to do if I see he's at home? Will he think it weird if I show up knocking on his door? Will I look like a stalker? Will he feel obligated to ask me in just because I came by? Should I go in? What am I even doing out here walking at night just to look at his house?*

When she's one house away, she hears a commotion coming from the direction of his house. Then she spies him rolling a garbage can toward the street. Her heart catches in her throat. She calculates the speed the two of them are walking and predicts she will arrive at the end of his driveway at about the same time he does.

One of her feet wants to keep going and the other wants to turn around and quickstep back to Justin's. The one that wants to turn around is just about to win when Michael's head comes up, and he looks in her direction. There is a street light above him, but she is in the shadows, so he shields his eyes with one hand and stops.

She stops, too, and takes a small step sideways to get in a darker shadow. She can't make out his features, and so can't tell if it's a curious look or a look of alarm he's giving. *If I move forward now and walk up to him, I will look like a nutcase. There's no way he can recognize me from where he is. I just need to casually turn around and walk away, as if I am walking a measured distance.* She turns around and starts to take a step when Michael calls out, "Hope, is that you?"

Hope feels like an escaped prisoner spotlighted by a police helicopter and that she should throw up her hands in a sign of surrender. She slowly rotates until she faces Michael's direction. "Who are you?" she calls to him.

Taking a step in her direction, he answers, "It's Michael, Michael Trent."

She walks toward him. "Oh, I didn't know who you were," she lies.

He meets her halfway. "What are you doing walking around here at night?"

Of course, she hasn't thought through how she will explain her presence. The truth would be easier if she hadn't moved out of Luther's and in with Justin, a truth that makes her sound like a woman who sleeps around, *which is exactly correct.* She can think of no other explanation, so she tries sharing half the truth. "I've left Luther. Like I've told you, I just wasn't happy with him. I know you disapprove, but I didn't know what else to do." She tries to read his face, but there are too many shadows.

"You know your situation better than I do, Hope. If you did what God would have you to do, then there can be no fault in it."

I've never asked God for advice. I don't trust Him to have my best interests at heart. "I feel like it was His will that I leave."

"But why are you here?" he asks, pointing at the spot they are standing.

"I live just a couple of blocks away. I had no idea this is where you live."

"So, you have your own place now? Good for you; that's a big step."

She just can't bring herself to correct him, so she attempts to turn the conversation in another direction. "I'm sorry I couldn't come to your wife's funeral. I couldn't get off work; I've already missed too much. Was it a nice service?"

He nods. "It was. It seemed like the whole town was there."

"I figured that's what would happen." Laying her hand on his forearm, she says, "I've been worried about you and how you're doing. We haven't talked in a while."

"Oh my gosh!" He clasps her hand. "I just remembered that you and I were supposed to meet the night Sarah died. You showed up, didn't you, and waited? I am so, so sorry. It completely left my mind, and I didn't remember till this second."

At the touch of his hand sparks go off inside Hope. *Is it just a friendly gesture, or is it an invitation?* If it had been any other man, she would know his intent. But she's uncertain what kind of relationship the two of them have. *How does he really feel about me?*

He removes his hand, which gets her out of her head. "Do you forgive me?" he asks.

Lifting her hand off his arm, she replies, "Of course I do. Sure, I was upset at first, like upset-concerned because I knew something had to be wrong for you not to show up."

He leans his head to one side where more light filters through. Perhaps the angle of the light is causing his heavy eyebrows to cast shadows over his eyes, but the bags under his eyes are obvious. The lines across his forehead look deeper. "You came to the house that night, didn't you? I remember seeing you."

This pleases her. "I just had to come by."

"But you just told me you didn't know where I lived."

Mama T used to tell her, "You'd be better off telling the truth, Hope, because you're a terrible liar. You never keep your story straight." Hope now wishes she'd heeded that advice, trapped as she is by her own lies. Her mind races in search of a plausible explanation, picking them up and putting them down like a woman at a yard sale who has no intention of buying anything. She gives a little laugh. "Did I say that? That was silly of me. I guess the surprise of seeing you taking out your garbage rattled me a bit."

"I see."

He doesn't believe a word I said. It's time to unplug from this situation and get out of here. "I'm glad I got to see you, and I hope you are taking care of yourself. I'm going to head back to my place."

She turns to leave, but Michael grabs her arm and turns her around. Her heart stops.

He says, "I want to make up for standing you up the other night. Let's make an appointment to meet again. What about next Thursday?"

It takes her a second to find her voice. "Sure, sure, that'll be great. I'll see you then. Good night."

"Good night."

The walk back to Justin's is brutal as she beats herself up for being *a lying, stupid, immature, fool!*

CHAPTER TEN

Mark Rochelle strides through the busy school hallway, speaking and replying to classmates. The sounds of metal locker doors closing ricochet through the air as everyone hurries to get their books and head to the first class of the day. Mark, however, has other things on his mind.

He stops in front of Heather Brown, the Guidance Counselor's, office door. He knocks twice and waits.

It takes a few moments, but she finally opens the door. Smiling, she says, "Good morning, Mark. How can I help you?"

"I need to talk to you about something. Can we go inside your office?"

Stepping back to let him in, she says, "Of course, come on in and have a seat."

Once they're settled, she says, "Now, what's on your mind?"

"I've got an idea, a good idea, but I think I'm going to need your help in making it happen."

"Well, you've certainly got my attention. Tell me about it."

"Lisa Rodriguez's suicide changed everything for me. It made me grow up and quit thinking only about myself and my plans. I don't think I'm different from anyone else in that way; it's just how everybody is, trying to make it, trying to fit in, making a name for themselves. And that's one of the reason's Lisa killed herself, because nobody was paying attention to her. We all met her in class or in the hallway every single day, but no one paid enough attention to see how desperate she was." Tears sting his eyes and his voice catches.

"Mark," Ms. Brown says, "I think you're being too hard on yourself and everyone else. It's normal for teenagers to be self-absorbed. It's unfortunate, but it's normal."

He swipes at his tears. "Well that's not good enough for me. It's just an excuse so kids don't feel guilty. Well, I think every student in this school should feel guilty."

"Okay, I'm not going to try and talk you out of how you feel, but what has this to do with the idea you have?"

He reaches in his hip pocket and brings out a folded piece of paper. "I want to raise awareness about teen suicide by starting a campaign or a program." He unfolds the paper and holds it out for her to see. "And we're going to call it the Lisa Campaign. The letters of her name will spell Life Instead of Suicide Advocates. I've been online, and there's a ton of information on the topic that people need to hear, simple things they can do that can make a difference in a person's life." He unzips his backpack and takes out a thick folder of papers. "Look at all this stuff I've printed off. Maybe if we had had a program like this, Lisa wouldn't have taken her life."

Ms. Brown takes the folder and flips through some pages. Looking at him, she says, "I love your passion, Mark. It says a lot about you that you want to take a tragedy and use it in a positive way, and I think your idea has a lot of merit. But let me caution you about oversimplifying a suicidal person. For lack of a better way of putting it, I'm a trained mental health professional who has learned the warning signs to look for, but I didn't see any signs in Lisa, and I don't know if I'll ever get past the guilt of that." She snatches a kleenex out of a box and dabs at the corners of her eyes. "I'm sorry."

Mark leans forward. "You get it then, the feeling of 'why didn't I do something?' I don't want anyone else to have to feel that, and I know you don't either. So this is something we can do to prevent it from happening again."

She leans back in her chair. "What is it you want from me in this?"

"I want you to let it be known you are one hundred percent in favor of it. The teachers here respect you, and if you're for this, they'll get behind it, too."

She clears her throat. "What about Mr. Biddle? He'll have to be on board with it, too."

Mark waves hand. "None of the kids have ever cared what he said. But especially now, with all he's got on his plate, I don't think he can afford to be against it."

Just then, there's a knock on Ms. Brown's other door. It opens immediately and Biddle steps in. He looks in surprise at Mark. "Oh, I'm sorry. I apologize. I didn't realize—"

He doesn't get to finish his sentence because Ms. Brown jumps out of her chair and throws an ink pen across the room. "That's it! That's the last time you're going to barge in on a confidential meeting of mine. I've warned you and warned you. I'm taking this to the Superintendent and the school board." Her face is beet-red when she finishes.

"Now Ms. Brown," Biddle says, "I think you're forgetting—"

"I'm not forgetting anything," she says as she stomps toward him. "If there's something you're wanting to tell the public, you go right ahead. I'm tired of you blackmailing me."

Mark sits in stunned silence.

Biddle looks at him and tries in vain to give a fake smile. "I'm sorry you have to see and hear this, Mark. Blackmail is such a strong word. I don't think Ms. Brown really meant to say that."

"I'm sorry, too, Mark," Ms. Brown says, "that you were subjected to Mr. Biddle's completely unprofessional behavior and had to witness him threatening me. Why don't you tell Mr. Biddle about your plan that you were telling me?"

To have the conversation turned on a dime and thrown in his direction catches Mark off-guard. "You sure?"

"Yes, tell him all about it."

Mark delivers his talking points as Biddle listens. When he finishes, he waits for a reaction.

"Well, Mark," Biddle begins, "I think we're making too big a deal about all this. It's one suicide in how many years here? I don't see the point in talking up the topic. I think if we'll just keep it quiet, everybody will quickly forget about it and go back to their normal lives."

Mark falls back in his chair. He looks at Ms. Brown and raises his eyebrows.

She twists her mouth to one side and nods her head.

Slowly, he stands. Looking at Biddle, he says, "I cannot believe what you just said, not any of it. Shocked doesn't begin to describe how I feel right now. My parents always taught me to respect people in positions of authority, and I always have. But I'm telling you right now, I have zero respect for you. I can't wait to give them a full report on what happened here. You might have the bluff in on everybody else around here, but you will not bluff my parents."

Biddle's eyes dart around the room like a trapped animal. "Oh ... yes ... I ... I forgot ... I mean ... maybe I spoke too quickly. Perhaps there is sufficient reason to start this, what did you call it?"

"Lisa Campaign."

"Yes, this Lisa Campaign. Do mind if I take a day or two to think about it?"

Through gritted teeth, Mark says, "Here's the thing, this is going to happen with or without your approval. I will find a way to make it happen." Grabbing his papers and backpack, he storms out of the office and slams the door behind him.

CHAPTER ELEVEN

Hope parks beside an unfamiliar car in the employees parking lot at work. She glances inside and sees Carol Anne sitting behind the steering wheel and staring. Getting out, she taps on the passenger-side window.

Carol Anne jumps and recoils from the sound.

"Hey, hey," Hope yells, "it's me." She tries to open the door, but it's locked. "Unlock the door."

Carol Anne hits the lock button, and Hope gets inside. Once there, she sees Carol Anne's normally perfect makeup job is missing—no lipstick or eyeliner, and her hair looks like she barely combed it. "I didn't mean to scare you."

Carol Anne looks at her but her eyes look vacant, like she's not really there. In a voice devoid of emotion, she says, "It's okay. How do you like my rental car? It's until the body shop fixes my car. It's got some nice features, but I'm not even sure how to work them all. Is it time to go in to work?"

"Maybe you don't need to work today," Hope suggests. "You look like you're having a bad day."

Carol Anne blinks. "Bad day? What about a bad life? I'm having a bad life."

Hope feels like she's looking at a reflection of herself when she was so depressed. She can almost smell her friend's depression. "It's the Biddle lawsuit, isn't it?"

"I wake up thinking about it and go to sleep thinking about it. It is inescapable. I wish I could go into something like a witness protection program, get a new identity and move somewhere else. I never dreamed this would be so hard to do."

"Look, I'm the last person you should take advice from, not from someone who's made as many mistakes in her life as I have, but take it from the queen of running away, you can never run far enough—I should know. A geographical solution is not a solution at all. It's just a change of address. You cannot outrun what Biddle did to you. Now that you've let it out of the closet that you've kept it in forever, you've got to deal with it because it won't fit back in that closet."

Carol Anne sighs. "No matter what happens, to some people I will always be the woman who ruined Biddle's life."

"You're probably right. But the truth is Biddle ruined his own life, and it started years ago." Hope notices the car's clock. "Come on, we've got to go in. We're already late." Getting out of the car, she walks around to the other side and opens Carol Anne's door. She takes hold of her hand, and says, "Come on, let's go see how many dates Whitney had over the weekend."

Carol Anne gives a weak smile. "She's a mess, isn't she?"

"She is."

They make it to their office without running into any supervisors.

"Well it's about time," Whitney says. "I decided I was going to have to do everybody's work today. 'We don't have to go to work today. Ol' Whitney will cover for us.'" She stares at them with her hands on her hips. It's then she sees the state Carol Anne is in. She looks at Hope who gives her a concerned look, nods toward Carol Anne and shakes her head. "Looks like this is a morning for coffee all around. I'll be right back."

Hope follows Carol Anne to her desk, turns on her computer, and says, "You've got to at least look like you're working." She then goes and turns on her own computer.

When Whitney returns with coffee, Hope meets her.

Whitney whispers, "What's happened?"

Hope takes one of the cups. "Nothing new, that I know of. It's just wearing her down. She looks to me like she's lost weight."

"I think you're right."

"She told me she wants to run away, but I told her she can't run away from this, no matter how far she goes. I hope I told her the right thing."

"Oh, you did, girl. Good for you. She's got to see this through or she'll never have a good night's rest again."

"You know what he wants to do?" Carol Anne's voice interrupts them. "He wants to settle out of court, give me money to drop the suit. But if I agree, I have to sign a paper that I will recant my accusation and can never bring it up again."

They join her at her desk and Whitney hands her a cup of coffee, then says, "My Pops used to have a saying, 'You can't un-ring a bell.'"

Carol Anne looks up at her. "I've already rung the bell, haven't I?"

"Seems to me you have. He wants to pay you off because he knows he's going to lose this thing. He's scared, that's what he is. Tell me, how does it make you feel to know that you've made him afraid?"

Carol Anne sits a little straighter. "I hadn't thought about it that way. I've got him where I want him, don't I?"

"You've got his jewels in a vice, girl. Put the squeeze on him and make him squeal."

They all three laugh at the image Whitney paints.

"You and your mouth," Hope says.

"I just call it the way I see it."

Just then, their supervisor, Cara, sticks her head in the door. "Good morning everyone."

They look at her without responding.

"Carol Anne? Can we talk in my office? I've got some things I need to discuss with you."

Alarms go off in Hope's head. There's uncertainty and a little fear in Cara's eyes, something that's never there. Hope puts her hand on Carol Anne's shoulder and pushes down. "Why can't you talk to her here? We don't have any secrets among us. Anything you say, she's going to tell us anyway."

Clearly, Cara did not expect this, and her uncertainty grows. "I just think it's the kind of conversation that's best held in private." Looking at Carol Anne, she says, "Will you come with me, please?"

Carol Anne looks up at Hope who returns her gaze.

Whitney places her hand on Carol Anne's other shoulder. "What is it you call us? The Three Musketeers? All for one and one for all."

Carol Anne says to Cara, "Whatever you have to say, go ahead and say it."

"Are you sure?"

"Yes."

"First of all, what I'm going to tell you did not generate from me. As a matter of fact, I fought against it. It came from further up the ladder, and they made me the messenger." She pauses and draws a deep breath. "I'm sure you're aware of all the publicity surrounding your lawsuit against Mr. Biddle. It seems like the story keeps getting bigger and bigger. And even though the casino is a number of miles away from Bardwell, we have lots of customers from there and from the other places he's lived and coached. We have received some petitions demanding that you be fired from your job or the people who signed it will start picketing the casino. That's the kind of publicity we cannot afford. Carol Anne, I am terribly, terribly sad to tell you you're being let go."

The news has the effect of an atomic bomb, sucking all the air out of the room. It's like all four of them are waiting in silence, bracing for the sonic boom to follow.

The explosion though is the screaming and yelling voices of Whitney and Hope who step toward Cara and lambast her and everyone she represents.

Cara stands and takes it until they run out of wind and words. "Every single word you said is true," she says. "And if I wasn't raising two teenagers on my own, I would give them my resignation and walk out today. But I can't do that, not yet anyway. There's only one tiny silver lining in this, and it's really just guilt money—they are going to continue to pay you for the next 90 days."

Carol Anne stands up and wavers a bit.

Hope thinks she's about to faint, so she braces her shoulder against her. Whitney follows and does the same thing on the other side.

"When am I supposed to leave?" Carol Anne asks.

"Right now, I'm afraid. Justin is waiting in the hallway to escort you to your car. Not that it matters to you or will make a difference, but I'm truly, truly sorry. And I hope you nail Biddle to a wall."

CHAPTER TWELVE

Michael ends the phone call with his father and leans back in his desk chair. Slowly, he swivels his chair round and round, thinking about his father's advice: 'There are two kinds of decisions a pastor has to make—a scriptural one and a political one. It sounds like you need to make a political one.'

The pending meeting he has with the Board of Deacons to decide Jed's fate prompted him to reach out to his father, which he hates to do because his father still has the ability to make him feel like he's ten years old and incapable of doing anything right.

Earlier in the day he decided to trust his secretary, Helen's, discretion to keep their conversation confidential and asked her opinion on what he should do.

After he laid the situation before her, she said, "I am sorry to learn about Jedediah and Elizabeth, but I'm not surprised. He's always thought too highly of himself, and that clouds his judgment. That she has tolerated him as long as she has speaks to her determination to make it work or to her willingness to accept being miserable."

Michael was shocked at her summary of their marriage because he hadn't had an inkling there was trouble. But he wasn't surprised by her bluntness because more than once he'd been on the receiving end of it.

"Our church," she went on, "came about because of the growing dissatisfaction of attending a church that was governed by creed books, conventions, and superintendents, institutions that had become insensitive to both the needs of people and the Bible. I was one of the original people that put forth the idea to create a new church, not that that matters. I simply say that to emphasize I know what this church's direction was to be from the beginning."

Michael hung on her every word, knowing she was building a case for whatever piece of advice she was going to give him.

"Therefore, your decision is both easy and difficult. It's easy because you don't have to research a creed book or submit a question that has to work its way through various boards and committees that could take weeks or months to provide an answer. And it's difficult for the same reason. As pastor, the decision is yours to make, and it's the members obligation to obey it."

Michael mulled this over. "But my understanding is that when you appointed your first deacons you took a literal view of what the Bible says about that office."

"That is true."

He tiptoed into his next question. "So, how would everyone react if a new pastor, like me, decided to take a more liberal view? Not that I'm saying that's what I would do. But if I did?"

She looked at him the way he imagined she looked at a truant student when she was an educator. "I would say if you came to that conclusion after much prayer and study, you have no choice but to go that way. However, if you're doing it for convenience sake or personal reasons, you'd better think twice about that. And here's why: A well-thought-out reason will give you the conviction to help everyone understand how you arrived at your decision. But a personal or selfish reason will be like building a house on the sand. Your ministry will end up crashing down on you."

It was so like her to speak straight to the core of what his struggle is, knowing that he and Jed had become good friends. He told her, "I really appreciate you sharing with me. I value your opinion."

She neither thanked him nor acknowledged the compliment. Instead, she said, "Then I'll give you one more thing to think on. I love Jedediah, I truly do, but he is better at making new friends than he is at keeping them. He's his own worst enemy. And that's all I'll say about that."

Now, as he sits at his desk and looks at his clock, it seems the second hand is spinning rather than ticking, taking him closer to the time of the meeting. Getting out of his chair, he paces in an attempt to reduce his level of anxiety. His mind wanders to his secret phone and the satisfaction he would get from looking at some porn. *The Pastor Who's Addicted to Porn, that should be the title on my office door. Jesus, will that ever get out of my head?*

Back sitting at his desk, he opens the bottom drawer and stares at the Strong's concordance. He hasn't turned the phone on since Sarah's death because he didn't want to deal with whatever garbage Brittany has been texting him. *I wish I could turn it on without seeing all that. I guess I could and just not open her texts.*

The idea cinches it for him. He reaches down, takes out the phone and powers it on. After a few seconds, he sees his messages icon indicating fourteen messages, and his voicemail alert is flashing. Disregarding both, he opens the browser and instantly lands on his favorite site. He scrolls through images as his heart pounds and blood surges to his groin. There are no other thoughts in his head except his fantasies and the desire to pleasure himself.

Carrying the phone with him, he goes into the bathroom. Excitement and anticipation pulse through his veins just like it did when he was a kid and would sneak his father's Playboy magazines. Just as he's about to unzip his pants, the nude picture on the screen of his phone disappears and is replaced by the message of an incoming call from Brittany. It startles him so badly he nearly drops the phone.

Without thinking, he answers the call, but immediately regrets it.

"Well it's about time," she says. "If I didn't know better, I'd say you've been intentionally ignoring me. What's the matter, the grieving husband too overwhelmed with grief?"

Her sarcastic tone grates on him. "How do you know she's dead?"

"You're not going to trick me with that question. Are you recording this?"

"I wouldn't know how to."

"Well, I know about it because I get the local paper from there and keep up with what's going on in your little world."

"You shouldn't have done it, Brittany. There was no reason for you to take things that far. I told you I was working on things. You're just too impatient."

"I don't know what you're talking about. Done what? Take what too far?"

"I know you killed Sarah."

Brittany laughs loudly. "If you think that, then you're the one whose deranged. How could I have done that? The paper said it was an overdose on pills. You think I went into your house and somehow forced her to take those pills? If anybody made her do it, you did because you were such a crappy husband. You're just not husband material, Michael."

He has no defense against her accusation because it is true. If Brittany really didn't do it, then he was the major contributor to her death. He leans back against the bathroom wall, then slides down until he is squatting on the floor.

"Uh-oh," Brittany says, "is somebody feeling guilty? Is somebody crying? You need to snap out of it! It was the best thing that could have happened to us because now the door is wide open for us to be with each other, and nobody can say a thing about it."

Michael bangs the phone against the side of his head, furious with himself and with her but uncertain what to do about it. "Look, no matter what you think or what I said, I loved Sarah, and I'm sad about her death. And, yes, I feel guilty about it. I've got to have some time to get my head sorted out. So don't start making big plans."

"Okay, I can do that. I'll give you a little time, but don't be surprised if I drop in and check up on you to make sure you're not already screwing somebody else. The last time I dropped in things went pretty well, if I remember correctly."

He starts to let his mind wander down that memory road and relive the excitement, but stops himself with the image of Sarah's dead body lying on their bed. "That won't happen again, Brittany, at least not for a while."

She sighs heavily. "Okay, Mr. Party Pooper. I'll be a good girl and try to be patient."

"Listen, I've got to go. I'm late for a meeting."

"Okay. Just one more thing."

"What's that?"

"You're welcome."

Michael exits the bathroom shaken by Brittany's last words, but he's startled to see Price Jenkins standing in his office.

"Who were you speaking with, pastor Michael?"

"Oh...uh...no one...well, someone because I was talking to God. I know it sounds silly, but I go in there sometimes to pray."

"Enter thy closet and pray," Price says. "Sounds like a biblical concept. I only came into your office because you're late for the deacons meeting. I wanted to make sure you hadn't forgotten."

"No, no, not at all. As a matter of fact, that's what I was praying about. I'm ready to go, if you are."

Eager and concerned faces greet him as he enters the conference room. He smiles and nods at them. "Brethren, I will get right to the topic at hand, that is, should a man be allowed to serve as a deacon if he is divorced. My position on this topic has come about as a result of much prayer and study and listening for the Holy Spirit's direction, and because of that, I can share my position with a great deal of confidence. I believe the scriptures are clear as to the qualifications for deacons, the same qualifications this church used in appointing all of you. I see no justification for allowing Jed to continue serving as a deacon."

Jonathan Williams speaks up, "There's going to be members who will not like that position, pastor."

"You're right," Michael agrees.

"If Jed quits coming to church and goes somewhere else," Price Jenkins says, "it will have a dramatic effect on our budget. Jed is a significant contributor to the work here."

A general mumble rolls through the room as different men speak to their neighbors in low tones.

Lester Wade raises his hand.

"Yes, Lester," Michael calls on him.

"I don't think we should be swayed one way or the other just because of money."

"And I agree," Price says. "But there's a practical side to everything, and I thought everyone should know the implications."

"Honestly," Michael says, "I had thought about that. I don't want to lose Jed as a member of this church. He's always been an asset, and I believe he can still be an asset."

"How do you mean?" Ron Winters asks.

"I propose we create a position for Jed, that we put him in charge of member recruitment. We can offer him a small honorarium for his service, but I predict he'll decline it, that just being able to continue be a part of this dynamic church will be enough for him."

Smiles break out like corks popping out of champagne bottles, coupled with a chorus of "Amens".

"I knew you would make a wise decision, pastor Michael," Price speaks for the group.

"Thank you," Michael says, feeling proud that he was able to make both a scriptural decision and a political one at the same time.

CHAPTER THIRTEEN

Carrying the last box of her belongings, Hope closes the door to Luther's house and heads to her car. She gives the scene one last look, taking in the fields of soybean stubble, the cypress trees in the distance, and a pair of wood ducks flying by. *This is what I will miss most about living here.*

As she sets the box in the backseat of her vehicle, the sound of a car driving up the driveway draws her attention. It's Luther. Hope swears over her bad luck. She had hoped to be finished and gone without crossing paths with him.

Instead of getting in her car and driving off, she decides to face him and talk things out.

He parks beside her and gets out smiling. "Boy am I glad to see you." He embraces her and kisses her, but she doesn't reciprocate his enthusiasm. "You feeling okay?" He looks at the boxes in the backseat of her car. "What's going on? Isn't that your stuff?"

Hope stands and looks at him. *How many men have I done this to? And how many different ways have I said it?* "I'm moving out and going to live with Justin."

"Aw, man, please don't do this to me, Hope. I've never loved somebody like I love you. What can I do to make you stay? I'll do anything, just name it."

"It's not so much you as it is me, Luther. You knew how I was when we met, remember? I left Frank to come live with you. It's just what I do."

"Maybe it's just because of losing Lisa. You need to give yourself more time to deal with that, maybe even see a counselor or something. Maybe with a little time you'll feel differently about staying here."

Shaking her head, Hope replies, "Maybe, maybe not, it's hard to say. But this is what I'm going to do for right now. We've had some good times, just remember those."

He reaches for her, but she holds him back with her hand. "What am I going to do without you, Hope? You're the only reason I look forward to getting off the boat. You make everything better for me. I just don't know what I'll do with myself without you."

"I know it hurts," she says, "and I'm sorry for that. I'm always sorry for hurting people when I leave."

"Doesn't it hurt you? Don't you feel anything for me?"

She shrugs. "I've kind of grown numb to all that. Like I said, I'm sorry you're hurting. I like you, Luther. You're not a bad person. You just picked the wrong person to love. I'm the bad apple, the rotten banana. You're going to be better off without me, you'll see." She gets in her car and closes the door.

He dashes over and puts his hand against her window. She hears his muffled, "Please don't."

Putting the car in reverse, she turns around and heads out the driveway. Giving one last look in her rearview mirror, she sees him standing with his hands at his side, looking like an abandoned dog.

You really are cruel, she says to herself. *You're like a black-widow spider with a long trail of heart-broken men in your wake. And you'll do the same thing to Justin, eventually.* Sadness and aloneness, two familiar foes, surround her, drive tent pegs in her heart and set up a tent. A wave of depression like she hasn't had since the days after Lisa's death hits her, wiping out any signs of light or life. A sharp pain strikes her chest, and she has difficulty breathing. Then, unexpectedly, she begins to cry.

*****

By the time she reaches Justin's trailer, her tears have dried, and she's put Luther out of her mind. But depression still has its arms wrapped around her. She speaks to it, *I thought I was rid of you. Are you ever going to leave me alone? You're like a cancer that goes into remission but never disappears and then comes roaring back like a lion.*

Leaving her things in the car, she goes inside, crawls in bed and pulls the covers over her head. *At least Justin won't be home for a few more hours.*

Sleep comes quickly but brings with it twisted and tortured dreams from which she cannot escape. Therefore, when Justin comes home later and shakes her by her leg, she flings the covers off and screams, prepared to fight a dragon.

He backs up against a wall, eyes wide. "I'm sorry, I shouldn't have woke you up. I was just going to ask you what you wanted for supper."

Hope stares around the room in which nothing looks familiar. Looking back at Justin, she finally comes fully awake and rubs her face with her hands. "That's okay," she tells him. "I was in the middle of a nightmare when you woke me up. I wasn't sure where I was for a moment."

"Can I sit on the edge of the bed?" He asks.

"Sure. I'm not going to bite you."

The bed sags when he sits down, so much so that Hope, who was sitting on her knees, nearly loses her balance. Instead, she falls against him. He puts his arm around her and tries to kiss her, but she pushes away from him. "Stop. Not now," she tells him.

The corners of his eyes turn down. "But I thought when you leaned on me it meant you wanted to fool around."

Shaking her head, she says, "I wasn't coming after you. I fell against you because I lost my balance when you nearly turned the bed over by sitting on it."

He stands up, looking dejected.

"Look," she says in a conciliatory tone, "I didn't mean to hurt your feelings. I've just had a bad afternoon, was having nightmares, and suddenly I'm woken up by a man as big as a grizzly bear. We can fool around tonight, how's that?"

Justin's eyes light up and a smile explodes onto his face. He looks like a kid who won a prize at a carnival, always hoping but never expecting. "That sounds great. What do you want me to fix for supper?"

With no appetite, Hope has difficulty thinking of anything that would taste good, so she says, "I'll eat whatever you want to fix."

He claps his hands together. "Great! I'm making mama's special chili recipe." He turns and rumbles out of the bedroom toward the kitchen.

I better make sure we have plenty of Tums on hand tonight. She lies back down on the bed. *I was feeling so much better for the past few weeks. How can I get back there?*

Like following a trail of bread crumbs, she retraces everything that has happened over the past weeks, looking for clues that will reveal to her how she was able to throw her depression into remission. Sooner than she expects, the path becomes clear. *When I opened up completely to Whitney and Carol Anne and took our friendship to the next level I felt a weight had been lifted. But the biggest thing that helped was talking to Michael.*

A feeling of warmth spreads through her as she pictures him sitting in his chair, his eyes glued to hers, like what she has to say is the most important thing in the world to him. She's never interacted with anyone who made her feel that way. It boosted her self-confidence, and those weekly meetings gave her something to look forward to.

She suddenly remembers they made an appointment to meet again, but she can't remember what day today is. "Hey Justin," she calls out, "what day of the week is today?"

"It's Thursday," he responds. "Remember, you get every third Thursday off at work."

Thursday! I'm supposed to meet him tonight! She jumps out of bed and hops in the shower, feeling as if she's escaped depression's grasp.

CHAPTER FOURTEEN

Michael is unsure if he should or no, but he's eagerly looking forward to seeing Hope. He's really had no one to talk to since Sarah's death, especially since Jed has been consumed with his divorce from Liz. That reminds him that Liz is coming to his office tomorrow to discuss her position as music director, the question being—should she continue to serve in that role even though she's going to be divorced.

I never dreamed I'd be having to make these kinds of decision so soon into my ministry here. The decision about her was much easier for him to make than the one about Jed. *This decision is selfish. I'm not about to let anything come between me and spending time with Liz.* He's been thinking about her a lot. Fantasizing would be a more accurate description. *Is it possible she and I could end up seeing each other and getting married?*

He keeps telling himself he needs to move slow and carefully with Liz. What bothers him the most is he can't figure out exactly how she feels about him. She keeps her emotions in check except when she's directing the music, and then she emotes through every part of herself, which is why he loves watching her.

All of this brings him back to Hope. *She gives me what no one has ever given me—the feeling of being heard.* It's different than when church members listen to him. They do it because he's the pastor. And then there have been those who pretend to listen to him, but they are really wanting something from him, a favor of some kind.

With Hope, she's unimpressed with his position and acts like they are equals. *That could be my fault because I've shared so much about myself with her. I might call it a counseling session, but it really isn't. It's connecting with each other at a deep level.*

He hasn't seen her since Sarah's suicide, and he wonders how he'll feel when he's alone with her.

He smiles as headlights spread across the church parking lot, and the car parks next to his. Hope gets out and heads toward the door. She's so thin and her movements so smooth she looks like she glides across the pavement. His heart quickens as she nears the door.

When she enters, he barely restrains himself from throwing his arms around her and holding her like a long-lost friend. They stand and look at each other, her eyes searching his face and he trying to read her.

"It's good to see you," he says.

She twists the blue streak in her hair around her finger. "It's good to see you, too."

"I've been wanting to ask you about that blue streak in your hair."

She lets go of it and looks self-conscious. "What about it?"

"I know you don't like drawing attention to yourself or people looking at you, so why do that and the piercings?"

She smiles. "Because it works."

"Works? How do you mean?"

"You notice my blue hair and my piercings, so do other people. That's what they focus on, which is okay with me because when they do that they really aren't looking at me. It's like a Christmas tree. When people say you have a pretty Christmas tree, they're saying they like the ornaments on the tree. They don't really look at the tree itself, don't notice if it's a scotch pine, cedar, ponderosa pine, or blue spruce. You get it?"

Michael chuckles. "I never thought about it that way, but you're right. Well, when people don't look at you or give themselves the chance to know you, they're really missing out."

Even in the dim lighting of the lobby, he can see she's blushing. "Come on, let's go to my office."

They assume their accustomed positions, she on the loveseat with her legs pulled up under her and he in an armchair.

"I'm not going to ask you how you're doing," Hope says, "because I got tired of hearing the question. How ever you're doing that's just how you're doing, right?"

Michael nods. "That is so true, because it can change from moment to moment."

"Yes. Just like me today. I had a wave of depression hit me, hit me hard, so hard it swallowed me. I haven't had that feeling in some time." She looks down. "It's hard."

"I'm sorry you feel bad. I guess I misread you, I thought you were in a pretty good mood."

Her head pops up. "Oh, I am in a good mood. It's crazy how emotions can pick you up and throw you down from one moment to another."

"How did you do it, go from being depressed to being in a good mood."

She gives him a knowing smile. "It changed when I remembered I was meeting with you tonight."

Her answer warms him. "I'm glad."

They sit quietly for a few moments, as they often do. Then Hope says, "Do you want to talk about it?"

He crosses his legs and feels a little guarded. "Talk about what?"

"You know what. The suicide."

He thought he'd be prepared for this because he knew she would ask him. But now that the question lies in his lap, he feels uncertain. "I haven't really talked about it with anyone, except when I answered the cop's questions."

Hope unfolds herself and holds him with her eyes.

"It was weird, strange, shocking, unbelievable when I walked in the room and found her lying there on the bed."

Hope nods.

"At first, I thought she might be sleeping. No, that's not true. I knew she was dead; I just hoped she was sleeping. The first thing I thought of was what are people going to say."

Hope frowns at that. "Why did you think that?"

"It's what I always think in every situation. That's all I heard from my parents growing up. What people thought was paramount. And now I see why, because when you're in the ministry your livelihood is dependent on people viewing you in a positive way."

"Wow, I could never live in that kind of circumstance. Here's the funny thing about me, I don't care what anybody thinks about me, but at the same time my social anxiety is all about me worrying what people are thinking about me. That's what I call crazy in the first degree."

Michael laughs.

Silence descends on them again.

"Quit wondering what I'm thinking," Hope says.

"How'd you know that's what I was doing?"

"I can just tell. Tell me about Sarah dying." She scoots to the edge of her seat and rests her elbows on her knees. "And don't try to be careful with what you say. Say whatever is in your heart."

Her persistence and insistence pull him toward her. He feels like the floor is opening up under him and that he's going to lose control. Emotions begin bubbling up into his throat and Hope's image blurs as tears fill his eyes. He opens his mouth to speak, but nothing comes out. Clearing his throat, he tries again, "I was scared. When I left that morning, everything seemed as usual and then she was dead. Dead—there's no way to fix or undo that." His voice begins to squeak as he has trouble pushing the words past the big bulge in his throat. "But the hardest thing to get past is the...the guilt."

As if that word was the proverbial finger in the dike, suddenly he begins to sob uncontrollably. Wave after wave erupts from him, causing his body to spasm. He tries to rein it in, but it is more powerful than him.

Without warning, he feels Hope's arm around his shoulder as she sits on the arm of his chair. She pulls him toward her, and he gives into her, pushing his face into her chest. He is a child, a child who's been seeking comfort and reassurance most of his life. And now he's found it in the unlikeliest of places. He throws his arms around her and holds on for dear life.

When Michael is cried out, he draws a deep breath and lets it out. He unwraps his arms from around Hope, sits back and looks at her in surprise. "I'm sorry. I don't know what came over me. I shouldn't have done that."

Hope looks down at her tear-stained shirt and touches it. "Why not? What's wrong with you being human?"

"I feel emotionally naked and vulnerable."

"Scary, isn't it? I felt the same way after I recently told my friends my story. But once I realized I could trust them; the fear went away." She puts her hand on the side of his face. "You can trust me."

The sound of doors closing rings in Michael's head as he shuts the openings to his compartmentalized life. As he does so, he begins to feel more in control of himself and the situation. "I need to stand up and walk around a bit."

When he jumps up, the move is so unexpected Hope nearly falls off the arm of the chair. "What's wrong? What happened?"

What IS wrong? Normally I would have taken advantage of a situation like that and had sex with the woman. It would have been easy. Why didn't I? He looks at her uncertainly. "I think...I think it's getting late, and you have to go to work in the morning. Let's wrap this up. I look forward to seeing you in church this Sunday." He walks to the office door, opens it and waits for Hope to leave.

CHAPTER FIFTEEN

As soon as Justin finishes having sex with Hope, which took less than five minutes, he rolls onto his side and almost immediately begins snoring. Thankful she's rid of him for the rest of the night, Hope gets out of bed and slips on jeans and a hoodie. Sleep is the last thing on her mind.

Ever since she left her meeting with Michael this evening she's been unable to think of anything else. *I've never experienced such an intense and intimate conversation. There were moments I could hardly breathe. I don't think I've ever felt so close to someone.*

She replays the scene in her head. She was surprised to learn how insecure he is, always worrying about what others think of him. She had always figured when a person was as successful as he appeared to be, that would produce a tremendous amount of self-confidence. *Things are not always what they appear to be, that's for certain.*

When she moved to sit on the arm of the chair with him it felt completely natural, and she did it without thinking. Once there, though, she feared she'd invaded his personal space, and he would be offended or make her move. *If he'd made me do that, I think I would have run out the door and never gone back.*

Putting my arm around him was an even bigger risk, but it felt wonderful. The warmth of his body...she closes her eyes and relives the electrifying feeling. *I never wanted to kiss somebody so badly in my life!* But before she could act on her urge, he collapsed onto her chest and began to sob.

At that moment, everything had shifted for her. Rather than being a woman intent on an episode of passion, she was a mother comforting a child. *If I'd done that more with Lisa, maybe things would have been different for us...for her.*

When she'd come home, she removed her tear-stained shirt and carefully folded it and placed in her drawer. *I may never wash it again.*

What troubles me, though, is how everything ended. One second we were as close as two people can be, and the next moment he was showing me the door. It reminded her of her early years in Paducah when she had to trade sex for money so she could feed herself and Lisa; as soon as the transaction was completed, both parties went their separate ways.

Questions plague her:

Did I do something that offended Michael? Did I give off the wrong kind of signals?

Was he mad? He didn't look mad, but he acted mad.

Does he not feel about me the way I feel about him? What if he doesn't; what will I do then?

Is this the end? Will he ever want to see me again? Sure, he invited me to church, but did he really mean it? And do I want to go to church there if things between us have changed?

Like a dog chasing its tail, round and round she goes with these questions but gets nowhere.

Depression begins seeping back into her bones. It is a feeling so familiar a part of her welcomes it because living in that darkness, that place of not caring, although it is filled with self-inflicted pain, makes her impervious to the pain that comes from being hurt by others.

Sadness envelopes her so tightly, she finds it hard to breathe. She jumps out of the chair, grabs her keys, and heads out the door. The cool night air shocks her, but it helps her get a breath.

She hears the river calling her, and she pulls out of the driveway intent on going there. Instead, though, she finds herself stopped in the street in front of Michael's darkened house. Sitting there, staring at the house, her chorus of questions catches up with her, demanding answers.

She considers going to his door and waking him up. Her imagination plays out every possible scenario to such a bold move—*What will he do i ...? What will I do if...?*

Just as she's about to open her door and walk to his house, flashing blue lights light up the street. Panicked, she looks in her rearview mirror and sees a police car stopped behind her. Evidently, the officer had approached her with headlights off.

Her heart beats so fast it feels more like a hummingbird's wings beating than the pulse of a drumbeat. She watches the officer approaching her car. *What am I going to say? How do I explain why I'm sitting here? How long have I been sitting here? Long enough that someone saw me and called the police?*

The policeman taps on her window with his flashlight and then shines it in her face, blinding her. She rolls the window down.

"What seems to be the trouble, ma'am?"

She squints at him. "I'm sorry, I honestly stopped in the street and got lost in my thoughts. I know it makes me sound crazy or drunk. While I might be called crazy by some, I am not drunk."

He shines his flashlight throughout the interior of her car. "I need your license and registration, please."

Hope's heart sinks. "I left the house in such a hurry I forgot to get my billfold with my driver's license. I just live two blocks from here. If you'll follow me there, I can get it for you. Please don't give me a ticket."

The officer replies, "Keep your hands where I can see them, and step out of the car, please."

Trembling, Hope gets out.

"Empty your pockets."

"I don't have anything in my pockets."

"Then turn them wrong side out."

Hope complies.

"Turn around and put your hands on the hood of the car." When she does he kicks her feet back until all her weight is on her hands. Then he frisks her. "Stand back up," he says.

A familiar voice says, "Excuse me officer, can I do anything to help?" It is Michael.

Hope sees him standing on the sidewalk in front of his yard, hair askew and wearing a bathrobe. She is mortified.

The officer looks at him, and says, "Oh, hey pastor Michael. What are you doing here?"

"I live here. Is that you, Harold?" He approaches the policeman.

"Yes, it is."

Michael looks at Hope, then turns to the officer. "What seems to be the problem?"

"I found this woman sitting in her car in the middle of the street."

"Hello, Hope," Michael says.

Hope's shame deepens.

"You know her?"

"Yes, absolutely. She's one of my church members."

The policeman guides Michael out of earshot from Hope, and they engage in a conversation.

Hope wishes she could disappear, evaporate from view. *He'll never want to see me again.*

The conversation between the two men is brief, and they approach her. "I'm going to give you a free pass this time," the officer says. "You're lucky Pastor Michael showed up and said he'll vouch for you. Next time, you need to be more careful and aware of what you're doing. And always have your license with you."

Hope feels relieved but not as strongly as she feels embarrassed. She can't bring herself to look at Michael. "Thank you, officer," she says. "I promise it'll never happen again."

"Okay. Get in your car now, and be on your way."

She mumbles a thank you to Michael, and quickly as she can gets in her car and drives slowly away. In her rearview mirror she watches Michael and the officer talking and watching her drive off. Her heart aches as she says to herself, *Things will never be the same between us.*

Instead of driving home like she knows she probably should, she heads toward her original destination—the river.

Driving the backroads, she remembers a spot Luther took her to one time and turns off on a dirt lane. She only drives a short distance until the lane ends, and she gets out. The smell of water and the sound of croaking frogs greet her. She climbs up a bank and reaches an abandoned railroad track.

The moon shines through broken clouds and reflects off of the steel rails. Taking her time, she walks between the rails until she spies what she's looking for—the iron skeleton of a bridge that crosses a feeder stream of the river. The rails end abruptly as the floor of the bridge rotted away long ago.

A sense of calm resignation comes over Hope as she grips what's left of the bridge, and she scoots along a rusty beam. When she reaches the middle, she stops and looks down into the inky blackness below. She knows what lies forty feet below—mangled pieces of the bridge and rails, small boulders, and a rippling stream.

Without Lisa and without Michael, what's the point of going on? No one will notice or care. I just can't do this anymore.

CHAPTER SIXTEEN

"Suicide is the second leading cause of death for young people between 10 to 24." Liz looks up from her notes and scans the faces of the students sitting in their desks. Surprisingly, they appear to be giving her their rapt attention. "Sometimes your struggle can be underestimated because of your age, but we want you to know we hear you, and we want to help."

She continues, "I'm going to give you a phone number, and I'm going to repeat it more than once in my presentation. It is a number you can call twenty-four-seven. It is the number for the National Suicide Prevention Lifeline 1-800-273-8255. We're going to have the number posted everywhere we can: in the school, in your churches, in businesses in town. Please share it on your social media, too. 800-273-8255."

She pushes a key on her laptop and a picture of Lisa appears on her PowerPoint. She turns to the movie screen, and says, "You all know who this is. Lisa Rodriguez is why we are here doing this. A new group is being started in school called LISA, which stands for Life Instead of Suicide Advocates." She turns back to the students. "We want all of you to be a part of this group. We've created a Facebook page by the same name. Please join the group.

"One thing that's important for you to know is how to take care of yourself. First of all, ask for help. Don't be afraid to let your friends, family, or teachers know what you need when they ask; they want to help.

"Secondly, remember that whatever you are feeling, it can be overcome: family conflict, relationships, grades, and the loss of important people can seem impossible to deal with. But with support from others, you can.

"And in the third place, evaluate the relationships in your life: love and friendship are all about respect. Toxic or unhealthy relationships can negatively affect you. Whether you're dating or building new friendships, remember your rights. If you're being bullied, help is also available."

A girl holds her hand up.

Liz prompts, "Yes? Do you have a question?"

"You say if we're being bullied, there is help. What kind of help are you talking about?"

Liz has spent hours preparing for this presentation and felt she could handle any questions about suicide, but this is a question she wasn't expecting. "I'm sure if you tell a teacher about it, they will address the problem and give you the help you need."

Several in the room laugh out loud.

A boy in the back called out, "Lady, you don't know this school very well, do you?"

More laughter.

The girl who asked the question, says, "Bullying goes on here all the time and has ever since I've been here. But the ones doing the bullying have parents who are rich and powerful, so nobody does anything about it."

Liz notices three attractive girls on the front row exchange devious smiles and winks. She turns to Heather Brown, the guidance counselor, who agreed to sit in on this meeting. "Would you like to respond to this, Ms. Brown?"

"Ms. Brown's not the problem," the loud boy says. "She's the best."

All the kids nod in agreement.

"It's old man Biddle that's the problem," the boy goes on. "All he cares about is keeping the rich folks happy and keeping his job. Although it looks like that's going to come to an end pretty soon. I hope they cut his balls off."

The room erupts into applause and students high five each other.

Liz recognizes she's lost her audience, and she waits for the burst of energy in the room to subside. When quiet returns, she looks at them steadily, then puts Lisa's picture back on the screen. She turns her back to the room and looks at the picture. "I can't help but wonder, would Lisa still be with us if when she was being bullied, a classmate had walked up to her, linked their arm in hers, looked at the bullies and said, 'I'm with Lisa. Why don't you bully me, too?' And what if it had been two fellow students who had stood up for Lisa, or five, or ten? Instead, though, people saw it happening and did nothing, which made Lisa feel like she was facing everything alone."

Turning back around, she says, "You see, putting all the blame on the school staff is an easy way to keep from accepting any responsibility yourselves; it keeps you from feeling guilty."

The room becomes deathly quiet.

Liz lets her words sink in. "Life is hard for all of us, and we shouldn't have to do it alone." Her voice catches, and her eyes grow misty as she remembers her pending divorce. "We all need each other." She advances her PowerPoint to the next slide.

"Here's how to help: If your friend confides in you they are having thoughts of suicide, believe them and get help, even if it's just calling 800-273-8255. Be a better listener. Whatever your friend is going through might not seem like a big deal to you, but it is to them and that's the only thing that matters. Tell them you are there to help. And don't keep suicide a secret. No matter what you've promised, if they say they are thinking of hurting themselves, you need to involve other people."

She advances the next slide. "Lastly, these are some warning signs to look for. If you or someone you know exhibits any of these, call the Lifeline."

The students stare at the information on the screen.

- Talking about wanting to die or to kill themselves

- Looking for a way to kill themselves, like searching online or getting a gun

- Talking about feeling hopeless or having no reason to live

- Talking about feeling trapped or in unbearable pain

- Talking about being a burden to others

- Increasing the use of alcohol or drugs

- Acting anxious or agitated; behaving recklessly

- Sleeping too little or too much

- Withdrawing or isolating themselves

- Showing rage or talking about seeking revenge

- Extreme mood swings

As Ms. Brown escorts the students out of the room to their regular classes, several of them pause long enough to thank Liz and vow to help make a difference.

Over and over Liz shares her presentation until, by the end of the day, all the students have heard her. She turns to Ms. Brown and lets her shoulders sag. "I am exhausted. As a matter of fact, I can't remember when I've been so exhausted."

Heather walks up to her and gives her a hug. "You were unbelievable. I promise, no would could tell you were getting tired. You showed as much energy and passion for the last group as you did for the first. I can't thank you enough for doing this."

"The thanks goes to Mark. I probably would never have gotten involved if he wasn't as fervent about making a difference as he is. I just hope these kids take it seriously and really start changing how they treat and relate to each other."

"Well, I can tell you I was watching the students as you spoke, and they were indeed taking it seriously. They hung on your every word. Some made notes. I've got to believe this is a start of something big. Maybe other schools will start doing something similar."

Mr. Biddle walks into the room, rubbing his hands together. "How did things go today? From what I saw, the kids seem pretty excited about all this."

Heather answers, "I think it's one of the most important things that has happened since I've been in this school."

Biddle is taken aback. "Well, I'm sure it was important, but we've done many tremendous things here through the years."

"Whatever you say," Heather replies.

Liz sees his eyes narrow as he looks at Heather. Even though it only lasts a second, it makes her uneasy, and she wonders what the history is between the two of them. She says, "I want to thank you for letting me speak to the kids today. You didn't have to do that, even though you were opposed to the idea."

He does his best to smile at her, but the effort fails miserably as his eyes are dark and wary. "I hold you in high esteem, Ms. Rochelle, and trust you to always do the right thing."

Liz wishes she could throw up on his shoes for being so two-faced. Instead, she gives him a steady gaze and waits for him to blink first. At first, it appears to be a Mexican stand-off, but after several seconds, his face turns red and he looks at his watch. "Well, I have another meeting I need to get to. You ladies have a nice rest of the day."

They watch him leave then look at each other. "Reminds me of a weasel," Heather says.

Liz says, "Or a poisonous snake."

CHAPTER SEVENTEEN

Michael checks the time: 4:24 p.m. *She'll be punctual, she always is.* He walks to his office door and watches Helen turning off her computer and gathering her things. "I trust you'll have a good evening," he says.

Ignoring his comment, she says, "I can stay later, if you'd like me to, at least until you finish meeting with Liz."

If Sarah wasn't dead, I would be suspicious she told you to say that. "That's quite all right. We have matters to discuss, and I'm not sure how long it will take. You go ahead, and I'll see you in the morning."

Walking past him, she says, "Whatever you say."

Truth is, he's been eager to meet with Liz outside regular office hours. After his evening with Hope last night, he never went back to sleep, and it's been on his mind all day. Liz, though, will be able to take his mind off of whatever it was that happened last night.

No sooner does Helen exit the offices than Liz walks in. Immediately, he senses something is amiss. There are lines on her face he's never noticed before, and her hair lies uncharacteristically limp around her face and on her shoulders. Her gait and movements lack the crisp confidence they usually project. Without any energy, she says, "Hi, Michael."

"What's the matter, Liz?" he asks, then turns and leads her into his office.

Sitting down, she says, "I'm just exhausted, that's all. I spent all day at the school talking to students about suicide. It was a wonderful day but a fatiguing day. And then, on my way here, I learned Jed has hired Adam Cartwright to represent him in our divorce proceedings. He's known as 'The Barracuda' and deservedly so. I'm more than a little surprised Jed hired him because he always spoke of him in disparaging terms, but also because I thought he and I had agreed we would keep lawyers out of this and work out the terms together. My hope was that we could divorce without it turning into an out-and-out war."

This is not what Michael anticipated when he asked her to meet with him to discuss her role as Minister of Music, a role he most certainly wants her to continue in. *But maybe I can take advantage of her vulnerable state.* "I'm sorry you've had such a challenging day. But I'm so proud of your willingness to tackle the suicide problem and take it into the schools. It will be impossible to measure how much lasting good you did today. It's conceivable there was someone who heard you who was contemplating suicide, and your words made them relook at that option and feel hopeful."

A gentle smile takes the edge off the sharp features of her face. "I really appreciate you saying that. Jed was opposed to the idea from the start, which is one of the main reasons I decided to divorce him. It's like I don't know him anymore. We used to always be on the same page together, working to help make this a better place to live." A solitary tear slips out of the corner of her eye.

Michael watches it slowly run down her cheek, over her jawline, and down her neck. He wishes he could use his finger to trace the track of that tear and touch her face, her neck and the tender place between her breasts where he imagines the tear disappeared to. "I am very sad that you and Jed are divorcing. It's proving to be unsettling to many people. I'm new here, but it's obvious you and he are held in high esteem by people around here and are looked up to as models to emulate."

Liz sits a little straighter. "I shouldn't be talking to you about Jed and me. I know you and he have become good friends, and it puts you in an awkward position."

Leaning forward, he replies, "It is true Jed and I are friends. He's the first one who really embraced me as a newcomer and helped me learn the community and begin to fit in. But I don't feel you're putting me in the middle. I've learned over time there are many sides to a situation, so I don't try to choose sides or lay blame. I just try to lend a sympathetic ear to those involved, which I'm willing to do for you." He hesitates a second, then adds, "Besides, I would like for you to view me as a friend, as well." He holds his breath to see how she receives the last comment.

She gazes at him with an expression he can't interpret. "If you can remain impartial, as you say you can, I admire that, I suppose. I tend to be more passionate about things and try to figure out which is the side of right, and then I defend it with all my might."

He winces inside at her insinuation.

She continues, "I've always viewed our relationship as more professional than personal. Our discussions have always centered on how the music can enhance the worship experience of our church members and how it can reinforce the message you present."

Michael feels like the fisherman whose big catch is about to slip off the hook. "I see what you're saying. I guess I always felt like we had a special connection because whenever I have an idea about the music you're there before I get there. The music you select is always so perfect, as if your spirit and mine are one in our desire to glorify God in worship." To elicit feelings of sympathy, he adds, "But evidently you view all that differently than I do." He sits back in his chair as if wounded.

She quickly responds, "I didn't mean to hurt your feelings by anything I said, Michael."

I love hearing her use my name.

"It's just that after our last pastor violated so many women in our church, I'm extra, extra cautious. Please don't interpret that as me not caring about you or especially my having a dislike for you because actually the opposite is true. I've never felt the passion I feel for the music like I do since you arrived. You've kindled a fire in my soul, a fire I've longed for all my life. I'm certain God sent you to us because you are exactly what the church needed. It's an honor for me to be connected with you in serving our Lord."

As she speaks, color comes to her cheeks, and her eyes have a fire in them, both of which excites and gratifies Michael.

But the fire quickly goes out. "I suppose though," she says, "all that will have to come to an end because of the divorce."

Michael feels a little panicky. "What do you mean? What are you talking about?"

"There's no way you can let a divorced woman serve as the Director of Music. I understand the why of it, but it still makes me sad."

"Well, let me quickly set your mind at ease about that. I do indeed intend for you to continue in your current position."

"But —"

"No," he cuts off her protest. "There are no buts about this. I've spent much time in prayer and study over this, and my conclusion is God wants you in the role. If we are to be a community of believers that teaches people about the grace of God, then we certainly need to be practicing it. How hypocritical it would be to remove you just because you're going through a difficult time. What message would that send, that people have to be perfect to attend church here? 'We're all fellow strugglers' is the message I want people to hear and know."

Tears pool in her eyes, telling him his words have found their mark.

He reaches his hand toward her, and she takes it. "Liz, God has given you a special talent. You have to use it to glorify him. You hear me? You have to. And here is where you are going to do it."

She puts the back of his hand to her lips. "Thank you, Michael. We are so blessed to have you here."

A smile stretches across his face.

CHAPTER EIGHTEEN

Whitney looks across the office at Carol Anne. "Why do you think they gave you your job back?"

"I think it's the national focus on the MeToo movement. If word got out they fired me because of the lawsuit, it would start a firestorm of negative publicity, not just for this casino but for all the company's casinos."

"I'm glad you're back."

"I guess I am. It's just bittersweet, that's all."

"I get it," Whitney agrees. "Have you heard from Hope?"

Shaking her head, Carol Anne replies, "Of course not, that's not how Hope is. And it's pointless to call or text her because she never responds."

"I know. But it's been two days since she's shown up at work. You think it's her depression that's got her again?"

"Could be. Sometimes it really brings her down, but she's been so much better for the past several weeks. Should we go see about her?"

"I think we should. She'll get mad about it probably, but if she does I'm just going to tell her she needs to use her phone like regular people do. Just send a text telling us she's all right, that's all it would take."

"Okay then, we'll go right after work today."

The soft clicking of their computer keys rules the silence as they return to work.

After a few minutes, Whitney asks, "How about you? How are you doing? You don't talk much about the Biddle thing."

"I turned down his offer to settle out of court."

"Good for you! Keep up the pressure. He's wanting to keep it quiet and believes it will all die down and he can keep doing what he does. Are you having to go it alone or are there still some others who are sticking with you?"

"There are four others besides myself. It looks like they are going to see it through, but you never know, they may drop out like the others."

A few minutes pass as they focus on work. Then Whitney asks, "Can I ask you a question?"

"Sure you can."

"Why haven't you said anything about Biddle before now?"

Sighing, Carol Anne answers, "It doesn't make sense, does it? My lawyer says that is where Biddle's defense team is going to attack my story. You know, when I was involved with him during high school, I didn't tell because I knew it would bring it to an end and that's not what I wanted. I thought I was in love with him and he was in love with me. I thought we would have a life together." She shakes her head. "Saying it out loud it sounds crazy, doesn't it?"

"I think I get that," Whitney replies. "But when you figured out he was just using you, why didn't you tell then?"

"Shame, embarrassment, and guilt. I was humiliated by what I'd done. I just knew everyone would point at me and tell me how foolish and stupid I'd been, like I was the one to blame. Don't you know, it's always the female's fault. As time passed, there were periods when I told myself it didn't really happen and periods when I put it completely out of my mind like it never happened. But all that changed when Lisa committed suicide, and I heard he was her principal. If I ever learn that he was taking advantage of her and that was why she killed herself, I could never live with myself."

Whitney jumps in, "Hold on now, don't start blaming yourself for what Lisa did."

"But if I'd said something before now and helped bring him to justice, maybe she'd still be here."

"My granddaddy used to say, 'If ifs and buts were candies and nuts, we'd all have a merry Christmas.' You can't let yourself live in that place. Suicide is much more complicated than you're making it out to be. You just focus on doing everything you can now to stop Biddle, and put all that 'what if' stuff away."

*****

After work, they get in Whitney's car and head toward Luther's place. As soon as they pull in the driveway, he exits the house and walks toward them.

Not waiting for them to get out of the car, he stops beside Whitney's window and motions for her to roll it down.

"What in the world?" Whitney says as she lowers it.

"What are y'all doing here?" Luther asks. "You come to rub my nose it in?"

"Rub your nose in what?" Whitney replies. "What are you talking about?"

"You've got no business here. You know she's not here."

Carol Anne leans over and looks at him. "Are you saying Hope isn't here?"

"Of course she's not. You both know that."

Whitney says, "Neither of us have a clue what you're talking about. We came over to see Hope because she hasn't been to work the past two days. We're worried about her."

"She packed her stuff and told me she was going to live with Justin."

Whitney and Carol Anne look at each other. "Justin?!"

"Yes, fat-ass Justin."

Carol Anne says, "Then why hasn't he said anything to us about her not being at work?"

"She's not been working?" Luther asks.

Whitney whips out her phone. "I'm calling Justin right now. If there's something going on and he hasn't told us, he'll be sorry."

She pauses as the phone rings. "Justin! I'm fixing to find you and beat you like a child. Is Hope living with you?" She listens to his answer. "Why haven't you told me and Carol Anne, and why hasn't she been at work the past two days? Is she sick?"

This time she listens for several moments then ends the call. Looking at Carol Anne and Luther, she says, "She moved in with him, but he hasn't seen her for two days. He figured she came back here to be with Luther."

Luther swears, then says, "Well, she isn't here."

Carol Anne says, "Then where is Hope?"

CHAPTER NINETEEN

A shriek of pain rips from Hope's mouth and echoes down the small ravine as searing pain shoots through her left ankle and up the side of her calf. The pain throws her onto the ground. Reflexively, her mud-smeared hands, with their broken fingernails, rush to comfort the ankle that she has decided is broken. The empathetic part of her wants to caress her ankle, but the logical part of her steps in and stops her because it remembers how badly it hurt the last time she grabbed it.

Holding her leg up, she rolls onto her back and slowly lowers her leg until the shoeless heel of her foot touches a rock. Even that light pressure sends a jolt of pain through her ankle, and she nearly passes out.

This is the perfect example of my life. I try to kill myself and, of course, don't succeed, and end up with more problems than I had when I decided to kill myself.

Jumping from the abandoned railroad trestle had been neither planned nor well thought out. It just made sense at that moment. She wasn't sure what she expected would happen but certainly didn't expect how bad it would hurt when she landed on the rocks protruding from and lying just below the surface of the stream. Even though it was nighttime and the area remote, there was an explosion of light when she landed. Then she sank under the water. *Yes, Poseidon, if you rule the waters here, take me, please take me.*

To her disappointment, her body rose to the surface, and she began floating downstream on her back. She made no move to chart her course, instead, she gave her will to the will of the stream. The only thing that kept her alert was the fiery pain in her ankle and leg. She was certain she had other injuries, but none of them screamed loud enough to match the decibel level of her ankle.

She imagined floating down the Mississippi River and into the sea, which would surely swallow her tiny life. But her dream was interrupted when she got entangled in the limbs of a tree that had fallen across the length of her exit-from-life stream. At first, she tried to pull herself through the twisted limbs, but the pain from her ankle nearly made her pass out. The same thing happened when she tried to go under the tree. So, she lay there skewered by the tree, neither above the water nor under the water—a perfect metaphor of her life with depression.

For most of the next day, she was content to lie in the embrace of the tree and let the cool water help anesthetize her ankle. Mostly, she thought about Lisa and what it might be like to be reunited with her. *If she's in hell because she committed suicide, then I'll join her there, and it will make hell bearable. But if God's the merciful God Michael says he is, and she is in heaven, then surely he will take me there, too.*

It's that last thought that brought tears to her eyes. *When I see her, I will hug her like I should have hugged her when we were living. I will apologize for being a horrible mother and making her life so complicated. And I will cover her face with kisses.*

As the day wore on though, her thoughts turned to Michael and how loving and kind and warm he is. She longed to be held in his arms and began to imagine it happening. The warmth of his body flowed into her and made her smile.

Then a troubling thought occurred. *If I die, will he blame himself for it? Will he feel remorseful about how he ended our last visit and believe it was the cause for me taking my life?*

The more she ruminated on it, the guiltier she felt. Feeling responsible for how someone else feels will eventually crush even the strongest of persons. Thus, her decision to crawl out of the stream and try to find help. *I'm doing this for you, Michael.*

Shifting from passive suicide to active survival mode, she righted herself and tried to touch the bottom of the stream. What she didn't expect was how numb her entire legs and feet were. They were like logs attached to her torso. So, she used her arms and hands to pull herself along the length of the tree, until she made it to shore. Exhausted, she lay there until she recovered her breath.

Putting her good foot on a rock, she tried to stand up. But the algae-covered stone proved too slick, and her foot flew out from under her, causing her to land on her back. Her head struck the flat side of a rock, and she saw stars just before passing out.

When Hope came to, night had swallowed day, and the air was filled with nighttime sounds—croaking bullfrogs, tree frogs and spring peepers, a pair of owls calling each other in hopes of a romantic encounter. Her head and torso rested on the rock-strewn shoreline while her legs and feet lay half-submerged in the water.

Sitting up, she pushed against the ground and scooted on her butt until she was completely clear of the water. Just as she cleared it, her ankle bumped against a rock, sending jolts of pain through it. She grabbed her ankle to stop the pain, but all that did was make it worse. When the pain subsided, she screamed for help.

In spite of her dire situation, the irony of it did not escape her: a woman who tried to commit suicide crying out for help.

She had no idea where she was without knowing how far she had floated down the stream. Whether there were any houses or roads close by was impossible to tell. So, she continued crying out for help, until finally she was so hoarse only a whisper escaped her lips.

Exhausted, she leaned down to the water and slacked her thirst. Then, finding a space with no protruding rocks, she curled up and went to sleep.

Now, she sits on patch of moss-covered ground and looks at the bank of the stream she has managed to climb over. The sides of it are covered by sharp limestone rocks that were purposely placed there to prevent erosion but unfortunately tore her clothes and flesh and broke her fingernails. She turns her head and considers the distance to the top of the ravine. *I have got to make it to the top, so maybe I can figure out where I am.*

She spots a piece of a tree limb lying ten feet away. Hoping she can use it as a crutch, she crawls to it. Luckily, it isn't rotten, so she uses it to stand upright. *Finally! Something works in my favor.*

She estimates the length of the uphill climb to the top of the ravine. *Thirty feet that might as well be thirty miles. I don't think I can do it.*

Not for the first time during this event, she considers praying and asking God for help. *But how can I ask God to help me when I tried to take my own life? He's probably turned his back on me like I did him.* So, she sets out to make it on her own.

Keeping her foot high enough that it doesn't bump the ground proves more difficult than expected. Even the slightest touch sends shockwaves of pain through her ankle and leg. Once, she nearly passes out but shakes her head to clear away the blackness that threatens to take her down.

The morning sun finally chases away the clouds and beams brightly, warming her back. *Is that God putting his hand on me to encourage me?* She pauses in amazement at the question. *Such a thought would never have occurred to me if I hadn't met Michael. How different the world seems to me now. In the midst of all the mystery there is an element of certainty.*

She thinks about standing on the railroad trestle, feeling overwhelmed and hopeless. *It's these damned waves of depression that overwhelm me and drive me to the point of desperation. I've got to learn to manage that better.*

Lifting her face to the sun, she says hoarsely, "God, if you're here with me trying to help me, I want to thank you. And if you're not, I sure wish you would, even though I don't deserve it."

She focuses on the top of the ridge, and with a sense of renewed strength she continues toward it.

When she finally reaches the summit, she is shocked to see an RV sitting among a grove of pine trees forty feet away. She yells, but it only comes out a whisper.

Adrenaline shoots through her veins, and she quickens her pace, ignoring the pain of her ankle.

She raps on the door of the camper with the end of her stick and waits. Several moments pass with no sounds of anyone inside moving around. Wondering if they might be asleep, she strikes the door harder. Still no one answers.

Turning the nob does no good because it's locked. *Just my luck!* Despair begins creeping in until suddenly she hears a sound inside. A soft, *muffled?*, high-pitched sound.

Hope holds her breath to help her hear better. In spite of her hoarseness she manages to call out a raspy, "Is anyone in there? I need help."

Immediately there is the same muffled sound from inside.

She presses her ear to the door. *Is it a voice? A child?*

The noise sounds more desperate. There's a thud from inside.

Hope's imagination cranks out scary scenarios, all of which involve someone who is need of help. She cranes her neck to look in a window. Blinds cover the window, but they aren't completely closed. Hope squints to see between the slats. Her heart jumps at what she sees.

A little girl, wearing panties and a t-shirt, and with a gag around her mouth, trying to jerk free of something. *Is that a handcuff on one hand?* The girl's eyes are wide with terror as she looks toward the window.

CHAPTER TWENTY

Feeling fearless and fierce, Hope swings her stick at the window of the camper door until a bottom corner of it breaks through. Reaching inside she unlocks and opens the door. She makes it up the four steps to get inside and will later say she has no memory of doing it or how she managed doing so on a broken ankle. But when she gets inside, she doesn't see the girl anywhere.

"I'm not going to hurt you," Hope says. "I'm here to help you. Where are you?"

Suddenly, there's a whimper from underneath the pedestal meal table. With difficulty, Hope lowers herself to the floor and looks into the shadows. There, curled into a tight ball, with her knees to her chest and her arms hugging them, squats the child. Her head is hidden behind her knees.

"My name is Hope. I know you're scared. I know what it's like to be scared, to not know who you can trust, because I've felt that way before."

Slowly, the girl lifts her head just enough that she can look over her knees at Hope.

Hope reaches out her hand. "We've got to hurry. Let me take that off your mouth." Inching forward on her butt, she keeps her voice even. "I don't know who's done this to you, but they are a bad person. Let me help you get out of here. I'll protect you."

A small hand and thin arm reach out from underneath the table. Hope takes the hand and gently squeezes it. "Come on, let me help." She gives a slight pull on the girl's hand and is relieved she responds by easing toward her.

Hope edges toward the table until the girl crawls onto her lap and lays her head on Hope's chest. A wave of emotion so strong it nearly pushes Hope over hits her as images of Lisa at that age flash through her mind. She swallows hard to keep from being overwhelmed and focuses on untying the girl's gag.

Then she says, "Show me how you're tied up."

The girl shakes the hand with the handcuff on it, and Hope hears the other handcuff clanging underneath the table. Squinting, she sees that it is attached to the metal pedestal holding up the table. Panic grows. *How am I going to get that loose from there?*

Grabbing the pedestal, she jerks on it and makes the table wiggle a bit. She jerks harder but with no better results.

"No," the girl says. She crawls underneath and, grunting, pushes up on the table, but nothing happens.

Hope stares at her, then the girl motions her to help push up. The pain in Hope's ankle is returning, and every movement she makes is taking its toll. She lies down on her back so that her shoulders are underneath the table. Reaching up, she shoves against the table. Immediately, it pops off the pedestal and tumbles on top of her and the girl.

Quick as a wink, the girl slides the handcuff off the pedestal and smiles at Hope.

"Okay," Hope says, "let's get out of here. But I need to tell you I've hurt my ankle and can't go very fast."

A look of concern briefly appears on the girl's face, then she scampers to another room but is back in a second, carrying a bottle. She hands it to Hope who recognizes it is whiskey. Uncertain what the girl is wanting her to do, she raises her eyebrows.

"Drink it," the girl says. "He says it helps the hurt."

Hope quickly decides she doesn't have time to ask her any of the dozen questions that come to mind, but she does accept the truth of her statement. So she grabs the bottle and takes two big gulps. The burn and cough that follow are familiar to her from the period in her life when she was drinking too much. She says, "Help me stand up, and let's get out of here."

Once they're outside the RV, Hope realizes she doesn't know which is the best direction to travel and find help. There is a dirt lane leading through the trees. *Whoever owns this camper uses that to travel to and from here. He could be on his way back right now.*

"Where is your car?" the girl asks.

"That's the problem. I don't—" *Is it possible to follow the stream back to where my car is?* She thinks about the treacherous limestone rocks along the bank and if she can traverse them again with her bad ankle. But there's a clock ticking somewhere inside her that tells her the owner of the camper is on the way back and will be here any second.

Clutching her makeshift crutch in one hand, she grabs the girl's hand with her other, and says, "This way," and heads toward the ravine that holds the stream.

Stopping at the precipice, she looks upstream. Crossing the rocks and walking along the stream will leave them completely exposed, but the area between the top of the ravine and where the rocks start is littered with small trees and brush they might use to keep hidden.

Behind her, the rattling sound of a diesel engine approaching snatches her attention. With her heart in her throat, Hope says, "We've got to hide!"

Thankfully, a new surge of adrenalin takes the sharp edge off the pain from her ankle, but she refuses to take a chance on walking on that foot. Moving sideways, as much as forward, she looks like a crab.

Behind her, the engine roars louder until it suddenly stops. *He's reached the camper.*

Hope and the girl start through a patch of thick brush but are jerked to a stop by the thorns of a wild rose bush.

"Ow!" the girl cries.

Immediately, Hope claps her hand over the girl's mouth. "Shhh! He'll hear you." For the first time, she takes in the girl's features: dark hair and eyes, olive complexion. "What is your name?" she whispers.

"Montana."

"Montana, we have to be quiet so he can't find us. Okay."

Montana nods.

Hope leads them around the wild rose and moves through some chest-high shoots of elm trees.

A man's roar echoes through the trees above the ravine. "Montana, where are you?!"

Montana squeezes Hope's hand tighter. "Please, don't let him get me," she whispers.

Hope longs to stop, sit down, and take Montana into her arms. Squeezing her tightly, she would say, "I'll protect you. I love you. We're going to make it." Tears sting her eyes at the thought, but survival mode will not give her room for sentimentality, so she keeps moving.

"Come back here!" the man's voice booms, but he sounds farther away.

Thank you, God! Please keep him looking in the other direction.

Keeping her balance on the incline of the ravine while trying to move fast proves more difficult that Hope expected. Already, she feels blisters on her hand from having to rely on her crutch. An open stretch of ground with scattered patches of sagebrush looks invitingly easier than forcing their way through thick and sometimes prickly brush.

Just as Hope starts through it, she stops and looks around. *If he looks in this direction, he'll see us easy.* But to go around it will take precious time and keep them from reaching her car more quickly. "Okay, so look," she says to Montana, "I want to get across this patch without being seen. To do that we're going to have to lie on our bellies and crawl across. You understand?"

Montana nods, then says, "I've got to pee."

"Okay, pull your panties down, squat and pee here."

"It hurts to pee."

"What do you mean?"

"It hurts...burns really bad when I pee."

Bladder infection? Kidney infection? From what? From what he has been doing to her?

"I'm sorry it burns, but I can't do anything about that. We'll have to get you to a doctor. You're either going to have to hold it, or pee while it burns. But make up your mind quick. That man could be coming any second."

Montana pulls her panties down her thin legs and squats. A look of fear squeezes her eyes together, and Hope turns her back to her to give her some privacy.

In a few moments, Hope hears her whimpering, then crying.

"It hurts so bad," Montana whines.

"I know, sweetheart. I've had the same thing before. It really does hurt. But you don't need to hold your pee in; it'll make it worse."

In a moment, Montana says, "I'm done."

Turning around, Hope says, "Okay, let's go."

Pushing her crutch ahead of her, Hope inches across the ground. Dragging the foot of her broken ankle proves too painful, so she bends that knee and keeps her foot in the air and hopes it doesn't stick up above the grass.

Montana keeps so close to her their sides touch, which makes it harder to navigate across the ground, but Hope reasons it's more important to help the girl feel safe. She tries not to think about the number of ticks that might be hitching a ride on her or the possibility of coming face to face with a snake. She never did believe Luther's admonition, 'Snakes are more scared of you than you are of them.'

It's been a bit since she heard the man yelling. *But maybe he's not yelling anymore. Maybe he's moving stealthily toward us, following our tracks.* "Stop," she whispers. "Let's just listen."

The only sounds she hears are the ones made by nature: grasshoppers rubbing their legs, song birds—a Cardinal close by, a Carolina wren, whose loud song contradicts its tiny size, a Kingfisher down by the stream, getting ready to catch a meal. "Do you hear him?" she asks Montana.

"No."

"Good. Let's keep going."

When they finally make it through the stretch of sage, they find they are surrounded by several cedar trees from three to six feet tall. Hope rolls onto her back. "Let's rest a minute."

Montana lays beside her, rests her head on Hope's shoulder, and both of them close their eyes.

CHAPTER TWENTY-ONE

Hope opens her eyes but can't see anything. Sitting up, one of the cedar limbs brushes across face, causing her to cry out.

Montana crawls onto her lap in an instant. "What happened?" she asks.

The shocking truth dawns on Hope. "It's nighttime. We fell asleep when we stopped to rest. I can't believe we slept that long."

"I'm thirsty," Montana says.

Her statement shifts Hope's attention to take stock of her own needs, and she discovers she, too, is thirsty—and hungry, too. Immediately, her stomach growls to provide proof of her assessment. *How long can Montana last without any food or water? Probably not as long as I can. God, I wish I knew how far away my car is from here.*

Montana tugs on her shirt. "I'm thirsty," she repeats.

"I know you are, but I don't have anything with me."

"What about the river? That's where me and that man got our water from."

"The man in the camper?"

"Uh-huh."

"Who is he? He's not your father, is he?"

"No!" Montana says quickly. "I don't know who he is. The other man gave me to him."

Hope's mind swirls in an attempt to make sense of what Montana's telling her. "So, somebody gave you to this man."

"Uh-huh."

"Well, how did that other man get you?"

"He said he would take me home from school. He said my mama told him to. He said she was too busy."

Hope begins to connect some dots. "How long ago did that happen?"

"It was right after my birthday."

"When is your birthday?"

"March fourth."

Nearly two months ago! Hope wants to know what has been done to Montana by these men, but at the same time doesn't want to hear it. She asks, "Where are you from?"

"On the farm."

"What do you mean?"

"Papa works on the farm for Mr. Compton every year. He let me and mama come with him this year."

The further Hope goes in this conversation the more unexpected turns it takes. *Migrant workers. They must have come from Mexico.* "So, where is Mr. Compton's farm?"

"It's in Mississippi. When can I have something to drink? And I'm cold."

Hope hangs her interrogatory questions on a hook to possibly take up again later. *But for now, I've got to take care of this girl.* She's already thought about the available water down below, but just thinking of traversing the rocks to get there makes her ankle hurt. *Grow up and quit thinking about yourself*, she chastises herself.

"Okay," she tells Montana, "we're going to go down there and get some water to drink. We still won't have anything to eat, but filling up with water will make us quit thinking about food. There's lots of rocks we're going to have to climb and walk over, so be careful not to slip and fall."

Taking hold of her stick, and with the help of Montana, she gets to her feet. Her hand feels raw, and she's certain the blisters on it have torn open and are bleeding. It triggers a memory of when she and Michael shoveled the dirt into Lisa's grave and all the blisters it created on her hands. She sways, trying to catch her balance, but Montana puts her hands on her and steadies her.

"Can you do it?" Montana asks.

Hope looks at the filtered light from the half-moon above shining in the girl's eyes. *I failed Lisa, I will not fail this little girl.* She answers, "With your help I can."

Leaving the shadows and safety of the cedars, Hope looks nervously back at the top of the ravine. She can't figure out what happened with the man at the RV. She figured he would be searching in their direction once his efforts in the other direction were fruitless. *Maybe he got scared he was going to get caught and has packed up and left from here. Or maybe he's called some of his buddies to help him start searching in the morning. Or maybe he's got night vision goggles on right now and can see us out in the open.*

She silently curses her imagination for putting that last thought in her head. But even if it's true, there's nothing she can do about it. As if she grabbed a broom, she sweeps all thoughts from her mind and focuses solely on getting Montana some water.

She tries to keep her eye on the child as they move across the rocks, but every time she does it causes her to make a misstep and stumble. Her entire left leg now throbs with pain, and in spite of the chilled night air perspiration dots her face.

Montana moves as effortlessly as a monkey across the difficult terrain, even coming back at times to help Hope get back up. *She's a tough kid. A kid whose probably not a kid anymore if what's been done to her is what I think it is.*

After what seems an interminable amount of time, Hope feels the moisture from the water on her face and the sound of croaking frogs reaches her ears. "We're nearly there," she says to Montana. "Be careful now, the water's really cold. I don't want you to slip and fall in."

"Okay."

"Hold my hand."

Walking together, they ease forward until Hope's foot splashes in the water along the shoreline. The moon leaves silver streaks on the dark swirling current further out.

"We'll get on our knees and cup the water to our mouths with our hands," she instructs.

As soon as Hope bends down, she hears a funny sound in the water in front of her. Then the loud report of a rifle echoes from behind her. She and Montana scream as another rifle shot rings out.

Grabbing Montana around the waist, she picks her up and wades into the stream, looking for deeper water. A bullet whizzes so close to her she hears its buzz. "Can you swim?" she shouts at Montana.

"Yes."

"Under water?"

"Yes."

"Good. That's what we've got to do. He won't be able to see us then. Give me your hand, and take a deep breath. We can't get separated."

Montana does exactly as told, and they disappear from view.

Stroking with one hand and one leg, Hope swims in desperation against the flow of the stream, knowing that her car lies somewhere upstream not downstream. She feels Montana gyrating along with her and hopes her efforts are propelling them in the same direction.

A number of seconds pass before she feels Montana trying to pull her to the surface. Hope is glad because her lungs are burning for fresh air. They break through the thin plane that separates water from air gasping for breath.

"Shhh, shh, shh," Hope cautions. "Don't let him hear us. Just get a deep breath because we've got to go down again."

Over and over they repeat the cycle without having any idea if they've moved farther away from where they first entered the water or if its flow has pushed them downstream in spite of their Herculean efforts. Hope notices her hands are growing numb and fears hypothermia could engulf Montana. So, the next time they surface, she locates the shoreline and swims toward it.

As soon as her foot finds the bottom of the stream she hobbles ahead until she stumbles onto the shore with Montana collapsing beside her.

CHAPTER TWENTY-TWO

Hope and Montana lie side by side gasping for air. Suddenly, Hope's stomach roils. Rolling onto her side, she vomits all the water she's swallowed while swimming. *Montana probably needs to do the same thing.*

In the dim light, she looks over and sees her lying very still. An arrow of fear strikes Hope's heart. She grabs Montana, bends her over and begins striking her between her shoulder blades.

Montana begins coughing, then, she too, throws up. When she's finished, she begins shivering so hard her teeth chatter.

Hope looks at the shoreline and opens her eyes wide in hopes it will reveal a safe hiding place for them. She spots something flat and wide tangled among low-hanging branches and tree roots but is uncertain what it is.

Hugging Montana to her chest, she creeps closer. Not until she puts her hand on it does she recognize it is the bottom of a jon boat. *Probably swept down here from upstream a long time ago and never found.*

With the bottom of the boat turned up and facing the stream, Hope squeezes past the limbs and roots to the opposite side. *A perfect hiding place! No one will find us here.*

"I...I...I'm freezing," Montana says.

"I know. I'm going to fix that. Take your clothes off."

The girl obeys without a word, and Hope takes hers off, too. Next, Hope wrings as much water out of each piece of clothing that she can and hangs them on the limbs around them. Laying her shirt on the ground, she sits on it and pulls Montana onto her lap, wraps her arms around her and hugs her to her chest. "We'll keep each other warm," she whispers.

At first, Montana's body feels cold, but slowly it begins warming as it takes in some of Hope's heat. The girl lies so still, Hope assumes she's fallen asleep. *Sleep would be nice, but I can't afford to. He'll keep looking for her.*

When you are hiding, measuring time becomes impossible. Sometimes moments crawl by and sometimes they fly. Hope keeps track of the familiar noises of the night, listening for any dissonant sound. Her entire body aches from the exertion of the day and from sitting tensely in the same position for so long. She wants to stand and stretch her legs and back but doesn't want to wake her charge.

She shifts her weight, and Montana mumbles something in Spanish. Hope is trying to figure out what she said when a twig snaps somewhere between the boat and the stream. She puts her hand over her mouth to stifle a cry. *No animals around here make that kind of disturbance. It has to be the man looking for Montana.*

She holds her breath as she listens for sounds of him passing on by. There are a couple of splashes further away downstream from her. *He must have started looking for us further upstream and is working his way down. Finally, a stroke of good luck.*

When several moments pass without any other aberrant sounds, Hope relaxes and lets her breath out. Her body had become so hyper-aroused a thin sheet of sticky sweat adheres Montana to her. She peels her off of her until she's sitting up. "Feel better?" she asks.

"Uh-huh."

"I think the sun will be coming up soon. When it does, we'll go looking for my car."

"I'm hungry."

"Me, too. But we'll just have to wait until we can go get something in my car."

"How far is it?"

"I really don't know."

"Far?"

"I wish I knew, but I don't. My hope is that it'll not be too far, and we'll get there some time today."

This less-than-encouraging assessment of their situation causes them both to fall silent and consider what might happen if it takes them more than a day.

How long does it take a person to starve to death? What about a child? Hope wishes she'd paid more attention to Luther when she went hunting and fishing with him as he pointed out wild vegetation humans can eat. She does remember him telling her certain things are poison, but, again, what they look like she cannot tell. *Best thing for us is to not eat anything, no matter how good it looks.*

It's not much longer until the dark of night fades to gray and the sun's first rays light the morning sky.

"Are you ready?" Hope asks.

"Are we going to walk naked?"

Hope laughs. "No. We'll put our clothes back on, even though they'll feel damp and cold."

Once dressed, they crawl out from behind the boat. Having lost her crutch, Hope finds it impossible to stand up without Montana's help.

"Do I need to find you another stick?" the girl asks.

"Maybe in a minute. Let me stretch for a second and look around. When she looks toward the stream she nearly shouts for joy—a tree is lying across the stream, undoubtedly the same tree she got tangled in in what now feels like forever ago. *My car can't be far away.* "We're going to make it!" she exclaims.

"Is he still going to try to kill us?" Montana asks.

Hope's feelings of excitement get pushed out of the way by fear. This time she scans the area around them, looking for any signs of danger. She sees their pursuer's heavy boot print in the mud where he passed by during the night. They are only going in one direction, which tells her he didn't return, at least not this way.

With no signs of danger lurking close by, she says, "Listen, I can swim faster than I can walk. I'm going to stay in the water, but I want you to follow along on the shoreline. Can you do that?"

"I want to be with you."

"I know, and I want you with me. But the water is too cold for you. I won't be that far away. You'll be able to see me. Doing it this way will mean we get to my car more quickly. Then we can turn on the heater and go find something to eat. Doesn't that sound good?"

Montana nods vigorously.

Smiling, Hope says, "Good. Let's get started." She hobbles deeper into the water until she's able to start swimming. The cold water is a shock. *I don't know about this.* Forcing herself to ignore the cold, she starts stroking against the flow of the stream. *I'm glad it's not swollen by recent rains or the current would be too strong.*

She finds there are enough tree snags to use to pull herself along at times to spell the burning muscles in her shoulders and to let her catch her breath. All the while, she keeps a watchful eye on Montana who mirrors her by keeping an eye on her, too.

For the first time since finding her in the RV, her thoughts turn to what's going to happen to her next. *I'm going to have to go to an emergency room with my ankle, and they'll have all kinds of questions about Montana.* Her heart sinks and tears sting her eyes at the thought of Social Services coming and taking Montana away from her. *I want her to stay with me. I can give her a good life. I'll be different with her than I was with Lisa.* But she knows her pleas and wishes will undoubtedly fall on deaf ears.

Maybe I could take her to Justin's before I go to the hospital, and he can watch her until I get out. Nobody has to know about her. She shakes her head at the craziness of such an idea and marvels that she would even think it.

At every bend in the stream she keeps expecting to spy her vehicle, hoping it will be soon because her hands are growing numb and her good foot is, as well.

As luck would have it, just when she thinks she can go no longer, her heart leaps at the sight of her car nestled among some trees. Pointing toward it, she calls out to Montana, "There it is!"

The girl claps her hands and her face lights up. "Come on." She motions for Hope to come to her.

At the shoreline, Hope gladly accepts Montana's help in getting out and then assisting her in reaching her car. They climb inside, and Hope cranks the engine. She leans back against the seat, giving her muscles a second to rest and relax. "I think there's a blanket in the back seat," she tells Montana.

Without a word, Montana climbs over the seat, grips the blanket and drags it with her to the front seat. Wrapping it around herself like a cocoon, she says, "This feels good. I love you."

Those three words unzip Hope's heart, and she begins to sob.

CHAPTER TWENTY-THREE

Panting, Whitney and Carol Anne half run and half walk through the hospital corridor.

Carol Anne says, "We're not supposed to be running."

"Nobody better try and stop us," Whitney replies. "That is, if they know what's good for them."

"How did Hope sound on the phone?"

"Her voice sounded tired and small."

"Small?"

"Yeah, like a little kid. It was weird. I didn't even recognize it at first."

They come to a T in the hallway and stop to read the signs.

"It's this way," Carol Anne says, pointing to the left. As they head in that direction, she asks, "And she didn't say where she'd been or what happened?"

"No," Whitney replies. "All she said was that she'd had an accident and was here at the hospital and could we come. I had dozens of questions but decided they weren't as important as getting hold of you and us meeting here."

"You did the right thing. It's a big deal that she even called."

"That's what I thought."

They come to a nurses' station and stop. A nurse is studying his computer screen but pauses to look up at them. "Can I help you?" he asks.

Whitney says, "Our friend was brought into your emergency room. Where can we find her?"

"What's her name?"

"Hope Rodriguez."

He stands up and comes around the console to stand with them. "I'll take you to her." He walks them to two large doors that say NO ADMITTANCE.

"Is she going to be okay?" Whitney asks.

He swipes his key card, and the doors swing open. "Yes, she'll be fine."

They walk into an area that is a half-circle of eight or ten exam areas separated by curtains. Hospital personnel move in and out of them seamlessly, paying no attention to Whitney and Carol Anne.

The nurse escorting them leads them to one of the curtains, and says, "She's in here."

Inside, they find a doctor standing between them and a view of Hope. The doctor is saying, "So, tomorrow we'll do the surgery on your ankle and hopefully be able to put a walking cast on your leg. But I won't know for certain how much ligament damage is done until I get inside. Hang in there. I'll see you tomorrow." He turns and almost bumps into Whitney. "Oh, excuse me, I didn't hear you come in."

Whitney gives him her best sparkling smile. "Honey, you can bump into me anytime you want to."

He gives her a look that's a cross between thank you and panic, then quickly steps around her and out through the curtain.

They turn their attention to get a full view of Hope. Her leg is in traction, keeping her foot elevated with thin ropes. Her forehead has a purple knot on it, and one cheek has an angry looking scrape. They move to opposite sides of Hope's bed.

"What in the world has happened to you?" Carol Anne cries.

"It's complicated," Hope replies. "But I'm sure glad to see you guys."

"With you it's always complicated, isn't it?" Whitney asks with a smile.

"That's not nice," Carol Anne chastises her friend.

"But it's true," Hope comments. "First thing, I found a little girl and brought her here with me. I don't know where she is or what's being done with her. You've got to find her and tell me what's going on."

They stare at her unblinking.

"Okay," Hope says, "I guess I better start at the beginning, if I can figure out where the beginning actually is."

The story she gives them is filled with partial truths. She leaves off the events that drew her to the railroad trestle, telling them instead she decided to go hiking by moonlight and fell, which resulted in her broken ankle and all the scrapes and bruises. "I don't know how long I was passed out or how many times it happened, but when I finally crawled out of the ravine I discovered this solitary RV. I thought whoever it belonged to would help me, but they weren't there. What I did discover was a little girl handcuffed to a table."

Carol Anne gasps, and Whitney places her palm on her chest, and exclaims, "Dear God in heaven!"

"The man who had her came back to the RV and tried to kill us. I'll tell you about that later. I'm worried about Montana."

Her two friends exchange a dubious look.

"I see you've got a pretty big knot on your head," Carol Anne says. "Have they done any tests yet to see if...you know...maybe it's affected you?"

Hope looks from one to the other. "You think I'm crazy, don't you, that I'm making this all up. Fine then, be that way! I'll get someone else to help me. I need a nurse!" she yells.

"Look, Hope," Whitney says, "you've got to admit this sounds like something out of a Hollywood movie or something. We just want to be sure—"

A nurse hurries in, cutting Whitney off. "You call for a nurse? Are you okay?"

"I remember you," Hope says. "You were here when I came into the ER, right?"

"Yes."

"Please tell my friends that I had a girl with me. They think I've been addled by this blow to my head."

The nurse looks at them. "She's telling the truth. There was a little girl."

Hope grabs her wrist. "Where is she? Where is Montana? I need to see her."

The nurse pries Hopes fingers away from her wrist. "She's okay, Hope. Children's Services is involved. She's in a hospital room for observation. We don't know anything about her."

"Her parents are migrant workers and were in Mississippi when Montana was abducted or bought or whatever was done. She's been bought and sold more than once before arriving here. I think she's a victim of the sex trade."

A wary look creases the nurse's features. "I will be sure and tell the social worker. I think there'll be police or sheriff deputies involved, too. Maybe even FBI, if what you say is true."

"You don't believe me either, do you?!"

"If I didn't, I wouldn't be taking the time to explain things to you and your friends. But that's all I need to say about it, or I might get in trouble." She pats Hope's shoulder. "You need to try to rest." She turns and leaves.

"Wow," Whitney says, "complicated doesn't begin to describe this whole story. I'm sorry we doubted you, Hope."

"It's okay. I know it sounds completely unbelievable. It even sounds that way to me when I tell it, but it's the God's truth. Will you please try to find Montana? That's the girl's name, or the name she told me."

"I'll go," Whitney says. Winking, she adds, "I can be more persuasive than little Carol Anne here." She turns and heads through the curtain.

Carol Anne asks, "Didn't we hear the doctor say you're having surgery tomorrow?"

"Yes. They're going to repair whatever is broken and torn in this ankle of mine."

"Does it hurt?"

"I think they've got me pumped up with pain medicine because it's for sure not hurting like it was." She snaps her fingers. "I forgot! I need you and Whitney to go get my car for me, or get someone to get it. I had to leave it because I was too weak and shaky to drive."

"Sure, we can do that. But what about Justin? Hadn't you rather he get it?"

Hope sighs.

"He doesn't know your here, does he? Why haven't you called him?"

"I didn't want him to come charging up here and be in the way. I'll let him come pick me up tomorrow after the surgery."

Suddenly, they hear Whitney approaching. "She's right in here. She'll tell you everything you need to know." The curtains part, and she leads a middle-aged woman into the area. "This is Hope Rodriguez."

The woman approaches Hope and offers to shake her hand, but Hope folds her arms across her chest. Seemingly unaffected by this brush-off, the woman says, "My name is Beverly Cotton. I'm a social worker with the Department of Children's Services. I'm seeing after Montana."

Immediately, Hope uncrosses her arms. "Is she okay? Where is she? What's going to happen to her?"

"First of all, physically she's going to be fine. She's a little under nourished but getting some good meals will take care of that. She's staying in the hospital tonight just to be certain she's okay, then she'll be released in the morning."

Hope smiles. "She's going to be okay. That makes me happy. I don't suppose there's any way you could bring her here to see me."

"Probably not, but I'll check on that for you. She's asked about you."

Hope's heart swells. She hadn't expected news like that. "She's pretty special."

"The other thing is," Beverly begins, "it may take some time to locate her parents, if, as I've been told, you're correct in believing they are migrant workers."

Everyone's eyes are on Hope. She holds her breath, believing something is about to happen but uncertain what it is.

"So," Beverly continues, "we need her to live with someone until we locate her parents."

It takes a couple of beats before Hope gets it. Her eyes grow wide. "Me? You want me to take her?"

"Yes, that is if after I interview you and feel you are a safe place for Montana."

"You won't have to worry about that," Whitney cuts in as she wipes tears from her cheeks. "That woman right there will move heaven and earth to protect that child."

Hope's throat is so full of emotion she cannot speak. Carol Anne takes her hand between hers, and says, "Oh, Hope, this is wonderful."

Beverly, says, "We can do the interview now, if that's okay with you, Hope."

Hope nods vigorously.

Looking at the other two women, Beverly says, "If you two can leave us alone..."

"Sure, sure," Whitney says, "we understand. We'll come back tomorrow, Hope."

"Good luck with the surgery," Carol Anne adds.

*****

Two hours later, Whitney and Carol Anne drive slowly along a gravel road.

"Do you think this is it, this time?" Whitney asks. "Because we've already had to turn around three times looking for Hope's car."

Carol Anne refers to a piece of paper she wrote directions on. "Honestly, you're guess is as good as mine, but I think this might be the right road."

"We are in the middle of nowhere. If we get lost, I'm going to blame you."

Suddenly, Carol Anne sees a flash of color among the trees to her right. "Stop! There it is!"

Whitney halts the car, and they get out. "What in the world is Hope doing coming to a place like this? It gives me the creeps." She looks around and sees Carol Anne following a foot path. "Hey, where are you going?!"

"I want to see where this goes."

"Well, wait for me." She hustles after her.

They don't go far before they find the railroad track and spy the railroad trestle. Stopping where the rail line ends, they silently take in the scene of the abandoned trestle and the stream below.

After a few moments, Carol Anne says, "Are you thinking what I'm thinking?"

Nodding, Whitney says, "Yeah. I don't think our girlfriend told us the whole truth."

CHAPTER TWENTY-FOUR

Hope lies quietly in her hospital bed, listening to the sounds of nurses in the hallway. *I'm glad they finally put me in a regular room, even if it's only going to be for one night.* She closes her eyes and tries to force her body to relax, but with her leg in traction, it is impossible.

Instead, she thinks about the interview and being told she was approved for temporary fostering Montana, "until we find her parents." To be given a second chance at being a parent would have been a wish beyond the limits of her imagination.

She remembers lying in the stream, wondering why jumping off the trestle didn't kill her, and asking herself if it was God intervening in her life. *Used to, I would say it was luck or fate, but since meeting Michael and going to church it makes me wonder if God has a purpose for me to fulfill.*

And now, that purpose has landed in her lap. *Another daughter.* Beverly's words of caution to not get too attached landed on deaf ears. All Hope could hear was that she was going to be a mother again.

She spends some time imagining what their life will look like together. But then, her thoughts turn to Michael and the aborted session she had with him. *I was just kidding myself in thinking there was something special between us. Who am I to him? Nothing, at least nothing special.* In spite of the hurt and disappointment, she smiles to herself as she remembers how moving it was the first time he called her by her name. 'Hello, Hope.' A tear trickles down the side of her face.

"Hello, Hope." *His voice sounds so real.* "Are you asleep?"

Her eyes pop open, and Michael is standing beside her bed. *A dream?* She reaches toward him, and he takes her hand. *Not a dream!*

"Hey there," he says quietly. "I hear you had a pretty bad tumble."

She finds her voice. "How did you know?"

"Your friend, Carol Anne, got in touch with me."

She pulls her hand back and slips it under her blanket. "Why are you here?"

"I wanted to see how you're doing and if you're going to be okay."

Confusion spins Hope's thoughts. "I don't understand."

"Perhaps I shouldn't have come. Do you want me to leave?"

"No," she answers more quickly than she would have liked. "I just...I mean, after our last meeting, I thought..."

He runs his fingers through his thick hair. "Yeah, about that. I'm sorry for how I acted. I got afraid. Truth is—you scare me, Hope."

"What in the world are you talking about? Why would you be afraid of me?"

"Ever since I was a kid, I've had to live a very measured life, always being careful to do and say the right thing. That means I've always kept my emotions in check, never letting my true emotions show without first figuring out an appropriate way of expressing them. But when I'm with you I feel so relaxed and comfortable in a way I've never felt with anyone else. That's why the other night scared me. I had never been so real as I was at that moment."

If that fateful meeting broke Hope's heart, his words now stitch it back together. She reaches for him with both arms.

He hesitates for a second, then eases into her embrace and gently returns it. He whispers in her ear, "I'm sorry I hurt you."

"It's okay," she sighs, as warmth fills her body. "Everything is okay now." *Do I dare kiss his neck? Will that be too much and it break this spell?* Before she can decide what to do, he loosens his embrace and lifts his head until he faces her. He's so close she can feel his warm breath brush against her lips. She tilts her head toward him and closes her eyes.

But instead of feeling his lips against hers, she hears him say, "I can't. Not here." And she feels him move away.

Opening her eyes, she sees his face is flushed and his eyes ablaze.

He takes a deep breath and lets it out slowly. "Oh my, Hope, you have cast a spell on me. What is it about you?"

She blushes. "I don't know. I do know I've never behaved around other men the way I am when I'm with you. I'm ashamed to tell you I've been with lots of men, but I was always a chameleon with them, being the way they wanted me to be, or at least the way I thought they wanted me to be. But it was all an act. With you though, I'm me...real, and it feels nice. No, better than nice. It feels unbelievable."

They look at each other for a few moments uncertain what to say next.

Finally, Michael points at her ankle. "Why don't you tell me what happened?"

Hope relays to him the same version of the truth she told her two friends. "I feel awfully foolish about it all now. A small thing turned into a big thing, but I'm going to get to be a mother again."

He holds her eyes with his, and says, "I don't believe you."

Frowning, she says, "Don't believe what?"

"I don't believe your story about the hiking accident because I don't think you're telling all the truth. I've no doubt there's truth in it, but I suspect you're leaving things out."

She tries to tear her eyes from his but can't escape the grasp of his stare. She tries to sound indignant, "I don't like being called a liar." But her voice lacks conviction.

"I'll make you a promise," he says. "If I'm wrong in my suspicions, I will apologize all over myself and beg your forgiveness. Just tell me I'm wrong."

She turns her head, looks at the wall and bites her bottom lip. "Why don't you believe me?"

"Because I know how upset and hurt you were after our meeting, and then there was the scene when you stopped in the street in front of my house and the policeman came. I know that humiliated you."

Tears sting Hope's eyes, and she squeezes her fists. She feels him lay his hand on her shoulder, but she refuses to look at him.

"Hope," he says softly, "I think you tried to kill yourself by jumping off that railroad trestle."

"What makes you say that? I didn't say anything about a railroad trestle."

"Carol Anne told me. She and Whitney saw it when they went to find your car. They both believe, as I do, that you jumped off in an attempt to end your life."

Turning her head toward him, she presses her cheek against the back of his hand. "It's true. But I didn't go there intending to do it. It was just a spur of the moment decision when my depression told me everything was hopeless. It's scary how despondent I can feel in one moment and in the next moment everything can be wonderful—like right now." She gives him a weak smile.

"It makes me sad that you would feel so desperate. But you've got to remember and think about the people you would leave behind if you killed yourself, how awful they would feel. I've seen it before. The friends and family of the victim are left with a tremendous load of guilt because they feel like they should have done or said something to save the one they love. Don't misunderstand me, I'm not trying to make you feel guilty about what you did. I'm just trying to help you remember that there are people who do care about you, like Whitney and Carol Anne, and now this little girl...and me, too."

Hope hangs on every word and holds her breath to see if he will include himself in the people who care about her. "I had decided you didn't...care about me, other than I was just one of the members of your church. I've come to view you as my anchor, the one who helps me feel secure and safe. You don't understand. I've not had that since my parents died when I was a teenager. I do love Carol Anne and Whitney, they are like my family, but they don't give me what you do. Does any of this make sense?"

"Yes, I think it does. It's just I'm not the one you should rely on as your anchor. Especially when I don't feel like my own life is anchored." He pauses before adding, "You don't know everything about me and wouldn't feel the same about me if you did."

Hope tries to unzip his last comment to see what's inside but finds nothing. "I cannot imagine anything that would make me change how I see you."

"That's another conversation for another time. Right now, what you need to do is go to sleep and rest." He drags the heavy reclining chair over to her bedside and sits down. "I'm going to stay here with you tonight."

Hope makes no pretense of hiding her surprise. "You don't have to do that for me. You need your rest, too. You can go home; I'll be fine."

Crossing his legs, he leans back and says, "Nope. I'm staying. You close your eyes and sleep."

She closes her eyes and after a few moments says, "Will you read to me?"

"Read what?"

"I don't care. I just like the sound of your voice."

Michael gets up, looks in the drawer of her bedside table and pulls out a Gideon Bible. Flipping some pages, he begins reading, "The Lord is my Shepherd, I shall not want..."

CHAPTER TWENTY-FIVE

At 7:00 the next morning, Michael pulls out of the hospital parking lot and heads home. His back and shoulders ache from trying to sleep in the chair in Hope's room, and it feels like he has a pinched nerve in his neck, which makes it difficult for him to turn his head.

When he went to visit her, it wasn't his intention to stay the night, but it seemed like the natural thing to do, more natural than the thoughtful things he used to do for Sarah. Being kind to Sarah was hard work because she could be so defensive and could find an ulterior motive in anything he did. Plus, she was so exacting in how she wanted things done. *Hope is nothing like that, which is why she is so refreshing.*

His conscience taps him on his shoulder and asks, *But what are your intentions with her?* This is not the first time he's posed the question to himself. His answers to it have ranged from *I don't know,* to *continue to deepen our relationship,* to *seduce her and get her in bed,* with multiple variances to each of those thoughts.

When he finally arrives at his street, he forces his body to relax. *A long, hot shower. That's what I need.* But as he spots his house, a bolt of electricity shoots through him, stiffening every part of his body. Sitting in the driveway is a police cruiser.

His initial thought is to drive past and avoid whatever is awaiting him. *Maybe the officer won't notice me.* Unfortunately, that idea gets shot down when officer Jessie Pinkston steps out of the police car and looks right at Michael's approaching vehicle.

Reluctantly, Michael turns into his driveway and stops. His heart is racing, as a sense of impending doom floods him.

Jessie's expression appears disinterested, but Michael doesn't trust it. *Be careful, look out for a trap.* He forces his face into a smile, and says, "Officer Pinkston, good morning."

Pinkston gives him a once-over look, making Michael painfully aware of how disheveled he must look.

Pinkston says, "I thought I might talk with you before you left for work. But, apparently, you didn't spend the night at your house last night." His words are delivered calmly and politely, but Michael hears the accusation just the same.

Keeping the smile pasted on his face, Michael says, "Yeah, last night was a bit unusual. One of the members of my church had a bad accident, and I stayed the night at the hospital to make sure they were going to be okay."

"And?"

"And what?"

"Are they going to be okay?"

"Oh, sure, sure, they're going to be fine, though they'll have to get used to walking with a cast on their leg."

Pinkston purses his lips. "I see. You must be talking about Hope Rodriguez. I heard some of that traffic over the police scanner last night."

This unsettles Michael even more, though he's not sure why.

"Small towns," Pinkston says. "Everybody pretty much know everybody's business."

"Or at least they think they do," Michael replies. He hears the defensive tone in his voice, and quickly adds, "I'm not saying there's anything wrong with that, it's just there are times people might be mistaken in their interpretation of what they see or hear. Wouldn't you agree?"

A smile pulls at one corner of Pinkston's mouth.

Is that a smile of agreement or a smile of a cat about to catch a mouse?

"Can we talk inside?" Pinkston asks.

"Uh, sure, if you think that's best. The place may be a mess. You know my wife died, and I haven't really been keeping up with the housework." His last words are his attempt to soften Pinkston and at least get some sympathy from him.

Whether it works or not, he can't tell because the officer makes no reply. Instead, he reaches inside the police car and retrieves a leather bag. Motioning toward the house, he says, "You lead the way."

Michael walks up the sidewalk as his mind peppers him with possible reasons why the policeman wants to talk with him. His conclusion is it has to have something to do with Sarah's death.

He takes his keys out of his pocket to open the front door, but his hands are so sweaty the keys slip and fall to the ground. Bending over to pick them up, he says, "Lack of sleep has me all thumbs this morning. You ever try to sleep in a hospital room?" Again, trying to elicit at least a thread of compassion from Pinkston.

"Yes," he replies. "My wife died with cancer last year, and I spent the last three months with her in the hospital."

Michael's hopes for sympathy evaporate immediately. "I'm so sorry," he mumbles as he opens the door.

Once inside, he motions toward the couch. "Why don't you have a seat? You want some coffee or water or something?"

"No, I'm fine," Pinkston says. "You've got me curious though."

"Curious about what?"

"When my wife was sick, our preacher came to visit regularly, but he never spent the night. Isn't that a little unusual?"

Michael's failed attempts to get ahead of the conversation compound his anxiety and fear. *How do I answer his question without it leading to more questions or suspicions?* He decides saying little is better than launching into an elaborate explanation. "That's a fair assessment," he says.

Pinkston opens his mouth to say something, then closes it. With a wave of his hand, he says, "Doesn't matter. That's not why I came anyway."

Here it comes.

"I want to talk with you about your wife's death."

Just what I expected. Rather than saying anything, Michael holds his tongue and waits for Pinkston to proceed.

"Here's the thing," Pinkston says, "I keep wondering why your wife didn't leave a suicide note. Not that it's terribly unusual. As a matter of fact, about fifty percent of the time there isn't a note. But a woman like your wife, a woman who used to work at a library and must have valued the written word—I just think she would have left a note."

Michael is so floored by Pinkston knowing this about Sarah he can't get his breath. He simply returns the officer's intense gaze until he can find some air and his voice. Coughing to clear his throat, he says, "I can see why you'd feel that way, but for some reason she chose not to leave a note. To do such a horrible thing to herself says to me she wasn't thinking clearly anyway. I guess the last thing on her mind was writing a note of explanation."

"Well," Pinkston draws the word out, creating the effect of a maestro stretching out his arms before an orchestra before delivering the downbeat to begin. "The problem is, I believe there was a note, a note you evidently didn't want anyone to find."

Michael's heart beats like a big bass drum. "I...I don't...I mean...why..."

Pinkston says, "You remember when you dropped your glass in the kitchen when I was here that night, and Liz swept it up?"

Michael stares mutely.

"Remember that little piece of paper I pulled out? That little piece of paper really got me thinking, thinking so much that I decided I would try to find if there were other pieces that might go with it."

Michael tries to swallow, but his mouth is as dry as the Sahara.

"Turns out," Pinkston continues, "there were some pieces that belonged to the piece I found. It wasn't easy because I had to wait for the lab to compare them to determine if they were indeed the same kind of paper." Reaching in his leather bag, he pulls out a large Ziploc bag that has a sheet of paper in it that has been taped together. He lays it on the coffee table between them and turns it so Michael can read it.

Michael feels the blood draining from him. It is the note he found beside Sarah, the one he tore up and threw away. He looks up at Pinkston and tries to form a question, but his brain won't work.

"You're wondering how?" Pinkston reads his mind. "I got nosey and went through your garbage can outside. It took a while to find them all and then another while to put them together so they formed the original note." He sits back on the couch while the heaviness of the evidence settles on Michael's shoulders.

Michael looks from him to the note and back at him but still can't figure out what he should say.

Pinkston says, "What I can't figure out is why you didn't want anyone to know about the note. 'You're welcome' seems like such an innocuous message. What were you afraid of?"

It strikes Michael that what he says next may be the most important words of his life. He hangs his head and in a small voice, says, "I was afraid people would say the suicide was all my fault, that Sarah killed herself as a favor to me. And if that happened, it would ruin my ministry."

The silence that follows Michael's confession lasts so long he looks up at Pinkston to see if he's still there.

When their eyes meet, Pinkston says, "That makes sense, I guess, in a pitiful, selfish way."

'Pitiful' and 'selfish' are like nails, pinning Michael's hands to a cross.

Pinkston continues, "Now we've come to the real problem. You see, Sarah did not put that note together. Her fingerprints were nowhere on it. Your fingerprints were on it because you found it and tore it up. But there are fingerprints of someone else, too. What I want you to tell me is, who is that other person? And what does 'You're welcome' mean?"

CHAPTER TWENTY-SIX

"How are we supposed to work on our marriage when we never talk or visit with each other?" Jed asks.

Liz hears the agitation rising in his voice. "Jed, we spent our entire marriage working on it, or at least I did."

A butterfly zigzags its way between them as they sit on one of the park benches placed on the town square by the local V.F.W. It's Saturday, so the courthouse is closed, and there's very little traffic in town.

Pulling her eyes away from the butterfly, Liz looks at Michael, and says, "I only agreed to this meeting in hopes it would help you better understand my position, even though I've stated it to you repeatedly."

Jed rubs his hand over the beard stubble on his cheek, stubble long enough that his action produces a scraping sound. That, and the bags under his tired, bloodshot eyes, prick Liz's conscience as she knows she's the reason for his mental anguish.

"I'm sorry," he says. "I just can't get my head wrapped around the fact we're getting a divorce. Me—you and I—getting a divorce. It's like an oxymoron. People who've heard about it have told me they can't believe it. Some of them are really shaken."

Nodding, Liz says, "I know. I've heard the same kinds of comments. And ... honestly, I'm having difficulty getting used to the sound of it myself."

He reaches for her hand, but she leans away. Pulling himself back in, Jed says, "Then why are you doing it? It's not what I want. This divorce is because of you, not me."

"That's a very convenient way to think about it, isn't it? It absolves you of all blame and makes me the guilty party, as if you were the perfect husband. The public doesn't know the Jed that I know; the conceited, narcissistic, self-serving Jed. I've always protected you from letting that being seen. I allowed myself to accept those traits because you used them to better our town. I guess you could say I discounted them and made myself focus on your good traits, or at least on the good outcome of your bad traits."

Jed looks bewildered. "I don't know what you're talking about."

"I know. And that's what's so sad. It took me all these years to come to the realization that you don't see yourself the way you really are. Even when I've tried to, in a sense, hold a mirror up in front of you and tell you these things, you looked right through the mirror, shrugged your shoulders and said you didn't get it."

"This is about the affair, isn't it? You're still not over the affair."

"Oh my gosh!" Liz snaps. "This—this right here, this part of this conversation—that's one of the main reasons I'm divorcing you. You are not hearing anything I'm saying. It's pointless." She stops and stares at him.

Several moments pass, then Jed says, "Can we at least remain friends? Just because we're divorcing doesn't mean we have to become enemies."

"Well, you know...that's what I was hoping and felt like we had a verbal agreement we could settle the technical issues of the divorce between us. But that ship sank when I learned you hired Adam Cartwright to represent you. I mean, Adam Cartwright?! What are you wanting to get out of me?"

Jed cannot hide his surprise she knows this. "Now look, Liz—"

"Don't 'now look, Liz' me," she cuts in. "We both know exactly what kind of divorce lawyer he is. He will advise you to go for the jugular, whatever you think that might be."

"I don't blame you for being mad about that. I didn't seek him out, it just sort of happened. I was having a beer the other night at TJ's and Adam came in and sat down with me at the bar. We started shooting the breeze, one thing led to another, and I ended up telling him about the divorce. He said, 'Why don't you let me represent you?', and I said, 'Sure, why not?' I'll tell him I changed my mind if you want me to."

Liz sighs. "The problem with your story about you and Adam is I have no way to know if it's the truth or not. You are so good at twisting a story and still keeping it close to the truth." She stands up. "Here's my truth: You hire whomever you want to represent you, and I'll do the same. We'll end up spending all our money on lawyers' fees, and Mark will have nothing for college." Turning quickly, she walks to her car and gets in.

She watches Jed in her rearview mirror staring at her with his mouth agape as she drives away.

He is exhausting to talk to! He and Adam at TJ's—what a pitiful sight. Two middle-aged men, alone at a bar, especially at TJ's. The small tavern has a less-than-stellar reputation, having served alcohol to minors, bringing in a stripper on weekends, and, of course, the regular fights that break out between drunken friends.

She drives slowly and lowers the driver's side window. As the wind rifles through her hair, she tries to imagine it rinsing out the exasperation she feels. For the most part the exercise is helpful, but she's left with a sadness borne from the loss of a childhood dream of getting married and living with the same man into old age.

Knowing Mark is at a friend's, she dreads going home to an empty house. So, she drives through the streets of town, looking at Spring's improvement to the landscape. Redbuds and Dogwoods work their magic and draw her attention. Some daffodils and tulips are clustered around tree trunks while others have created their solitary pool of color in the middle of a yard. Robins hop through yards looking for a morning meal.

Suddenly, she thinks about Michael. *Maybe it would help to talk to him. It might get me out of this funk I'm in.*

She pilots her way toward the side of town he lives on and turns down his street. She sees the patrol car but misinterprets which house it is sitting outside of and believes it is Michael's neighbor.

When it becomes obvious where the cruiser is sitting, she remembers the last time a policeman was there. She pulls in behind the car and stops. *Surely Michael hasn't done something to himself.* Her imagination runs wild with horrible thoughts and images, and a feeling of trepidation takes hold of her.

Bracing herself, she gets out of the car and silently enters the front door of the house without knocking. She hears Michael's voice in the kitchen, "I know it sounds stupid. I just panicked."

She makes her way to the kitchen, causing Michael and officer Pinkston to turn to her.

"Liz?" Michael asks. "What are you doing here?"

"I was in town and decided to come by and see if you might, perhaps, have the time to discuss something with me." She looks at Jessie. "What brings you here?"

Tipping his hat to her, he replies, "Just following up with a few questions related to Mrs. Trent's death."

"You mean her suicide."

He sucks between his teeth, and says, "Maybe. Maybe not. There's been a new development in the case."

Confused, Liz looks from the officer to Michael and back. "New development? What are you talking about?

He flips through some pages of his notepad and begins relaying to her the details that brought him to Michael's house.

When he gets to the part about the letter and fingerprints he hands the ziploc bag to her. Liz's jaws pull taut, and her eyes burn holes in Michael's. "What is this about?"

Michael then picks up the story and explains his actions, trying hard to remember, word-for-word, what he told Jessie and making sure he punctuates the story with an appropriate number of tears. "I know I was stupid," he finishes. "But when I finally came to my senses, the lie was in place, and like a bell that's been rung, I didn't know how to un-ring it. What do you think I should do?"

Liz looks at Jessie. "What's next?"

"I want to know if he wrote the letter and what that message meant."

Looking back at Michael, she asks, "Do you know the answers? No, wait, don't say a word. I'm not a lawyer, but I think you shouldn't say anything else."

"Now wait just a minute," Jessie says.

"You haven't charged him with anything, have you?" Liz asks.

"No, not yet."

"Then he doesn't have to say a thing, does he?"

Jessie's face reddens, and he returns his notebook to his pocket. For a moment, he looks as though he's going to offer a rebuttal, instead, though, he walks past her toward the front door.

Once he's gone, Michael says, "Oh, Liz, I'm so glad you—"

She holds up her hand to cut him off. "Don't, just don't say anything. I'm going to leave now. I've got to have time to think about all this."

CHAPTER TWENTY-SEVEN

Consciousness comes slowly to Hope. She hears a word or two, then disappears into the dark. A flicker of light, a blurry image of someone in her room, both dissolve into blackness. Until finally, she comes fully awake. It feels like only moments ago that the anesthesiologist asked her to count backward from ten.

Whitney and Carol Anne stand side-by-side at the foot of her bed, smiling at her like two doting aunts.

"I think she looks good for what she's been through," Whitney says to Carol Anne. "Don't you think she looks good?"

Carol Anne replies, "I'll say she looks better than might be expected, given what she's been through in the last few days."

"No, no, she looks better than that. I bet she caught the eye of some of these men around here." To Hope, she asks, "Where's that good-looking surgeon? Is he single? Available?"

Carol Anne doesn't give Hope a chance to answer. "Hope's been awake less than a minute, and you've already turned the conversation toward sex. Honestly Whitney, you need to take something for your libido."

Looking at Hope, Whitney says, "Somebody else in this room might need something for their libido." To make certain the target of her comment is clear, she nods her head toward Carol Anne.

Hope gives only a small laugh for fear of irritating her bruised ribs. "You two need your own YouTube channel."

"YouTube?!" Whitney exclaims. "Did you hear that? Our friend who still lives in the 1900's, as far as technology is concerned, actually knows about YouTube."

"That is a surprise," Carol Anne agrees.

"Okay, I give up," Hope says. "I don't have any fight in me right now."

Her two friends separate and step forward to opposite sides of her bed. Hope offers them her hands, and they eagerly take them. "I really appreciate you all being here for me."

"That's what friends do for friends," Whitney says as she squeezes her hand.

Carol Anne asks, "How are you feeling?"

"Still a little groggy, but my ankle isn't hurting."

"Yeah, we talked with your surgeon who told us he did a nerve block to cut down on pain, but after it wears off, it could bark at you a bit. The good news is the ligaments he was worried about weren't torn badly enough to do anything to them. They'll heal on their own."

"And my ankle?"

"A couple of screws should hold it together so it can heal."

Whitney comments, "No weight bearing for two weeks, so you'll be using crutches or a wheelchair. Then you'll have a walking boot."

"You can forget about the wheelchair!" Hope answers sharply. "I won't use a wheelchair."

"Okay, okay," Whitney says. "What's that about?"

"I lived with a man for a little while who was wheelchair bound and had people waiting on him hand and foot. Then one day, when he thought I'd gone to the store, I caught him walking out of the bedroom into the kitchen. There was absolutely nothing wrong with him physically. So, I won't be using a wheelchair."

"Whew, that is messed up. Don't worry, no one can make you use a wheelchair. But you'll have to practice some with the crutches. I had to use them one time, and it's a lot harder than you might think."

"I guess you were by yourself last night," Carol Anne says.

Hope starts to lie about Michael but stops herself. "No, I wasn't. Michael stayed with me last night."

Her friends look at each other and smile.

"All night?" Whitney asks.

"All night."

Whitney rolls her eyes. "Hope and the preacher man...mmm, mmm, mmm. I don't know what to think."

Carol Anne, says, "I called him just because I thought a visit might cheer you up. I never thought he'd spend the night. Why didn't you tell him to leave?"

"I didn't want him to leave," Hope replies. "I'm more comfortable around him than any man I've ever known—ever."

"So, what are your plans for him?" Whitney asks.

"I don't know. Right now, I just like being around him."

"You know, his wife hasn't been dead that long," Carol Anne comments.

"What's that got to do with it?" Whitney asks.

"I mean, the man needs time to grieve. I don't want people getting the wrong idea about Hope."

"You worry too much about what people think, but that's your business. Life's short. If you see what you want, I say go for it."

"Okay you two."

Carol Anne looks at her. "I called Justin this morning, so you know he's going to come rolling in here like he's the hero or something."

This time, Hope rolls her eyes. "He is such a child. But he'll do anything I ask, so that's worth something."

"You better believe it is," Whitney says. "Of course, Luther was the same way. And I'll bet you that preacher will be eating out of your palm pretty soon. You need to give me some lessons on how you do it."

Hope and Carol Anne laugh.

As if he was waiting on his cue, Justin barrels through the door, huffing and puffing. "Oh my God, you're alive!" he exclaims and rushes to Hope's bedside, almost knocking Carol Anne down in the process. "I thought you went back to Luther. Then, when I found out you hadn't, I went wild with worry. What are you doing here in the hospital? Carol Anne just called and said you were here, she didn't say why. What happened? Are you okay? Did someone kidnap you? Were you in a wreck? Oh my God, I'm so glad you're okay." He bends over and smothers her not only with kisses but his girth as well.

"Okay, okay, okay," Hope cries out. "You're going to kill me if you don't give me some air."

Snapping back up, Justin says, "I'm sorry. I'm just so glad to see you. Tell me what happened."

"Y'all are going to have to excuse me," Carol Anne says. "I've got someone I'm supposed to meet. I'll touch base with all of you later."

"Well I'm not going anywhere," Whitney says. "'Cause I want to see this show. Go ahead, Hope, tell him what happened."

As Hope begins the story, Carol Anne slips out and heads to her car. She takes a moment to try and steel her nerves for the meeting she's going to. It's completely against her better judgment to be going because she doesn't know who the person is that she's meeting. It was a late-night phone call last night that set the plans in motion.

Carol Anne stared at the number on her ringing phone but didn't recognize it. *Probably another prank call about the Biddle lawsuit.* So, she ignored it. Several seconds later, she got a notification of a voicemail. Her experience with the prank calls was if they didn't get the satisfaction of giving her an earful live, they hung up.

Opening her phone, she pressed the button to play the voicemail.

A woman's voice said, "You don't know me, but you're going to want to because I'm going to join your lawsuit against Lloyd Biddle. And I will be the star witness. If you want to discuss this with me, meet me at Bob Noble Park in Paducah, tomorrow at one o'clock. Meet me on the south side of the pond."

Carol Anne starts her car and punches the park address into her GPS. Taking a deep breath, she heads that way.

To her relief she finds several people are making use of the park: bicyclists, joggers, moms pushing strollers, people having picnic meals in the pavilions. *They say there's safety in numbers. Even if this woman is some kind of psycho, surely she won't try something in front of all these people.*

She follows the drive to the pond and parks, then checks her directions and takes the walkway that circles the pond. As she gets close to the south side, she spies a woman sitting on a bench, wearing a jogging suit and large sunglasses.

The woman's head turns in Carol Anne's direction, but it's impossible to tell if she's looking at her or not. When Carol Anne gets closer, the woman pats the spot beside her as if inviting her to have a seat.

Carol Anne's nerves are pulled taut as she tries to be prepared for anything. She sits down and looks at the pond.

"Thank you for coming," the woman says. "My name is Heather Brown. I'm the Guidance Counselor at the school where Lloyd Biddle is the principal."

Her voice is shaking, indicating to Carol Anne she's as nervous as she is. Carol Anne holds her breath in anticipation of what might come next.

Heather continues, "When I was a student in high school, Lloyd Biddle was my principal."

Carol Anne turns and looks at Heather, who takes off her glasses and returns her gaze. No amount of makeup can hide the fact she's spent a number of hours crying. Carol Anne's mind races ahead, wondering if—

Nodding, Heather says, "Yes, what he did to you, he did to me. Like you, I believed all his lies. I gave him my virginity, and he broke my heart. I've let him blackmail me with the threat of firing me if I ever told."

Carol Anne starts to speak, but Heather stops her. "There's more. I knew Lisa Rodriguez was being bullied, I knew she was seeing Mark Rochelle and I knew she was pregnant.

CHAPTER TWENTY-EIGHT

Hope rests on her hospital bed, waiting for Justin to return from buying a pair of sweatpants that will fit over the cast on her leg. Whitney had offered to do the shopping, but Justin was insistent he be allowed to do it. "It's the least you can let me do, since you didn't even try to call me when you got to the hospital." He looked so pitiful Hope agreed to give him the job.

The longer he takes to return, the more apprehensive she gets. *There is no telling what he will bring back.* Besides, Beverly is supposed to be bringing Montana to her room to go home with her.

Just then, there is a tap on her door, and it swings open. A slightly-built woman, barely five feet tall, walks in. Her white hair sits in a bun on the back of her head. She reaches in the over-sized pocket of the white physician's coat she wears and pulls out a pen as she approaches Hope's bed. From the other pocket she retrieves a rolled-up sheaf of papers. Taking hold of the rolling overbed table, she lowers it and unrolls the papers on the table. Then she looks Hope straight in the eye.

Hope squirms. The woman's eyes are the color of slate and seem to hold a wisdom Hope has never encountered. She feels exposed, as if those eyes are looking inside her like an x-ray. On closer inspection, Hope notices deep crow's feet accenting the woman's eyes and lines on her cheeks that probably reveal dimples when she smiles.

Without preamble or warning, she says, "You have experienced much pain."

Hope is caught off guard by this and by the woman's accent, which Hope can't quite identify. "Well...yeah...I fell and broke my ankle...and—"

"That is not what I am talking about." She points at Hope's cast, "Anyone can see you have had a recent injury." Then, pointing at Hope's chest and head, she says, "I'm talking about pain there and there."

Hope winces as a sharp pain strikes her chest, and she feels the beginnings of a headache. Flashes of memories fly through her mind, as if this unknown visitor has triggered a tornado. A panic attack approaches.

At that moment, the woman rolls the overbed table out of the way and takes Hope's hand between her small, warm hands. "It's okay. I am here. Let the storm come so that it will pass."

Anxiety thrusts its arm up from Hope's chest and into her throat where it threatens to squeeze it shut. She tries to get a breath but can only gasp for air. Her heart beats with the force and speed of a jackhammer. She looks up at her visitor and sees the calm confidence in her eyes.

"It won't last forever," her visitor says. "Let it come, let it pass."

For what seems like forever, but in real time is only minutes, Hope's symptoms rage through her body. Several times she thinks she is going to die. But, eventually, the panic attack subsides, and her breathing and heart rate return to normal.

"You see?" the woman says with a small smile, "You survived." She lets go of Hope's hand, and says, "My name is Dr. Miller. I am a staff psychiatrist here at the hospital. I am very pleased to meet you, Hope. It is a lovely name you have, a name full of promise and expectation. But I sense those promises and expectations have yet to be fulfilled. Am I right?"

At the title psychiatrist, Hope pulls the protective iron wall around herself that she has used half her life. However, when she visualizes her wall she is shocked to see Dr. Miller standing inside the wall with her. Dozens of questions jostle for position as she tries to figure out what's going on. Wary and skeptical, she asks, "Who are you, and why are you here?"

With an inscrutable expression in place, Dr. Miller answers, "I believe I have already answered the first question. And you know the answer to the second one, so why don't you tell me?"

"How do you know so much about me?"

"So, you want to avoid my question. That's okay. I don't know details about you, other than what the doctors have told me about your recent injuries. But I am seventy-two years old and have been doing this work a long, long time. I trust my instincts. You, Hope, have been damaged, perhaps by the choices of others, perhaps by your own choices, or perhaps by both. If I am wrong, please be honest and tell me so."

Hope wants to tell she is completely off base, but for reasons she doesn't understand she can't get the words out of her mouth. Instead, she gives silent assent to Dr. Miller's assessment.

Sitting down on the edge of the bed, Dr. Miller says, "Good. Your silence tells me I'm right, but it also tells me you want to be honest, in spite of the fact you have lived a somewhat dishonest life."

Hope starts to protest, but Dr. Miller continues, "I don't mean you've engaged in criminal activities and are wanted by the law. I am simply saying you've not always been honest with others, with those you've had relationships with. For instance, this story you told the E.R. doctor that you fell while hiking. He does not believe that is true, and neither do I. And quite honestly, that is why I am here."

Finally, Hope connects the dots and understands why Dr. Miller's visit occurred. Hope looks at her for a second before saying, "Have you ever made a decision to do something in a moment and in the very next second regretted doing it?"

A smile broad enough to show her dimples spreads across Dr. Miller's face. "Oh my, yes, many times. I dare say anyone who denies such a thing is a liar. For certain, anyone who grew up in South Africa when I did would have to admit they've done it. We are imperfect people making imperfect decisions, living with unwanted consequences."

Hope marvels at her words. "I've never heard such a succinct description of my life."

"Your life? Oh, I thought we were talking about mine."

Hope's walls move in closer, bringing her face to face with Dr. Miller. But instead of feeling claustrophobic and uneasy, she relaxes and returns her smile.

"Thank you," Dr. Miller says.

"For what?"

"For letting me in."

A comfortable quiet fills the space between them.

Dr. Miller says, "I'd like to hear your story, if you'd like to share it."

In a response that shocks Hope, she opens her mouth and tells her life story, every good and bad thing that's ever happened to her, every good and bad thing she's ever done. Tears and smiles punctuate the story. Her heart swells with joy, and it aches with pain, like a rising and falling tide.

Dr. Miller alternately pats her hand, hands her a tissue, smiles with her, and shares a tear.

When Hope finishes, she feels exhausted but lighter, as if some unknown weight has been lifted from her shoulders. "Thank you," she says.

"No, thank you," Dr. Miller replies. "You've honored me by sharing your story. What I would love is if you would perhaps come visit with me after you leave the hospital. But experience has taught me that no matter what you might promise now, you probably won't follow through with the visit. I look at this as my one shot with you, and I've got to make the most of it. So, with your permission I'd like to give you my reaction to your story and how it has impacted you."

"I would love for you to do that," Hope answers.

"That's because you don't know what I'm going to say, for I don't intend to give you an assessment that's intended to make you feel better, though it might. But what I will say to you is completely honest. Are you still willing?"

Nodding, Hope says, "Yes, please."

"You have abandonment issues, Hope. Your parents' lives were snuffed out in an instant, leaving you on your own. Your grandmother, a poor soul in her own right, did what she thought was helpful, but in the end, it traumatized you even more. Therefore, you have felt insecure ever since. You've looked to men to give you a sense of security, going from one to another, initially feeling good about it, but it never satisfies. So you move on to another one.

"You are involved with this pastor in the same quest for security. He makes you feel like no other man has. That feeling is security, not love, although love can be a part of it. But you must be very careful, for my gut says he is not a man that can be trusted.

"The answer to your issue is to quit looking outside yourself for a sense of security. That is something that needs to come from within you. That needs to be your quest—to dig deep inside yourself, to find something that can fill you and satisfy your longing for security." She reaches inside her pocket and pulls out a business card. Laying on the overbed table, she says, "If you want to see me again, call me."

Hope tries to embrace everything Dr. Miller has said, but like trying to pick up an armload of clothes out of a clothes dryer some of the points escape her.

All of a sudden, Justin comes barreling through the door with four or five Walmart bags in each hand. "I wasn't sure what you'd like, so I—"

Seeing Dr. Miller stops him short.

"You must be Justin," she says.

"Uh, yes ma'am."

"It's nice to meet you." Turning back to Hope, she says, "Be good to yourself, Hope. You deserve it." And she exits the room.

CHAPTER TWENTY-NINE

Like two boulders, fear and dread sit atop Michael's shoulders as he walks from his car to the church building. Officer Jessie Pinkston's visit has upturned his world, leaving his future uncertain. *Should I run away, move across the country, change my name and start a different career?* Absurd as it sounds in his head, he turns the idea over a few times before he decides to shelve it, at least for the time being.

He was so shocked and surprised at Pinkston's finding the pieces of the letter and fitting them together he probably would have confessed everything he knew if Liz hadn't shown up and told him to stop talking. *And now that she knows how I handled things after I found Sarah, will I still have a chance at having sex with her?*

He shakes his head. *I could possibly be facing a charge of covering up a murder, and yet I'm thinking about having sex with a woman I've barely even touched? That's insane!*

Hmmm, 'insanity.' Would it be possible for me to use temporary insanity if I get charged with something? And if I plead insanity, will anyone around here still be interested in hearing 'that preacher who admitted he was insane'?

Why don't I plead ignorance about all of it? I don't know for certain where the note came from. And the same goes for the message. It's enigmatic.

He wishes he didn't have to walk past Helen to get to his office. She'll for certain have something to say that won't set well with him. The problem is, the things she says to him are usually incontrovertible. *At least I now have a key to the door and don't have to go through an inquisition from her in order for her to buzz me in.*

When he enters the office complex, Helen is standing by the copy machine as it spits out copies. She turns and gives him an appraising view. "I won't state the obvious, but I will volunteer to fix you some coffee, if that will help."

He figures she's referring to his haggard appearance but doesn't give her a chance to elaborate. He replies, "Coffee would be very nice. Thank you." Then he heads into his office and shuts the door.

For the next few hours, he drinks coffee and tries to decide what topic he should preach on Sunday, but his thoughts are like marbles on an uneven table top, skittering this way and that in unpredictable directions. Intrusive images of Hope, then Liz, then Jessie Pinkston, then Brittany distract him.

Finally, he closes all the books scattered across his desk, leans back in his chair and closes his eyes. *Lord, I need your help here. What is it you would have me preach about this Sunday?*

Taking slow, easy breaths, he waits for an idea to come to him. But nothing happens.

He opens his eyes, and they immediately focus on the bottom drawer of his desk. Pleasure and relief are that close. Before any rational thoughts can give him pause, he jerks open the drawer, grabs the phone out of the concordance and hurries into the bathroom. Like a shark in a feeding frenzy, he jumps from one pornographic site to another, filling his head with lewd images. He holds off masturbating as long as he can, knowing he will most certainly crash once that release passes.

Just as he's about to unzip his pants, he hears a noise coming from his office. It's the sound of his office door opening and closing.

"Michael?"

Is that Liz? "Be out in a second," he answers through the bathroom door. Closing and pocketing the phone, he flushes the toilet and runs water in the sink to complete the charade as to why he's been in the bathroom. Liz is standing on the other side of his desk when he steps out. Still sexually aroused, he immediately undresses her with his eyes. In a husky voice, he says, "Hi, Liz. I must confess I'm more than a little surprised to see you."

"I can understand why," she replies. Glancing at this sitting area, she adds, "Can we talk?"

A lascivious answer perches on the tip of his tongue. Only at the last instant is he able to swallow it. He motions toward the chairs. "Sure we can." As he walks behind her, enjoying the view, he feels like a cougar crouched in a tree and ready to pounce. *Be careful. Don't do anything stupid.*

Once they're seated, Liz says, "I feel badly for how I acted this morning at your house."

He waves her off. "Don't worry about it, it's okay."

"No, no it's not. There you were, in need of a friend, an ally, and what did I do? I turned my back on you. That was wrong of me, and I want to apologize."

Internally, Michael breathes a sigh of relief that she's not there as an antagonist bent on pursuing officer Pinkston's insinuations. "I'm certain you were shocked, and probably dismayed, at what I told you. Even though I lived it, it sounded unbelievable to me as I told it. You talk about feeling badly because you weren't there for me, but what about me and how I reacted to finding Sarah's body? I did nothing that a caring, loving husband would have. I only thought about myself." He hangs his head to give the appearance of being remorseful.

"I admit I was shocked," she replies. "It made no sense until I took some time to think it through. Who knows how they will act in a moment of horror like you witnessed? I might have done similar foolish things if I found Jed—"

When she stops in midsentence, he looks up and is surprised to see tears in her eyes. *Are they about feeling sorry for me or an expression of her disappointment in herself?* He's suddenly struck by a thought, "Why were you at my house in the first place?"

She appears to teeter on a precipice, trying to decide whether or not to open up to him, so he tries to give her a nudge. "Liz, anything you talk with me about is strictly confidential. I won't share it with anyone, even Jed."

Snatching a tissue from a box on the table beside her, Liz lays it on her thigh and folds it in half, then half again, and half again, then dabs the corners of her eyes with it. "Jed and I tried to have a meeting this morning. I mean, we did have a meeting this morning, but it didn't go well. He's not handling our pending divorce very well. He looks bad."

Michael asks, "What was the purpose of your meeting? Are you wanting to reconcile?" Part of him wants her to say yes for the sake of the church, but another part of him wants her to say no so he can pursue his lecherous desires.

Shaking her head, she answers, "No, I don't think I'll ever be able to be married to Jed unless God performs a miracle on him that produces some fundamental changes."

Her answer pleases him, but he doesn't want to appear so. "With God, all things are possible."

"Yes, but all things are not probable. A person has to be open to God changing them, which means they have to see their flaws. And that's the problem: Jed doesn't see himself the way he really is. I've tried and tried to..." Her voice trails off.

Michael waits for her to finish her thought, but she falls silent. He mulls over her statement about God changing a person and thinks about himself. *Maybe that's why God has never cleansed me of my sex addiction. He knows I really don't want to change.* He also thinks about Sarah and how he tried to get her to change, but to no avail. Absent mindedly, he says, "You can't make another person change."

"So true," she replies. "I've always known that to be true, but yet I kept trying. I kept thinking he'll finally see it and recognize the need." She pulls out another tissue as tears begin rolling down her cheeks.

"There are all kinds of tears, Liz, and they can mean a variety of things. Tell me what your tears are about."

"I feel guilty, even though I know I shouldn't."

"Guilty about what?"

"That I couldn't make the marriage work. Or maybe it's that I feel guilty for walking out on the marriage, because the marriage did work for Jed. He got out of it everything he wanted. I'm just tired of not feeling emotionally intimate with him."

"I'll state the obvious here," Michael says. "It takes two people to make a relationship work."

Liz nods. "But I also feel—" her voice catches in her throat, and she begins to cry harder. "I also feel so sad. This is the end of a childhood dream, of finding someone to spend the rest of my life with, to be married to forever." She buries her face in her hands.

Michaels eases forward in his chair and reaches toward her. *Dare I go sit beside her?* "I'm so sorry, Liz." She lifts her head slightly and takes his hand. He clasps it between his, hesitates for a second, then moves to the loveseat beside her. "Divorce can be harder than death," he tells her. "But you'll make it through."

She looks at him, and her eyelashes have tiny tears hanging on them like ornaments on a Christmas tree. "I don't want God to be disappointed in me."

Putting his arm around her, he says, "Oh, Liz, I don't think God is disappointed in you at all. I think he understands how hard you've tried and how unrewarding your life with Jed has been." A thrill runs through him as he feels the warmth of her body.

She relaxes against him and inclines her head toward his shoulder. "That makes me feel better because that's really the most important thing, isn't it?"

Michael feels himself getting aroused as his breath quickens. *How far should I go with this?* He gives her the slightest of hugs and is excited when she doesn't resist or protest. His head is filled with the scent of her. He feels her heart beating. Just as he's about to put his other arm around her and embrace her, a sudden thought brings everything to a screeching halt. He looks at his office door. *Don't forget, Helen could walk in at any moment.*

A sudden war wages in his head as part of him tells him to damn the consequences, that this is his chance with Liz, while another part cautions him to tap his brakes, that this step is sufficient and it will eventually take him to where he wants to land— between her legs. But nowhere is there even a whisper that what he's doing and what he wants to do is wrong.

CHAPTER THIRTY

Whispering into Hope's ear, Montana says, "He scares me."

"Who does?"

Montana points behind Hope to where Justin is standing.

Hope looks over her shoulder. "He's just a big teddy bear," Hope replies. "I know he's big and frightening looking, but he would never hurt you."

Montana looks toward the floor. "That's what they all said."

Hope feels as if she's drinking from two cups, one filled with empathy for this little girl, and the other filled with searing hatred for the ones who have hurt her. Giving her a hug, she promises, "I will never let anyone hurt you—never. Justin protects me, and he'll protect you, too. Look at him. Do you think anyone is going to get past him to where they can hurt you?"

Montana peeks around Hope as Justin steps back from the wheelchair and shifts his weight from his right foot to his left. Montana shakes her head.

"Exactly," Hope confirms. "You are safe with us. We're going to take you home where you will live with us. Does that sound like fun to you?"

Montana touches the wheels of the wheelchair. "Can't you walk?"

"I can with crutches, but the hospital wants me to leave riding in this just to make sure I don't fall and then sue them. Here, you hold my hand while Justin rolls me out to the car."

The three of them make their way down the hallway—a lost child, a woman wounded as a child, and an over-sized child—embarking on a new journey, each hoping for something different yet something similar: a sense of security.

When they reach the car, Beverly Cotton is there holding a child's car seat. "I didn't figure you'd think about needing one of these," she says. "And you practically have to have an engineering degree to learn how to fasten them in the car and strap the child in, so I'll give you a quick in-service." She smiles.

Hope likes the social worker's open and honest demeanor but also feels threatened by her because she will do everything in her power to find Montana's parents and return her to them, something Hope has decided she doesn't want to happen. *She's going to be mine. It'll be what me and Lisa never were. I know better now, and I'll do better.*

Justin rolls Hope to a stop beside the passenger's side front door. "No," she says. "I want to sit in the back with Montana." So he nudges the chair a bit further and helps her transition from chair to vehicle.

Meanwhile, Beverly has opened the other backdoor and lays the car seat inside. Step by step she shows Hope how and where all the straps go. Hope is certain she will not remember any of it and will have to end up looking for help on YouTube.

Beverly motions at Montana. "Come on, let's get you strapped in."

Quick as a monkey, she climbs inside and onto the seat. Grabbing the straps herself, she slips her arms in, pulls them tight then latches it.

"Somebody's done this before," Beverly beams. "Good job, Montana." With a small laugh, she adds, "You might have to teach Hope and Justin how to do it."

Justin gets in the driver's seat and buckles his seatbelt.

Beverly says, "You have my phone number, right Hope?"

"Yes I do."

"Call me if you need anything or run into something unexpected. And please keep your phone on in case I need to contact you about anything."

"Yes, I will for sure." Hope slips her phone out of her pocket and powers it on. She catches Justin looking at her in the rearview mirror with his eyebrows raised, and she makes a face at him.

"You're in good hands," Beverly says to Montana. "You can trust these people." She squeezes her arm then shuts the door.

Justin shifts the car into drive and eases away.

They ride in silence for a few minutes before Montana says, "My name's not Montana."

Hope twists her head so quickly she feels her neck crack. "It's not?"

"No. It's Gabriella."

Stunned, Hope asks, "Did you tell this to Beverly or to anyone at the hospital?"

"Nobody asked."

"Then why are you telling us now?"

"If you are my new mommy and poppy, I want you to use my real name. I think it's pretty."

"It is a beautiful name," Hope says. "I love it, Gabriella." Her heart soars at the sound of being called 'mommy'.

Justin speaks up, "Guess you better call Beverly and let her know. It's probably important to the investigation."

"I'll call her when we get home," Hope replies. *Or maybe I'll forget to call.* She deliberately turns the conversation toward learning what Gabriella's favorite foods and snacks are, and she makes mental notes of what needs to be bought at the grocery store.

Justin's phone rings. He looks to see who it is, then puts it to his ear. "Hello, mama." He listens for a moment, then replies, "Yes, she's in the car with me and Hope right now. We're taking her home." This time he listens a little longer before answering in a hushed tone, "Yeah, she looks kinda like a Mexican, but she's as cute as a bug." His mother's words are not intelligible, but her voice is so loud he jerks the phone away from his ear and Hope hears her screeching. When the receiver goes silent, Justin puts it back to his ear, and says through clinched teeth, "This is mine and Hope's business." Then he ends the call.

Hope cuts her eyes toward Gabriella and sees she's fallen asleep, so she leans forward and whispers, "What was that about?"

"I don't want to talk about it where the girl can hear it."

"She's asleep."

"Are you sure?"

"Yes! Now, what was that about? I know it was your mama."

Justin sighs. "You're going to get mad about it."

When he doesn't continue, Hope pops him on the back of his head. "Tell me!"

"Mama don't like me taking in a Mex kid. She says people will talk."

The only thing that keeps Hope from lunging over the back of the seat is her seat/shoulder strap. "How can she say that when I'm half Hispanic? My father was from Honduras."

Justin does not answer her.

"You mean, she objects to you being with me, too?"

"It don't matter, Hope."

"How come you've never told me your mother is a racist? Why has this never come up?"

"'Cause I knew it would upset you. Mama's kind of complicated."

"No, no she's not. She's just the opposite. Being racist is quite simple—you hate someone just because of their skin color or where they come from." She falls back against the seat, muttering to herself. Then she sits back up, and says, "We're not done talking about this," before settling back in her seat.

During the rest of the trip home, silence rules.

As soon as the car comes to a stop at their trailer, Gabriella comes awake. At first, she casts her eyes about in a panic until Hope takes her hand. "It's okay," Hope tells her. "Remember? You're with me now."

"Is this where you live?"

"Yes. You'll have a bedroom all to yourself. There's not much in there right now, but we can have fun fixing it up. Won't that be fun?"

Unbuckling and extracting herself from the car seat, Gabriella asks, "It'll be all mine?"

Hope reaches for her crutches and opens her door. "It sure will."

The two of them exit on opposite sides of the car as Justin gathers all the Walmart bags in one hand. Hurrying to the other side of the car, he says, "Wait until I can help you, Hope."

For once, she gladly accepts his help since she can't quite figure out how to get out of the car. "This is going to take some practice," she says, as she takes hold of his offered arm, pulls herself out and stands on one foot.

"You'll be surprised though how quickly you'll get used to using your crutches. I hurt my knee playing football in high school and was on crutches for a while. At first, it took me forever to get from one place to another, but pretty soon I got the hang of it."

Gabriella eyes her cautiously. "Can I help?"

"Why don't you open the front door for us?" Justin tells her.

She smiles and dashes to the door.

Hope moves carefully passed Gabriella and over to her recliner, which she collapses onto. Meanwhile, Gabriella races through the house yelling out excited questions to Hope who hollers back the answers.

"That is one excited little girl," Justin observes.

Hope smiles. "Yes, she is. I hate to ask you, but you're going to have to go to the store and buy some more things. I'll make a list for you."

"Why do you feel bad for asking me? That's why I'm here. I mean, we're here for each other, aren't we? Isn't that how couples do?"

Hope starts to remind him of what she told him when she moved in, that nothing is permanent when it comes to her and relationships, but at that moment Gabriella comes rushing toward her.

"I love it here!" the girl says. "Everything is so clean." She reaches for Hope who leans to one side so Gabriella can hug her neck.

Maybe it's time for me to quit being a serial monogamist. Maybe, for the sake of Gabriella, I need to stick with Justin. "Did you figure out which room is your bedroom?" Hope asks.

"Yes, but there's nothing in it."

"That's because we didn't know you were coming home with us, and we didn't have time to buy anything. But Justin is going to go to the store and get some things for you. It'll take us a little time, but we'll have it looking really special for you."

Justin hands her a notepad and pen. "Write the stuff down that I need to buy."

Without hesitation, Hope creates a rather long list and hands it to Justin.

He eyes it and scratches the back of his neck. "Uh, Hope, I'm not sure..." He stops and looks down at Gabriella. "Have you looked in the freezer?" he asks her. "There's some ice cream sandwiches in there, if you want one."

Hope is touched by his willingness to give up one of his favorite treats.

Gabriella turns and skips toward the kitchen. As soon as she's out of earshot, Justin says, "I don't have enough money to buy all this Hope. I want to get it, but I just don't have the money."

This is a topic Hope has been intentionally ignoring ever since the decision was made to bring Gabriella home, but now it has to be addressed. "First of all, you can use my debit card. I'll give you the PIN number. But also, we've got to come up with a plan whereby I can stay home with Gabriella. I don't intend to send her to daycare while I go to work."

Justin swallows hard. "I'm not sure I make enough money to support all three of us, and I sure can't ask mama for no help."

Hope bites her tongue at the reference to his mother because there's nothing else to be said about it.

Justin asks, "So, are you quitting your job?"

"I don't want to. I know I need to work, but I can't stand to think about leaving her. I wonder if they'd just give me a leave of absence or something like that until school starts in August. I'll be okay working while she's at school."

"Yeah...but what about the money? How are we going to afford for you to not get paid?" He falls silent, then says, "Maybe I could get a second part-time job."

For the second time, Hope is touched by Justin's willingness to sacrifice for her and Gabriella's benefit, but it also makes her uneasy to become so dependent on someone else. It's a mistake she's made in the past that always led to trouble.

Gabriella comes dancing back into the living room, cradling ice cream sandwiches to her chest. "Everybody gets one!" she sings.

Hope whispers to Justin. "Just use my debit card for now. We'll figure things out later."

CHAPTER THIRTY-ONE

Hope looks at the digital clock: 5:43 A.M.

Her right arm and hand are numb due to falling asleep while holding Gabriella in her arms.

Everything had seemed okay last night when she tucked Gabriella in bed and kissed her goodnight. Gabriella hugged her neck and kissed her on the cheek. Hope then joined Justin, who was already snoring, in their bed.

He stirred when she got in. "Everything okay?" he asked.

"Yeah. She went right to bed. No problem."

"Can we talk about money?"

Hope didn't want to but knew the subject had to be addressed. "I should have talked to you first before agreeing to take on Gabriella, and I apologize for that. It's just that everything happened so fast and—"

He interrupted her, "That's okay. You did the right thing. It's for sure not how I saw our life together, but who can refuse to help a kid in that situation."

His words touched Hope's heart. *He's really a decent guy.* Scooting closer to him, she said "Thank you for understanding."

"We just gotta figure out how we can afford to take care of her."

"One thing that completely slipped my mind is Beverly told me foster parents get money for raising a child. I don't remember how much, but that'll be something we can count on."

"That's great."

"I hope you understand why I don't want to go to work. I don't know if you can appreciate how much this chance means to me. The number of mistakes I made in raising Lisa would fill this bedroom and more. It's like before she died I was blind, but afterwards I could clearly see where I failed her." Her voice cracked as emotions rushed forward.

Laying his hand on the side of her face, Justin said, "Aw, Hope, don't be so hard on yourself. What's done is done and can't be undone."

"I wonder if the casino would give me something like a leave of absence until Gabriella starts to school without it costing me my job? I like working there with Whitney and Carol Anne; we've grown really close."

"Isn't there some kind of program that lets people do that?"

"Not that I know of."

Justin raised up on one elbow. "Yeah, it's called F L A...F A L...F M L A, that's it! I overheard somebody talking about it at work."

"But you don't get paid while you're not working, do you?"

"Probably not, but at least you'll still have your job."

"Will we have enough money to live on with your job and what we get from Social Services?"

"Don't you worry about that. I can get a second job."

Hope was moved by his offer. "I don't want to ask you to do that. It's not fair."

"You didn't ask me to do it. I'm doing it because I want to, and that's it."

Leaning up, Hope kissed him. "Thank you, Justin." She knew what the kiss would lead to but was okay with it because she knew having sex is what makes him happy. The cast on her leg made it extremely awkward for her, but he was like a buck in rut and unfazed by the cast.

Afterward, she lay there thinking about Gabriella and wondering what horrors she must have lived through since being taken from her parents. *What kind of parents does she have? Did they sell her to someone, or was she kidnapped? Are they afraid of being found, or are they frantic over their lost daughter?*

The question that left her the most conflicted was what she would do if Gabriella's parents are found. Even though she knew it was irrational, she thought of running away with Gabriella and giving them both new identities.

As she was entertaining this last thought, Gabriella screamed, "Help! Please help me!"

Completely forgetting about her broken ankle, Hope jumped out of bed and immediately fell on her face.

Her cry of pain cut through Justin's sleep. "What's happening? Hope, where are you?"

"Run see about Gabriella!" Hope cried. "She's in trouble!"

"I don't have any clothes on!"

Hope swore at him. "Then put your shorts on, and hurry!"

Another cry for help from Gabriella had the effect of a cattle prod on him. He sprang out of bed, slipped on his shorts and ran toward her bedroom like one of the bulls on the streets of Pamplona.

Meanwhile, Hope crawled to her crutches and pulled herself to a standing position. She took a couple of steps toward Gabriella's room when she heard Justin coming toward her, talking in soothing tones.

"It's okay," he said. "I've got you. I'm going to take you back here to where Hope is."

Gabriella was whimpering.

Hope turned on the lights as he entered the room cradling the child to his chest. The contrast in size between the two of them reminded her of pictures she'd seen of gorillas holding their young. "What happened?" Hope asked.

"She had a nightmare," Justin answered. He held Gabriella toward her so she could give her a kiss.

Gabriella threw her arms around Hope's neck, nearly causing her to fall.

"Careful," Justin told her. "Let's let Hope sit back down so she can hold you."

Hope made her way to the bed and sat down on the edge. Justin placed Gabriella in her lap, and Hope hugged her. "Now, now," she whispered in her ear, "your safe. Nobody's going to hurt you. Justin and I won't let that happen."

"I'll go sleep on the couch," Justin said. "You all sleep in here. Just holler out if you need something."

How a man treats a child goes a long way in influencing how a woman feels about him, and Hope was no exception. She felt her heart being knitted to his in a way she didn't think possible. She mouthed a thank you toward him just as he was turning out the lights.

"Sure thing," he said, then he closed the door.

Now, Hope tries slipping her numb arm out from under Gabriella without waking her up, but she stirs and opens her eyes. "Good morning," Hope says.

"I had a bad dream."

"I know. But it was just a dream. You're safe now, nobody's going to hurt you." Even though she's not sure she wants to hear it, Hope asks, "Do you want to talk about your dream?"

"It was one of the bad men who hurt me. He smelled bad."

Hope cringes but then feels rage over what was done to Gabriella. "I'm sorry he hurt you."

Gabriella closes her eyes and snuggles up against her. "There were lots of them."

Oh dear God, dear God! What has happened to this child?

Gabriella continues. "They said it would feel good, but it didn't."

Hope hears the floors creaking as Justin approaches from the other end of the trailer.

In the doorway, he whispers, "You awake?"

"Yes," she whispers back.

Gabriella sits up and smiles. "Me, too."

Justin says, "I've gotta get a shower and go to work. What are you going to do?"

Hope replies, "I'm going to work, too, and find out about this F M L A."

"What about Gabriella?"

"Yeah, what about me?" the child chirps.

Hugging her, Hope says, "Well, you're going with me. I'll let my friends meet you."

Gabriella jumps up and starts dancing on the bed. "Yea!"

"Ain't she the damndest thing," Justin smiles. "Like she ain't got a care in the world. But do you think you'll be okay to drive? I mean, with your cast and everything."

"I'll go slow and be careful, maybe drive around here a little bit to be sure I can manage."

*****

Hope pulls to a stop in the employee parking lot.

"You work here?" Gabriella asks. "It's really big!"

"Yes, this is where I work. I've got to meet with a woman about some things, but we'll also go by and see my friends Carole Anne and Whitney. You'll like them."

Gabriella begins unsnapping the car seat's harness. "I'll get your crutches for you."

Hope smiles at how helpful she's wanted to be ever since they met. Opening her door, she waits for Gabriella to drag her crutches to her. Then, with the girl helping, she stands up.

Gabriella skips all the way across the parking lot, a perfect mirror of Hope's heart skipping for joy.

Inside the casino, Hope makes her way to Cara Hernandez's office. She stops at the door with the gold plate that reads *Human Resource Director*. She knocks and hears Cara invite her in.

Cara immediately looks at Gabriella. "So, this is the little girl everyone's been talking about." She kneels down in front of her. "Hi, my name is Cara. You must be Gabriella."

Gabriella looks uncertainly at Hope.

"It's okay," Hope says. "She's nice."

Gabriella gives Cara a quick "Hi."

Standing, Cara turns her attention to Hope and looks at her cast. "How in the world are you doing? I understand you nearly died out there."

"Let's just say, it was interesting," Hope replies. "I came by to ask you about F M L A. I've decided I'm not going to come back to work until Gabriella starts to school. But I don't want to lose my job. Is there anything I can do to make all that happen?"

Cara smiles from ear to ear. "No, there's nothing you can do, but there's something that your fellow employees have done for you."

Hope is confused. "What do you mean?"

"Everybody pooled their unused vacation days and donated them to you. You won't have to work until November, if you don't want to, and you'll still get paid as if you were working."

Hope teeters on her crutches as the full import of Cara's news sinks in.

Cara reaches out and steadies her. "Why don't you sit down?"

Still dazed, Hope takes a seat. "I...I don't understand."

"Amazing, huh? I knew you'd be surprised. Of course it was Carol Anne's idea; she's always thinking of others. I wish I had thought of it first, but that doesn't matter. When people started hearing the story of what happened to you and what Carol Anne was asking, they were lined up out my door. It's really very touching all the way around."

Hope chokes on the flood of emotions filling her. "I've never...nobody's ever...I...I don't know what to say."

Gabriella squeezes her hand, and asks. "What's wrong?"

"There's nothing wrong, sweetheart. Everything is so right, so perfect, it's like a dream."

"But it's a good dream, right?"

"Oh Gabriella, it's the best dream."

CHAPTER THIRTY-TWO

A buzz ripples through the audience as Carol Anne and her lawyer, Katrina Carson, walk into the jam-packed courtroom.

As spring has marched toward summer, the amount of gossip on the streets has heated up as well. Friends and houses have been divided by opposing views of who is the guilty party in this case.

Carol Anne has dropped fifteen pounds off her already slight frame, finding it impossible to eat anything more than snacks, and she's chewed her normally perfectly manicured fingernails to the quick. "I just want to get it over with," she has repeatedly told her Katrina. She even told her she was ready to settle out of court, but when Katrina told her she needed to talk to Heather Brown, and she did, Heather convinced her that settling out of court was the same as saying he won. And that was certainly the last thing Carol Anne wanted.

Now, as she sits down beside Katrina, she takes a look at the jury. They, in turn, stare at her. *Sizing me up, no doubt. Can I convince them my story is true?* Seven men and five women. She figured having that many men meant the deck was stacked against her, but Katrina told her it meant nothing, that juries are impossible to read.

The next three days are like a nightmare playing in a loop. Character witnesses praising Biddle, making him sound almost god-like in their depiction of him and how he helped set them on a path of success that served them to the present. Fortunately, Katrina dug up some people who have a very different view of Biddle that is separate and apart from any abuse at his hands. Those people describe him as a tyrant and narcissistic. And even though they never had a sexual relationship with him, he made them feel uncomfortable, like he was pursuing them to that end.

Objections are shouted from both benches, some sustained and some denied.

Finally, she takes the stand to tell her story. Katrina leads her just the way they practiced it. Standing close to the witness stand, she makes her feel less alone.

To cross examine her, Biddle's lawyer fixes her with a stare and walks slowly toward her.

If someone put a gun to her head after her testimony and asked her to tell what she said, she couldn't have complied. It was a surreal experience. Questions asked and objected to before she could answer. Something she said was ordered to be stricken from the record. She tries to look at Katrina, but Biddle's lawyer purposely places himself directly in her line of sight.

It feels like the time she went to the ocean with her parents. She fell asleep on a float and didn't awaken until she was far out from shore, so far out that her screams couldn't be heard. A fin cut through the water close by. She jerked her legs out of the water and onto the float. Just when she was certain she was going to be eaten alive, she heard the buzz of an approaching Sea-Doo. Relief flooded her when she recognized him as one of the lifeguards on duty.

Carol Anne can recite every detail of that ocean experience, but her experience in court is like static on a radio.

As she sits down beside Katrina, her lawyer places her hand on her shoulder and leans in. "You did great, just like I knew you would."

I hope that's true and she's not saying it just to make me feel better. She reaches for a glass of water, but her hands are shaking so badly she decides against it. Finally, she's able to take a deep breath and lets it out slowly.

This next step in the trial is what she's really been looking forward to. Up to now, Heather Brown has been an anonymous accuser who added her name to the lawsuit, allowed to do so by the judge because of fear of reprisal against her by Biddle.

Katrina rises, and says, "I'd like to call one more witness, your Honor. I'd like to call Heather Brown to the stand."

Carol Anne purposely keeps her eyes on Biddle to see his reaction to this surprise, and she gets what she was hoping for. Shock registers on his face, and he turns as pale as a sheet. Carol
Anne wants to jump up and yell, "Not so smug now, are you? You're finally going to get exactly what you deserve!"

Unlike Carol Anne felt during her testimony, Heather appears cool and calculated as she details everything about her relationship with Biddle, both then and now. The silence in the courtroom deepens. Her story, which Carol Anne has not heard before, is eerily similar to her own, as if Biddle had some kind of play book he was using with his victims.

And just as he did with Carol Anne, Biddle's lawyer tries to paint Heather as the aggressor, the willing and eager participant in the sexual tryst. Hearing it, as it were, in third person, Carol Anne sees how confusing it would sound to someone with no understanding of Trauma Bonds, as explained by the psychiatrist who testified on their behalf, or of the profiles of sexual predators and their technique of grooming their victims.

She looks at the jury. *How much weight will they give to the testimony of a psychiatrist? How many of the men on the jury have secretly done something similar to Biddle's crime?* Her hopes of victory in the case begin to wane like water going down a drain.

Finally, the closing arguments are given—the last chance to influence jurors who haven't already made up their mind.

When the judge leaves the room, the audience begins shuffling toward the exits. Katrina says, "Let's go get something to eat. I doubt there will be a quick verdict."

"Does that mean you believe we've lost?"

"No, it just means the jurors have a lot of testimony to sift through and debate. It may take them several days to reach consensus."

Carol Anne's neck and shoulders ache from the tension of the past days. She rises, and the two of them walk to a local downtown eatery.

"I know you're exhausted," Katrina tells her. "But you did it, you told the truth about a monster who preys on children, and that's what you wanted to do from the start, right?"

"But did anybody believe me? What if the jury finds him innocent? What will that say about me and how people view my story?"

"Look, there are people who will never believe your story because they never knew the side of him you did. You can't fix that, so just accept it. Going forward, at the very least, he'll have difficulty getting a teaching job anywhere simply because of the suspicion surrounding him. This lawsuit has put people on alert."

The server brings their food, dishes that look like they came out of a magazine. But Carol Anne has no appetite.

Katrina motions at her. "Pick up your fork and eat, even if you're not hungry. If you don't start eating, you're going to get in trouble physically. Come on, take a bite."

Carol Anne obliges her, only because she's too tired to argue with her. After swallowing a few bites, she says, "I don't understand why Biddle hasn't gotten fired."

"That's easy. The school board is protecting itself from a wrongful job termination lawsuit. Let's say they fire him based on the allegations by you and others, and he is found innocent. He could turn around and sue them."

Carol Anne accidently drops her fork. It ricochets off her plate and onto the floor. When she bends over to pick it up, she hears a familiar voice.

"Eating a victory meal, that's my girl," Whitney says as she rushes to their table. "Man, I hate I missed everything today." She pulls up a chair and looks at Katrina. "Did you stick it to him today? Push in that knife and twist it?"

"You remember Whitney, I assume," Carol Anne inserts.

Katrina smiles. "I don't think I could forget her if I wanted to. She is a force of nature."

Whitney beams. Looking from one to the other, she says, "Well, tell me how it went today."

"It wrapped up today," Katrina answers. "It's in the hands of the jury now."

Whitney claps her hands together. "That's the sound of the bear trap closing on Biddle's neck. His ass is toast."

Carol Anne looks around nervously. "Not so loud, Whitney. Somebody might hear you who doesn't share your view of Biddle. Then there'll be a confrontation and argument, somebody'll snap a photo or video, and the next thing you know it'll be plastered all over Facebook and Twitter."

"Okay, okay, I'll hush up. How will we know when the jury has reached a verdict?"

Katrina says, "The judge, or his clerk, will call me and give us a time to be in court, then I'll call Carol Anne."

*****

Twenty-four hours later, Carol Anne and Katrina sit alone in the empty court room. Carol Anne stares at the empty jury box and feels as if her bones have been filled with lead, making movement impossible.

"I know this doesn't help," Katrina says, "but I'm really, really sorry."

Carol Anne looks at her, and for the first time notices worry lines across her forehead and crows' feet framing her eyes. "Yeah, me, too." Looking back at the jury box, she says, "They didn't believe me, did they?"

Katrina doesn't answer.

"And they didn't believe Heather, either, did they?" She puts her palms on the table, and with great effort pushes herself to a standing position. "It's still a 'boys-will-be-boys' world, isn't it?"

CHAPTER THIRTY-THREE

Looking in the mirror, Michael pulls the bill of the baseball cap a little lower so that his face is more shadowed. Large-frame sunglasses complete his disguise. Convinced that anyone would have difficulty recognizing him, he walks out of his house, gets in his car and drives the dark highway to Paducah.

By the time he reaches the city limits, his body hums with excitement. He will finally meet Candy Carter face-to-face. Even though he doubts that's her real name, it doesn't really matter. *Besides, I didn't use my real name, either. Just so she looks like her profile picture and is willing to do the things she says she will.*

A few weeks ago, while searching for new porn sites, he discovered *friendswithbenefits.com*, a match-making service for people interested in casual-sex dates. What he found there were women who were eager to do the things that porn sites only teased about. And by typing in his zip code he could make his search more specific.

He was both surprised and pleased at how many women were within a short drive of where he lived. A couple of them even lived in Bardwell, but he was too afraid they would recognize him. However, that didn't keep him from being on the lookout for them as he went about business in town. A part of him suspected the details in their profile were intentionally manipulated to make it appear they lived in Bardwell, but his suspicion didn't match his fantasy, so he dismissed it.

They decided to meet up in a public place, just in case either of them wanted to back out at the last second. Candy chose The Spyglass, a tavern located on the riverfront. It's main attraction being live Blue's music by local bands.

Michael parks, gets out of his car and checks his reflection in the window of a closed antique store. *Relax, be calm, or you'll scare Candy off.*

Approaching The Spyglass, the air pulses from the deep bass of the music inside. And when he opens the door, it feels like the energy in the tavern will blow his cap off. People stand two deep at the bar, and the dance floor is jampacked. Dimly-lit booths line the walls where mostly couples are sharing drinks and food.

Stepping out of the way of people entering and exiting the tavern, Michael scans the room, looking for a woman wearing a bright red top and sporting a diamond stud on one side of her nose. His eyes are arrested when he spots her sitting a small table in the corner of the room. An electric charge of excitement runs up and down his spine.

In the tiniest corner of his mind he hears, *Are you sure you want to do this?* It is the last vestiges of his conscience that he has been searing over with a hot iron. *Leave me alone,* his addiction tells his conscience. *I deserve this. I'm a man who has needs, and I'm not hurting anyone by doing something about it.*

Suddenly Candy looks up and spots him. She smiles, revealing teeth that are less white than they appeared in her portrait photo, and it looks like one of them might be missing. *Maybe it's just the dim lighting in here.*

He crosses the room to her and takes a seat. They take a moment to size each other up. Her thick makeup up doesn't completely hide her pitted, scarred face, and he was correct about the missing tooth.

She tries to hide the missing tooth by cupping a hand over mouth. "Hi, I'm glad you came," she says. "Guys often chicken out at the last minute."

Michael is fascinated by her eyes, which are the palest blue he's ever seen. He lets his gaze wander south and notices erect nipples on her ample breasts. Immediately, all the imperfections he'd noticed on her face evaporate. "I'm glad I came, too," he says.

"Nervous, aren't you?"

"What makes you say that?"

Pointing to her eyes, she says, "The sunglasses. Who wears sunglasses in a dimly-lit bar?" She laughs. "You need to relax, or you're not going to have any fun tonight."

He removes the sunglasses. "I just don't want to be recognized by anyone. It would create trouble I don't want."

"What do you want me to call you?"

"My name is Jonathan."

She smiles. "If you say so, Jonathan. If you're so worried about being recognized, why don't we go ahead and find a motel?"

Without hesitation, Michael stands up, and says, "Let's go."

"You follow me in your car," Candy says. "Hampton Inn okay with you?"

He hadn't thought about choice of location. "Uh...sure, if that's okay with you."

"I know the night manager, and he'll give us a good deal."

On the drive to the motel Michael wonders if Candy does this often. She seems unaffected by the kinds of feelings he's experiencing. *And she immediately had a motel in mind. Is that where she always goes?*

He's suddenly struck by a thought: *Could she have a venereal disease?* He never even considered bringing a condom. He starts having second thoughts and considers turning and going back home. But the excitement of having sex with abandon with someone he doesn't know is too much to resist. *I'll just tell her I forgot condoms and will go get some.*

He parks beside her and gets out when she does.

"I forgot to bring condoms," he says.

She laughs. "Don't worry, I've got you covered." She pats her large handbag. "You wait here," she says, and proceeds to the lobby.

In a manner of moments, she returns waving a room key-card in her hand. "He gave us the bridal suite with jacuzzi and king-size bed."

Michael isn't certain, but Candy appears to be a little unsteady on her feet, like she's drunk, and her accent has taken on a nasal, country sound, something he didn't notice at The Spyglass.

Grabbing him by the sleeve, she pulls and says, "Come on, big boy, let's get this party started."

*****

When Michael awakens, there is a thin shaft of sunlight sneaking between the space where the motel curtains are supposed to meet, but like most motel curtains they never do. At first, he's confused about where he is, until flashes of memories from last night remind him. And flashes are really all he has—disjointed images of Candy in the jacuzzi, drinking something she got out of the motel-room refrigerator; her straddling him in bed; her laughing at something he did or said.

At some point she gave him something to drink, or, rather, forced him to drink by teasing and making fun of him.

The one thing he does remember is she looked uglier and uglier the longer the night went on and her makeup wore off. He's sure he saw track marks on her arms.

He sits up in bed and puts his hands on both sides of his head to keep it from exploding, so severe is the throbbing pain. "You got any aspirin?" he asks Candy.

When she doesn't answer he turns to nudge her and discovers she's not in the bed. He stumbles to the bathroom, expecting to find her there, but, again, she's not there either. In a way, he's glad. *I really don't want to ever see her again—ever!*

Suddenly, his stomach lurches, and he falls on his knees in front of the toilet. He grabs hold of that ceramic throne as his stomach violently empties itself.

Eventually, he heads into the shower to clean himself up from being sick and from the events of last night.

Standing under the spray, his conscience attacks him with a vengeance, beating him with a cat-o-nine-tails made up of guilt, shame, regret, self-hatred, and anger. A self-administered punishment that has occurred so many times in his life he is almost immune to it. Almost.

He crumples in the bathtub and begins to weep. *Dear God in heaven, Either take my life or take this demon from me, for I cannot keep living this way.*

Through his blurred vision he sees a safety razor lying in the corner of the tub, evidently left there by Candy. With a shaky hand he picks it up. He slams it against the tile wall until he is able to extract the blade. Then he slices the inside of his thigh. He watches with fascination as a bright red stream mingles with the water and flows down the drain. The psychic pain he was experiencing has disappeared, silenced by the sting from his self-inflicted wound.

He lies there until the water begins to turn cold, then turns off the faucet and gets out of the shower. The cut has stopped bleeding, but he's careful not to touch it as he dries off.

Back in the bedroom, he starts getting dressed and discovers his wallet is gone. He grabs the wooden chair from the desk and slams it against the floor, again and again until it shatters into pieces.

CHAPTER THIRTY-FOUR

"I chose to keep my nose out of our last pastor's business, even though I knew someone needed to. I don't intend to make that mistake again."

Michael looks up from the book he is reading: OUT OF THE SHADOWS, by Patrick Carnes, a book about sex addiction he ordered off the internet the day after the fiasco with Candy. He was so engrossed in reading something which described him to a tee that he didn't hear Helen come into his office. He casually slides his Bible on top of the book in order to hide it, and says to her, "I'm always interested in hearing your commentary, Helen, even though it might sting at times. I know you're just being honest with me."

"Good. All I want is for you to be the best person you can be and bring glory to God. You've been doing an amazing job as our pastor, delivering lessons that are drawing people to God. My concern is over what you do with yourself when you're not in the pulpit."

Alarm bells ring in Michael's brain. *Did someone see me at The Spyglass? Have they told her I was with a woman?* "Can you be more specific?" he asks.

"You're not taking care of yourself, and it shows. Lots of days you come in the office looking like you haven't slept a wink. You're losing weight, too. Both of which are symptoms of depression. And God knows you have reasons to be depressed."

Michael breathes a quiet sigh of relief. "You're very kind to take note."

She waves her hand at him. "Blah, blah, blah. I'm not interested in hearing you say what you think I want to hear. I'm not like most the people you preach to. I don't need you to stroke my ego."

Michael's face reddens, and he's suddenly a ten-year-old boy in the principal's office.

"What I want you to tell me," Helen continues, "is what are you going to do about the problem?"

He wants to argue over her assessment of him and tell her he's not depressed and he's doing fine. But, first of all, he knows it's not true, and secondly, she won't be convinced. Being cornered by his own conviction and by Helen's forceful nature, he gives in. "You're right, of course. I don't know what I'm doing. I feel like I'm sleep walking through my days. My focus and concentration have disappeared. I'm tired of eating alone, of going home to an empty house, and of sleeping alone." His eyes grow misty. Standing up, he paces back and forth a couple of times, then stops, and says, "Do I need to resign? Does the church need a new pastor?"

Helen shakes her finger at him. "What kind of poppycock is that? Of course you don't need to resign. You're the best thing that's ever happened to this church. People are being saved, new members are being added every week. God is using you in a mighty way. It would be disastrous if you resigned. No, what you need to do is start taking care of yourself. Twice a week you and I are going to eat supper together. You're going to join a gym and start exercising every day. You will go see a doctor and have a complete physical, including bloodwork. And..." Her voice trails off.

Michael soaks up all she is saying and hears truth and good advice in all of it. It's clear though she has something else on her mind but is uncertain if she wants to share it. "Don't stop," he says, "you've uncorked the bottle of wine. Go ahead and pour the rest of it."

"Then, with your permission, I will," Helen replies. "You need to quit having so many meetings at night with Liz and with that other woman, Hope. You're a young, handsome, single man. Liz is youthful, strikingly attractive, and now single. And Hope is a lost soul looking for an anchor. That, my young pastor, is a perfect recipe for disaster, disaster for you, for them, and for our church. There, I've said it, and I don't want to hear your thoughts on the matter. You just think about what I've said." Without another word she turns, walks out of his office and closes the door.

He moves back to his office chair and collapses in it. *I know she's right, but give up meeting with Liz? Hope maybe, but not Liz.* He reaches down, pulls open the bottom drawer of his desk and fishes out his phone from Strong's concordance. He's told himself it's silly to keep up the charade of the extra phone, but he likes the element of excitement he gets from it being a secret. The risk he takes in sneaking it out and using it right inside a church building gives him pleasure in and of itself.

He pushes a button and waits for the phone to power on. The green flashing light tells him he has a message, no doubt from Brittany. Turns out it's a video. Expecting it will be X-rated, he enters his bathroom and pushes play, eager to see what she's sent.

Brittany's face fills the frame. "Hey, preacher man, don't you want some of this?" She holds the phone farther way from her face, revealing her naked body lying on a bed.

Michael grabs his crotch in excitement and squeezes. But then he pauses. There's something familiar about the video.

"When are you coming home? I'm getting tired of waiting." She pans the camera around the room, and he realizes she's in his bedroom!

He swears at the phone.

"Yes," Brittany purrs, as she points the camera back at herself, "I'm in your house."

The video ends abruptly.

Michael stares at the blank screen. *When did she make and send this?* He goes back to the original message and sees it was sent less than an hour ago. Then he clicks the video to see if it has a time stamp on it. There, in the bottom corner, he sees what he's looking for. Panic and fear snake through him. *She's at the house right now!*

He rushes out of the bathroom and his office as fast as he can, not taking the time to close his door. "Something's come up," he says, as he passes Helen's desk. "I'll be back later."

Helen stands up with a look of concern. "Are you all right?"

Michael keeps moving without answering her.

She comes around her desk, moves to the lobby and watches him head toward the parking lot and get in his car. She mutters to herself, "What in the world could have happened? No phone call came through me, and I didn't hear the Amazing Grace ringtone of his cellphone through the door. Strange, very strange." Just as she turns around to head back to her desk, she hears an auditorium door open and sees Liz walking through it. "I didn't know you were here."

Smiling, Liz says, "I came through the east side door and have been in the auditorium making sure everything on the stage is setup the way it's supposed to be. You know how Jerry moves things around sometimes when he's cleaning."

"He is thorough, I'll give him that. I spent all morning one time looking for the paper cutter."

Liz laughs. "I can believe it." She looks toward the offices. "I was going to ask Michael if he's decided on his sermon topic for this Sunday so I can start picking out some complementary music."

"He's not here."

"But when I drove through the parking lot a little bit ago, I saw his car."

"Well, he's just now dashed off and didn't tell me when he'll be back. You can call him on his cellphone, I guess." She turns and heads toward her office.

Liz follows, and says, "But he told me he would have something for me this morning. He didn't mention anything to you about his sermon, did he?"

"He did not."

"His door is open. Do you think it would be okay if I just stepped in and looked at the top of his desk to see if he has made some notes?"

Helen considers her question before answering. "Why don't I go in there with you?"

"That's fine, but don't you trust me?"

"It's not that. It's just I want to be able to truthfully say I was with you, in case there's ever a question about something missing."

Liz shrugs her shoulder. "Okay."

Walking behind Michael's desk, Liz sees a cellphone lying on the floor and the bottom desk drawer pulled out. Bending down, she picks up the phone and shows it to Helen. "He left his cellphone, so there's no point in calling him."

"He did leave in a hurry," Helen says. "I don't know what it was about."

When Liz starts to close the drawer, she sees a large book lying open in it with a cavity cut in the middle of the pages, a cavity about the size of the phone she's holding. She looks at the phone again. "This is not his phone."

"How do you know?"

"Because this is an android. Michael has an iPhone." She goes ahead and closes the drawer before Helen can see the mysterious book. "Should I lay this phone on his desk, or do you want to keep it in case someone calls looking for their phone? It's obviously one that someone dropped it. I guess Michael picked it up and decided not to put it in our lost-and-found room."

"That's probably a good thing. That room has nothing in it but casserole dishes and Cool Whip tubs people have left after our fellowship meals and an occasional Bible. Just give it to me, and I'll be sure to have it announced on Sunday that it's been found."

Liz turns her attention to the top of Michael's desk where his Bible sits on top of an open book. Moving the Bible out of the way, she says, "Maybe whatever he's reading will give me a clue as to his sermon topic." Her eyes fall on a passage that has been highlighted: *Sexual addicts are hostages of their own preoccupation. Every passerby, every relationship, every introduction to someone passes through the sexually obsessive filter. More than merely noticing sexually attractive people, there is a quality of desperation that interferes with work, relaxation, even sleep. People become objects to be scrutinized.*

"Is it helpful?" Helen asks.

Liz doesn't reply.

"Are you feeling well, Liz? Your face is awfully flushed."

Liz puts the Bible back where it was, and says, "I think I saw what I was supposed to see."

CHAPTER THIRTY-FIVE

Panting in the dark, Michael pushes himself off of Brittany and stares down at her. "Man, have I ever needed that!"

Brittany smiles. "I know what my man likes. But now it's your turn to do something for me."

He smiles back. "You like lots of things. Which one of them do you want me to do?"

"I want to try something different. Have you heard of 'safe breath'?"

"No, what's that?"

"It's another term for erotic asphyxiation, where you choke me just to the point of my having an orgasm, then you let go of my neck."

"That's crazy, and sounds dangerous."

"That's what makes it so much fun, they say. I've read that the orgasm is like none other you've ever experienced. I've just got to try it."

"I don't feel comfortable doing something like that."

She slaps him across the face. "I don't care what you feel like. You're doing this with me!"

Rubbing the side of his face, Michael says, "I get tired of that, too."

"What? This?" And she slaps him on his other cheek. "You like it. You want to be punished for all the bad things you've done."

He feels himself getting aroused inside her.

She raises her hips against him. "That's more like it. Come on, do it to me."

Feeling hot, angry and aroused, Michael makes love to her. She reaches for his hands, places them around her neck, and he applies some pressure.

"Tighter," she says. "Squeeze tighter." When he doesn't comply, she slaps him again.

A surge of adrenalin courses through him, and he presses his fingers and thumbs deeper into her neck. He feels her body tensing as her climax approaches.

She closes her eyes. "Tighter," she squeaks.

He squeezes as tight as he can. Harder, faster, tighter—he makes love like he's possessed.

Finally, he explodes with pleasure and collapses on top of her.

"That," he says between gasps for air, "was unbelievable. You didn't tell me I would enjoy it, too." He climbs out of bed, and says, "I'm going to get us something to drink."

In the kitchen, he grabs two bottles of water out of the fridge and heads back into the bedroom. "You know," he says as he walks in, "when I first saw that video you sent me, it made me mad. You take too many risks. But I guess it was worth it because—"

He stops and stares. "Brittany?" She lies naked on the bed with her legs splayed. "Brittany!" he says more sharply. "Come on, quit messing with me." He pitches one of the bottles toward her, and says, "Catch."

The bottle strikes her shoulder, but she doesn't move.

Ice fills Michael's arteries and heart. The other bottle slips from his hand and lands on the floor with a thud. Memories of finding Sarah fill his head. Suddenly, his feet are loosened from the floor, and he rushes to the bed. He gets on his knees beside Sarah and begins chest compressions, counting silently to himself. At the proper number, he leans over, pulls down on her chin, covers her mouth with his and fills her chest with air. Then he returns to doing chest compressions. Like a machine, focusing only on his movements and neither thinking nor feeling, he keeps it up until exhaustion overwhelms him, and he crumples onto the bed beside her.

After a few moments, he looks at her lifeless face. He feels neither loss nor grief. "You were always reckless," he says to her, "reckless and foolish. Frankly, I'm glad to be done with you and not have to worry about you doing something stupid that will get me in trouble. But, as usual, here I am with you, having to figure out how to clean up a mess."

Getting out of bed, he looks at her again. He curls his fingers into a fist, grits his teeth and punches her in the face. "I've been wanting to do that for a long time." Then he throws the comforter over her.

He glances at the clock: 1:19 A.M. *Time to make a plan.*

After getting dressed, he walks into the kitchen where he scrambles some eggs and makes a cup of coffee in the Keurig. He places a yellow legal pad and a pen on the kitchen table and sits down to eat and plot his next steps.

He quickly discards any ideas related to calling the police or calling a friend. *There's no way I can explain finding two dead women in my bed. So, how do I get rid of a body?*

The speed with which a sudden idea comes to him makes him wonder about his sanity and if this is the way it is with sociopaths.

Walking through the house, he turns off all the lights, plus the outside motion-activated lights on the corners of his house. *Wait twenty minutes, just in case someone is watching the house, so it will look like I've gone to sleep.*

During the twenty minutes he busies himself wrapping Brittany in a sheet, then tying it with nylon cord. Checking his watch, he hefts her over his shoulder, carries her outside and puts her in the trunk of her car. Before closing the trunk, he retrieves some concrete blocks stacked outside the garage and places them beside her then tosses in the spool of cord.

Inside the car, he turns off the automatic headlights and starts the engine. Wiping sweat off his face with his handkerchief, he adjusts the air conditioner to high. *Either this plan will work, or it won't. If it doesn't, then I will finally be set free from my life as a chameleon.*

Putting the car in reverse, he maneuvers around his car, into the street and heads south toward the East Fork of Clarks River, a place he'd found by accident during one of his driving-the-backroads escapes from the pressures of his job.

Forty minutes later, he slows as his headlights reveal a bridge up ahead. Checking his rearview mirror to make sure no one is coming, he extinguishes his lights and stops in the middle of the bridge. He looks around. No lights are shining as far as he can see.

Getting out quickly, he opens the trunk, lifts Brittany out and carries her to the edge of the bridge. Then he carries the concrete blocks and ties them to her body.

Just before shoving her off the side of the bridge, he says, "Sorry, not sorry."

Comfortable in the belief no one saw him, he takes the next hour to drive to the casino. Parking Brittany's car among customer cars, he gets out, walks to the front of the casino, and hails a taxi. Inside the taxi, he gives the driver the address to Justin and Hope's trailer.

"That's a long drive," the cabbie says.

"I know. I'm paying cash."

The driver pulls out, saying, "Whatever you say, captain."

Most of the drive Michael spends sleeping and being awakened by nightmares.

Once he's deposited at Hope's, he walks the two blocks to his house, goes in and collapses on the bed.

CHAPTER THIRTY-SIX

Sitting in the corner booth of their favorite meeting place, Hope looks at Carol Anne and says, "Please don't tell me you're moving away. I know we haven't visited and talked as much since I've taken off work, but that doesn't mean I don't think about you every day and wonder what you're doing. You and Whitney mean the world to me."

Whitney says, "I've tried and tried to talk her out of it, but she won't listen."

"I love you both for caring so much," Carol Anne replies. "But I don't think I'll ever be healthy if I don't get away from here."

Hope can't deny what she sees: her friend's cheeks are sunken and her fingers bony, added to that, her sallow complexion makes her look like a cancer patient. *God, please don't let her have cancer.*

Carol Anne says, "Ever since I lost the lawsuit I can't keep paranoid thoughts at bay. Even if it's not true, I think everyone who sees me is talking about me behind my back and laughing at me. I'm paranoid someone is going vandalize my car again or worse break into my house and rape me. I knew it was a longshot to win the lawsuit, but still, the only thing that made the effort to sue worthwhile was getting Biddle convicted." She breaks down in tears.

Hope puts her arm around her and holds her until her crying stops. "Where will you go?"

"I've got a cousin who lives in Seattle and works for Amazon. She says she can get me a job there and that I can live with her until I get on my feet."

"That's a long way from here," Whitney says. "I'm afraid we won't ever see each other again. It's the breakup of The Three Musketeers." She gives a weak smile. "Imagine us being The Three Musketeers. I never would have expected it. Look how different we all are from each other, I mean, we aren't anything alike."

They all smile.

"I know when I first started working with you all," Hope says, "I didn't like you at all, Whitney."

This produces a laugh from Carol Anne.

Whitney feigns hurt. "How in the world could someone not like me?"

"You were so loud and opinionated. And nobody at work intimidated you. I thought you were hard and uncaring."

Whitney replies, "And I thought you were a stuck-up little bitch."

Carol Anne spits out her drink and dies laughing.

Peals of laughter ring out from their corner as they erupt in laughter, as much about Carol Anne spitting out her drink as about Whitney's description of Hope. They wipe tears with napkins and gasp for breath until they finally regain control of themselves.

Carol Anne says, "We're going to get thrown out of here if we don't calm down."

Hope hoists her drink in the air. "Here's to getting thrown out."

Whitney and Carol Anne clink their glasses against hers and echo the toast.

Silence falls on them in anticipation of the end of their get together.

Carol Anne says, "Hope, tell me how you're doing. How are things with Gabriella and with Justin?"

Hope beams. "Things could not be better with me and Gabriella. I'm such a different mom with her than I was with Lisa. I read to her every day, tuck her in bed at night, laugh and play with her. I can't tell you how good it makes me feel. Don't get me wrong, we've had a few bumps along the way. Nightmares haunt her while she sleeps. She's seeing a counselor, but it's not helped much yet."

"Has she told you much about what all happened to her?" Whitney asks.

"Not a word, and I don't ask." She looks at her hands. "Honestly, I'm afraid to hear it. I don't know how I would deal with it. I'm trusting she's talking about it with the counselor." Looking up, she says, "That's really bad of me, isn't it?"

"Don't be harsh on yourself," Carol Anne answers. "I can see why you're reluctant to dig into all that. I don't know what I would do if I was in your shoes."

Hope looks at Whitney, hoping for absolution.

"Hey, look, I'm not walking in your shoes, so I'm not going to say anything about it. I just know you're doing a wonderful thing in making a difference in the life of a child. There's no greater act than that. No matter how long or short her stay is with you, she will never forget you."

Hope frowns. "What do you mean, 'long or short'?"

"I'm just talking about when they find the girl's parents and reunite them with her, if that ever happens. And who knows, it may not happen."

Hope leans back. "You know, I haven't even thought about that, but you're right." Pain strikes in the chest. Putting her hand there, she says, "I don't know what I will do if they come to take her from me."

Carol Anne and Whitney exchange a look.

"I'm sorry I said anything," Whitney says. "It'll probably never come to that. Her parents will be very hard to find."

"I agree," Carol Anne says. "Don't be worrying about that. Just enjoy being with Gabriella. Tell me about you and Justin. How's that going?"

"Yeah, well, Justin is Justin and that's all he'll ever be. I swear he acts more like a kid every day. Gabriella picks up after herself better than he does. And don't get me started on his mother. Oh my gosh, she tries to stick her nose in our business all the time."

Whitney says, "Sounds like somebody's fixing to change partners."

"Oh, Hope," Carol Anne says, "I wish you could find someone you could settle down with permanently."

"What's going on with you and the preacher man?" Whitney asks.

Hope sighs. "Can I be honest with you two?"

"Of course you can," Carol Anne answers.

"Michael is who I want to be with. We could be so happy together, I just know it. He makes me feel complete. And he would be a wonderful father to Gabriella."

"Have you told him how you feel?" Whitney asks.

Hope shakes her head. "I'm afraid to hear his answer."

"Would you be happy going back to Luther?" Carol Anne asks.

"No. Once I've cut ties with a man, I'm done with them, no looking back. Maybe I should try living by myself, with Gabriella of course. I've never lived on my own."

"Never?"

"Never."

"You might be surprised how rewarding it can be," Carol Anne encourages her. "I love living by myself...well, until all this happened with Biddle."

"Life's complicated, isn't it?" Hope comments.

"For sure," Whitney agrees. "But I've got to tell you, Hope, sometimes you make your life more complicated than it has to be."

Hope lets her friend's comment sink in a bit. "You know, you're probably right. But complicated is all I know, all I've known since I was pregnant at fifteen. Maybe complicated is normal for me."

Carol Anne takes in a deep breath. "Girls, I hate to break this up, but I've got to go."

"I've been thinking," Whitney says, "once you get settled out there, Hope and I need to make a road trip to come see you."

Carol Anne's face lights up. "Oh, that would make me so happy!"

Hope says, "You, me, and Gabriella."

"Sure, why not?" Whitney exclaims.

Slowly, they get up and walk outside the restaurant. Standing on the sidewalk, they clasp each other's hands in a circle.

Hope says, "My father would never tell me goodbye when he left for work. He would say, 'I will see you again.' So, this is not goodbye for me, Carol Anne, but—'I will see you again.'"

With her eyes brimming with tears, Carol Anne replies, "I like that. Yes, we will see each other again."

They all exchange hugs, get in their vehicles and go their separate ways.

As Hope heads home, she says to herself, *I've got to make clearer to Michael what I want.*

CHAPTER THIRTY-SEVEN

Sitting at his desk, Michael smiles as he looks at the numbers Helen ran for him before leaving for the day. Church attendance continues to swell. Since he started preaching here, the numbers are thirty to forty percent higher than a year ago. It has especially jumped since Sarah's suicide. *The sympathy factor I was hoping for. Jed's prediction about having to expand the auditorium make him look like a prophet. I just never dreamed things would go as well as they have.*

If I could just get Liz to warm up to me a little bit, things would be perfect. He's been so afraid of making too obvious a move and offending her he's reluctant to try anything. He finds her very difficult to read. *She probably still loves Jed. I'm just going to have to wait until those feelings have waned.*

Picturing Liz in his mind, triggers images of what he'd like to do to her, which triggers the desire to look at porn on his phone.

He checks the time to make certain he'll have time to surf his favorite sites before Hope arrives for her evening meeting with him. Satisfied, he reaches down, opens the bottom desk drawer and flips open the cover of Strong's concordance.

His heart stops as he stares at the empty hiding place. He is so stunned he cannot think for several seconds. But when thought does return, it returns at breakneck speed.

With trembling hands, he takes the book out and fishes around inside the drawer in case he accidently dropped it in the wrong place. Disappointed, he sits back in his chair. *When is the last time I used it?* He searches through the timeline of the past few days, skipping quickly over the debacle with Candy Carter and the horrific event with Brittany.

Suddenly, he sits upright and snaps his fingers. *It was when I got that video from Brittany and then rushed home.*

Certain he is right, he wonders who found it. *The only two people it could have been are the janitor and Helen. Unless...unless Jed dropped by and found it, or one of the deacons...or...*

His confidence drains away as he realizes his 'open-door policy' to visitors expands the list of suspects exponentially. *But if they found it in here, what did they do with it? Why not give it to Helen? Would they put it in the 'lost and found'?*

Springing up, he races through the empty corridors to the Lost and Found room. Empty Tupperware dishes and plastic tubs bounce off the floor as he scatters them out of the way in desperate search for his phone. After several minutes, he stops and runs his hand through his hair. *It's just not here. Maybe the person who found it has stolen it.* His stomach lurches. *Could they possibly hack into it?*

He grabs the edge of a counter top to keep from collapsing onto the floor. *No, no, no—that can't happen!*

At that moment, his phone rings. His feet clear the floor as he jumps. He grabs his chest as he looks to see who the call is from. "Hi, Hope, I haven't forgotten our appointment. I'm in another part of the building. I'll be right there to let you in."

"If you've got something else you need to do, we can have our meeting some other time," Hope replies with a tone of disappointment.

"No," Michael quickly replies, "I was looking forward to you coming. I just had to run over here to check something out. I'm on my way to let you in." He hustles back through the hallway, fuming over his missing phone. *There's nothing I can do about it right now. I need to be focused solely on Hope.*

His mind eases and his heart slows as he thinks about her—how attuned she is to every word he says, those deep eyes of her that draw him in and make him forget about everything else except the two of them. *But where do I want things to go with her? Would having sex with her make the connection stronger or will it taint the purity of our connection?*

Turning a corner, he spies her standing on the outside of the glass doors. *Her looks are so deceiving. She's not the frail, child-like waif she appears to be.*

She faces the door and smiles at him as he unlocks it. "I was afraid I got our appointment wrong," she says.

"Absolutely not," he replies. "I've been looking forward all day to seeing you." Out of habit from shaking hands with people at church, he extends his right hand.

But rather than reaching to shake with her right hand, Hope slips her left hand into his palm, steps inside and stands beside him with their hands held between them. With their arms touching, she looks up at him and smiles. "Hi there. Are you ready?"

Her moves catch him off guard, but it also excites him. *What does this mean? What is she telling me?* "You know the way, I'll let you lead."

She surprises him again when she says, "I've always wanted to see what it's like to be in the sanctuary when it's completely quiet and no one is there."

"Well, let's just go see," he replies.

Still clinging to his hand, she gently tugs him toward the sanctuary.

The hinges give a tiny squeak when he opens the door. They step inside and are swallowed by darkness and silence.

Hope gasps and squeezes his hand.

Standing in a dark and silent sanctuary is not a new experience for Michael. But standing here with Hope transfixes him. The connection between their hands silently crackles with electricity. He looks toward her to try and read her expression, but his eyes haven't yet adjusted to the darkness and all he sees is her form.

Finally, the breath Hope's been holding escapes in a rush. "Oh, Michael, can you feel it?" She lets go of his hand and moves in front of him. "There's something special about the connection between you and me, you can't deny it. It's like we were meant to find each other, our hearts are so alike."

Michael feels as if he is in a dream, a dream he has no control over. He hears himself say, "I've tried to figure it out and understand why it is the way it is with us, but I can find no answers."

She caresses his face in her hands. "I heard someone say one time that explaining magic takes the magic away. What we have between us, Michael, is magic, and I don't ever want to lose it." Rising on her tiptoes, she pulls his face toward her and kisses him.

He wraps his arms around her, tugs her tight against him and kisses her back, his tongue dancing a duet with hers.

Somewhere in the farthest corner of his mind he hears a whisper of warning. However, that sound is no match for the shouting he hears from his loins, begging him to take her. He slides his hand down to her hips and squeezes as he grinds his groin against hers.

Hope gives a soft moaning sound. "Yes," she whispers. She unzips his pants and reaches inside.

Michael feels he may burst at her touch.

"Hello! Anybody here?" A loud voice sounds from the direction of the building entrance.

Michael jerks away from Hope and zips his pants.

She grabs his arm and whispers, "Don't. Let's just stay here and be quiet. Whoever it is will leave." She runs her hand up his thigh.

"They might come in here," he answers, as he pushes her hand away.

"Pastor Trent? Are you here?" the voice persists.

"I've got to see who it is."

"Please," Hope begs, "don't break this spell."

"I'm sorry, I've got to go. You stay here, and I'll be back after I get rid of them." But he already knows if he comes back, they won't pick up where they left off. He's completely in his right mind now, and he's scared at how close he came to being caught having sex with a woman in the sanctuary. *God, I'm such a fool! A damn fool! One of these days it's all going to catch up with me.*

Leaving Hope standing there, he exits the sanctuary, calling out, "I'm here! Who is it?"

Someone he doesn't recognize steps out from the lighted office area.

"Oh, hi," the man says. "I had decided no one was here." His clothes are mismatched and well-worn. His big toe protrudes from a hole in one of his tennis shoes, having escaped efforts to hold it in with grey duct tape. "You must be the Pastor," he says to Michael, as he stretches his hand toward him.

Something doesn't feel right to Michael, and he gives the man a wary look and a half-hearted handshake. "I don't recall meeting you before."

"No sir, no sir, I'd say you haven't. I've never been in these parts before. I'm on my way to Chicago to see my mother who is at death's door, God bless her. I'm her only son, and I think she's hanging on until she can tell me goodbye."

Tears well up in his eyes, but to Michael they seem fake. *Don't try to fake a faker.* "And where is your home?" Michael asks.

"Mississippi. I've lived in several towns along the gulf. You ever been there? It's beautiful to behold, but a man'll starve himself to death working there."

Michael senses he's about to launch into another story, *which will be just another lie,* so he cuts him off. "Why are you here? And why did you enter our building after dark when it's clear we are not having a service of some kind."

Wringing his hands, the interloper says, "Well, here's the thing, mama sent me some money to help me get to Chicago but I had car trouble a ways back and had to spend a good portion of the money on repairs. I was hoping maybe your church could give me some gas money. I read your name on the sign and saw the two cars in the parking lot. There also was a light on inside, so I thought I'd take a chance."

Suddenly, flashing blue lights burst through the glass entrance.

Michael spots a police car under the canopy.

The man bolts for the door and is about to shoot through it when an officer holds the door against him. His eyes dart around like a scared and cornered rabbit. "Why did you call the police on me? I wasn't going to hurt anyone."

Before Michael can reply, the policeman enters, grabs the man's arm and forces him onto the floor.

The man howls in pain.

"Are you okay, Pastor?" the policeman asks. "Did he harm or threaten you?"

"Uh...no... he just...uh...wanted gas money, I think," Michael stammers. He then relates the man's story. "But where did *you* come from? And why are you here?"

"Someone called in about a suspicious-looking man prowling around your church. I don't know what this man told you, but judging by the way he looks and smells whatever he told you wasn't the truth. I'm going to take him in and find out who he is. If what he told you turns out to be true, I'll give him gas money myself." He hauls the man to his feet and escorts him outside.

Michael stands, holding the door half open, and says, "I'm sure I need to thank you for coming. I guess I'm too trusting."

"There's just a lot more meanness in the world than there used to be. You have a good evening, Pastor."

He watches the officer drive away and notices as his headlights sweep the parking lot Hope's car is no longer there. *She must have eased out another exit and left without turning on her headlights.* What he's uncertain of though is how he feels about it.

CHAPTER THIRTY-EIGHT

Hope screams and slams her forehead against her steering wheel as the blue strobe lights from the police car ricochet off the church building and parking lot. In spite of being dazed from the blow to her head, she slams it again. She spews a stream of cuss words, aiming them all at God. *Thank you, God, for ruining everything once again! It doesn't matter how close I get to happiness, you always step in and blow it up. Yeah, thanks—thanks for nothing!*

Curious about what is going on with the police at the church building, but not curious enough to stick around and find out what it is, she starts her car, jerks the gearshift into drive and edges out of the parking lot without turning on her headlights.

She turns her mind back to the scene in the sanctuary. Kissing Michael was unlike anything she's ever experienced. It sent sensations all the way to her toes, which, up until now, she believed was an expression people made up. His tongue dancing in her mouth was like a hot poker and stirred her fire. She felt an aching between her legs. And when she reached inside his pants, there was no doubt he was ready.

And then! And then, just as we were seconds from having sex, "God blows it up!" she yells.

At least I now know Michael feels the same way about me as I do about him, or he wouldn't have returned my kiss. She imagines what it would feel like to have him inside her, which leaves her itching to be satisfied.

She hurries home to Justin with the intent of bedding him as soon as she gets there. But all that screeches to a halt when she remembers Gabriella, and she immediately feels ashamed. *How could I have forgotten her? My Gabriella.* She smiles at the thought of holding her and feeling Gabriella's arms around her neck. *That's magic, too.*

As she enters the house, she hears Gabriella back in her bedroom yell, "Uno!"

In the bedroom, Hope finds Justin and Gabriella on the floor, Justin lying on his side and Gabriella sitting on her knees. The girl's eyes dance with excitement as she squeezes her final card.

When Justin plays his card, Gabriella throws her card into the air and jumps up and down. "I win! I win! I win!"

She throws herself onto Justin's side, and he reacts by crying out in fake distress. "Help, help, somebody save me!"

Hope feels a tinge of guilt about the bad things she said about Justin to her friends. *He really does try, and he has a good heart.* She sheds her mantle of frustration over what happened at the church, and announces, "I'll save you!" Charging into the room, she grabs Gabriella in a bear hug but pretends not to be able to lift her.

Gabriella squeals with delight.

Hope says, "She's too powerful for me! We will have to use our magic weapon against her."

Gabriella wriggles to get free. "No, don't tickle me."

Hope grabs one of Gabriella's bare feet and begins tickling her.

The child bursts into laughter and contorts her body to get free. "I give, I give!" she cries.

Immediately, Hope relents and pulls her into her arms and kisses her cheeks. "I think you and Justin were having a great time, weren't you?"

Nodding, Gabriella says, "Yeah. He's no good at Uno, you know it? You could beat him if you wanted to."

Hope laughs and looks at Justin, who winks at her. "Poor Justin, is he good at anything?"

Gabriella pauses, then says, "Eating! He's good at eating."

Both Justin and Hope laugh.

Justin sits up, pats his stomach, and says, "I can't deny it. I do like to eat."

Holding Gabriella in her arms, Hope uses her butt cheeks to turn her back to Justin and move closer to him. Leaning back against him, it pleases her that he folds her and Gabriella into his arms and gives a gentle squeeze.

The room grows very quiet for several moments.

Gabriella speaks, "I like it here."

Tears spring up in Hope's eyes and roll down her cheeks. "I'm glad you like it here. I like you being here."

Justin's voice is choked with emotion, as he says, "And I'm gladdest of all that both of you are here." He gently rocks side to side.

Hope closes her eyes. *If my life ended right now, I would die happy.* "I hate to break up this little party, but someone needs to take a bath and get ready for bed."

"Do I have to?" Gabriella whines.

"Yes, you have to. You go get your pajamas while I start your bath water."

"Will you help wash me?"

"Yes, I'll help you."

Gabriella rises and heads to her dresser to get pajamas. As she does, Hope tilts her head back and says to Justin, "Kiss me."

He readily obliges her.

"Thank you," she says.

"I'll kiss you anytime you want to be kissed."

"That's not what I'm talking about. I'm talking about what just happened here—you playing games with Gabriella, holding us in your arms, making us feel loved and protected. I know it's a lot, being with me and taking on Gabriella. I just want you to know I appreciate it, and I'll never forget it." Unexpected emotions rise in her chest, and she's afraid she's going to cry. Quickly, she gets up and offers her hand to help him up.

Looking at her, he laughs, "It would take ten of you to pull me up. I better do it myself." Grunting, he stands. "Hope, I know I'm not good enough for you. But I want you to know I'll always do my damndest to make you happy."

Hope's heart balances on a razor with Justin's tender and sincere promise on one side and the memory of being with Michael on the other side. "Justin, you must always remember my pattern in relationships. I'm not good at sticking things out. I'm not saying I'm getting ready to leave you. I'm just saying you need to remember that about me. It'll be really helpful one day." Before he can reply, before she sees the hurt on his face, but mostly before she starts crying, she walks out and heads toward the bathroom.

Gabriella joins her as water rushes into the tub. "Can I have bubbles?"

"Of course," Hope replies, and she reaches for a pink bottle and squirts it underneath the faucet. Immediately, white mounds of bubbles erupt.

In a flash, Gabriella strips off her clothes and climbs in the tub. Scooping up a double-handful of bubbles, she blows on them, sending them into the air.

Hope says, "I used to do that when I was your age. It was so much fun."

"Don't you do it anymore?"

Hope smiles. "No."

"Why?"

"I don't know, I just quit doing it one day."

"Why?"

"I guess it seemed like a waste of time."

"Why?"

"There were things I needed to do."

"Why?"

"Okay, enough of the why questions."

"Are you going to leave Justin?"

Hope is taken aback. "No, of course not. What makes you say that?"

"I heard what you all said when I was getting my pajamas."

"That was just grownup talk. Sometimes grownup talk doesn't mean anything. It's just people talking, trying to get things out of their head, and the words they choose don't always do a good job explaining it. Don't you worry, I've told you many times I will always take care of you."

"But what about Justin?"

Hope reaches for a wash cloth and swishes it in the water. "Enough of your questions. Stand up and let's get you washed and in the bed."

After two bedtime stories, a goodnight kiss, a drink of water and another goodnight kiss Hope finally joined Justin in the living room. "Whew! That girl and her questions."

"I know," Justin agrees. "I didn't know kids asked so many questions, especially 'Why?'."

He hands Hope a cold beer. "Thank you," she says, and turns her attention to the TV screen. The images and storyline are familiar to her, but that's not what is on her mind. *How will it affect Gabriella if I leave Justin? Will Michael be willing to accept Gabriella when I go live with him? Does he even like kids?* She realizes she's never fully introduced Gabriella to him, only pointed him out to her when they were at church. *That's what I've got to do. I need to let him meet and get to know her. I'm sure he'll love her just like I do, and it might make him more eager for us to move in with him.*

Having settled on a plan, she closes her eyes and replays every detail of this evening's meeting with Michael. Her body grows warm and her nipples harden. She opens her eyes and looks at Justin. "Hey, let's go to bed and fool around some."

Without hesitation, Justin is on his feet, grinning. "That's what I'm talking about!"

In the bedroom, they quickly undress and crawl under the covers. She does everything Justin asks her to, and he complies with her every wish. A crescendo grows inside her, begging to reach the surface. When the orgasm comes, all she sees is the face of Michael.

CHAPTER THIRTY-NINE

Michael stands on one side of the church stage as all the deacons mount the steps to the stage and line up on the other side. His heart beats so hard he feels it pulsing in his ears. *This is it. This is the end for me.*

He searches the crowd for a kind face, but angry and accusatory looks are all he can see.

A somber-faced Price Jenkins approaches the lectern and taps on the microphone. Confident it is on, he unfolds a piece of paper and reads, "It is with utmost gravity that we assemble this evening to consider the fate of Michael Trent. As deacons of the church, we believe we must do what God would want us to do." He turns to the other deacons and holds out his hand. One of them steps forward and gives him a phone.

Michael swallows.

Price holds up the phone toward Michael and asks, "We ask that you answer truthfully, because the truth is what will set you free. Sir, is this your phone?"

Michael considers lying, but doesn't want to add that to his charges if they've unlocked it and already know it's his. "Yes, it is mine."

A low murmur moves through the audience.

Price turns back to his notes. "We paid a goodly sum of money to have someone break the code and get into this phone. What we saw there were the vilest examples of debauchery I personally have ever seen or heard of. The deacons discussed whether we should do something called a screenshot and then show them to the congregation, but that idea was voted down because we believed we would be committing a sin by putting such things on public display. However, we did put together a written summary of what was found and distributed it to the church membership just so they could understand the extreme action we were making."

Michael never felt so alone, and his eyes filled with tears. "Is there anything I can do or say?"

"No, sir, there is not," Price intones. Folding up the paper and returning it to his pocket, he says, "The Law says the sinner must be put outside the camp and stoned, and that is what we will now do."

Confusion mixed with horror races through Michael. "What do you mean?"

The deacons surround him and bind his arms and legs with rope, then hoist him onto their shoulders and proceed to the parking lot, with the audience following in their wake.

"No, no!" Michael screams. "You can't do this! It's madness!"

A solitary wooden pole has been erected in the parking lot, surrounded by piles of rocks. Michael is tied to the pole, and the deacons join the crowd surrounding him.

"Who will cast the first stone?" Price calls out.

"I will," a woman answers from the back of the crowd. The people make way for her and Brittany steps out from among them.

"You...you...can't be...," Michael stammers. "How..."

She hefts a rock in her hand and throws it with all her might.

Just before the rock hits Michael in the face, he wakes from the nightmare. Jumping out of bed, heart racing, he looks wildly around his darkened bedroom. His mouth is dry as he tries to catch his breath.

Moving to the bathroom, he turns on the light and splashes cold water on his face. As he looks at his face in the mirror, all he can see are questions with no answers. He stumbles back to bed and collapses onto the covers.

A few hours later, as he eats a toasted bagel with peanut butter on it, he turns on the local TV station, just as he has every morning and evening since killing Brittany, to see if there's any news of her body being found. *Even if they do find her, there's nothing around here to tie her to me.* When the newscaster starts wrapping up the morning show and segueing to the Today Show, Michael clicks off the TV, goes and brushes his teeth then heads to work.

On the drive there, he thinks about Hope and how close they came to having sex. *I've got to have sex with her, at least once, just to see what it's like. If kissing her was like being set on fire, I can't imagine what having sex will be like.*

But as he turns into the parking lot his thoughts turn to more serious matters. *I've got to find my other phone.*

Getting out of his car, he spots what looks like Jed's car careening off the street, bouncing over a curb and into the parking lot and speeding toward him. Petrified, he squeezes his eyes shut certain Jed is going to plow into him. But screeching tires cause him to open his eyes.

Jed's car slides to a stop. Smoke rolls from each of his tires and the smell of burnt rubber fills the air. The driver's door flies open and Jed stumbles out of the car. Unkempt would be a kind description of his appearance. It's so bad, Michael is alarmed.

Walking a crooked line toward Michael, Jed yells, "Have you been sleeping with my wife?"

Michael stares at him in disbelief. "What?" Jed grabs Michael by the front of his shirt. When he does, the smell of alcohol wafts over Michael. Now he sees Jed's bloodshot, bleary eyes. He puts his hand on Jed's shoulder. "Jed, come inside and let's talk."

Jed shrugs off his hand. "Answer my question. Are you the one who's been sleeping with Liz?"

"No, I'm not sleeping with Liz."

"Who is then? Somebody is."

Michael puts his hands on both sides of Jed's face and turns it toward him. "Look at me, Jed. You and I are fixing to go into my office and drink some coffee and talk our way through this. Okay?"

Jed doesn't answer but doesn't resist Michael leading him toward the building.

Inside, as they pass by Helen, Michael says, "I know I shouldn't ask, but would mind putting on a big pot of coffee for us? And I don't want us to be interrupted."

Helen stands and steps toward the coffeemaker. "I'll let you know when it's ready."

Ninety minutes and countless cups of coffee later, Michael escorts Jed from his office.

Jed stops at Helen's desk. "I'm humiliated and very apologetic for my behavior, Miss Helen. Please forgive me."

"There's nothing for me to forgive," she replies. "But if it makes you feel better, then I forgive you."

Michael lets out a big sigh as Jed leaves the building.

"Not the way you expected your day to start, was it?" Helen asks.

"I should say not. I'm already exhausted. Jed's just having a hard time coming to grips with Liz being through with him."

"Sorrow and hurt are around us every day, we just don't always see it. Because if we did, we'd be much less judgmental toward our fellowman and more loving and kinder."

Michael looks at her for a second. "That is beautifully said, Helen. With your permission, I'd like to use that in a lesson sometime and give you credit for saying it."

"If you think it will be helpful, then feel free to do so. Whether you give me credit for saying it matters not to me. I'm certain I'm not the first person to say it."

"Perhaps not, but you're the first person I've heard say it."

Feeling thoughtful, he turns to go in his office.

"Before you go back in," Helen says, "there's something I'd like to ask you."

He stops and turns around. There's a change in her tone that puts him on edge.

Sliding open the top drawer of her desk, she withdraws something and holds it toward him. "Have you lost a phone?"

Alarms and sirens scream in Michael's head. He tries to be calm, but his face burns. There's no doubt in his mind it is his phone, but he tries to play it off. "I'm not sure. Let me see." He turns it over in his hand several times as he crafts an answer to what will undoubtedly be her next question—'Why do you have two phones?'

"Where did you find this phone?" he asks.

"It was in your office. Liz was actually the one who found it."

This stops him. *Liz? How did she find it? What was she doing in my office?* He considers playing the indignant card but decides it will make him sound desperate. Instead he decides to give as little information as possible. "I believe it might be mine."

"I thought maybe it was one you found in the sanctuary and hadn't yet been put it in the lost and found room."

Why didn't I think of that?! He gazes at her, waiting to see if she's finished or wants to dig for more details.

She returns his gaze with a steady gaze of her own.

I'm not volunteering anything. If she wants to know something, she's going to have to ask.

Finally, she says, "Whether a man has one phone or five is his business and none of mine. What is my business, though, is the welfare of this church. That should be the business of every member of the church, to be invested in protecting each other from harm and to help heal the wounds of those who are hurting."

Michael has heard this kind of thoughtful and measured preamble from Helen before, and he's certain she's pulling back the string of a bow in anticipation of sending an arrow straight to his heart. He braces himself and says nothing.

"There's something off about you, Michael," she continues. "I haven't been able to figure it out enough to name it, but there is something. My gut tells me so, and I trust my gut. Don't misunderstand me, you are a gifted presenter of God's word, and you want to bring people to Jesus. However, I believe there's something you are hiding, hiding from us folks at church, maybe even hiding from yourself. It's that little bit that keeps me from trusting you one hundred percent. I've been praying about it, praying for you to work it out with the Lord. But that's not going to happen unless it's what you want."

Her arrow finds its mark but doesn't just sting him, rather it strikes what feels like a mortal wound. His heart quits beating, and he cannot breathe. The only thing that prevents him from blurting out the truth is Helen sits down at her desk and busies herself at her computer while saying, "That's all I've got to say. Now run along."

CHAPTER FORTY

Liz finishes the last page of the book she's reading, closes the book and turns it over to look at the front cover. OUT OF THE SHADOWS, by Patrick Carnes. The examples she read of people engaging in meaningless sex while in the throes of sex addiction nauseated her. She cannot fathom how a person could allow themselves to become so debased. More than once, while reading, she wondered aloud if Jed could be a sex addict. *He was always obsessed with having sex with me. Was it because he was acting out fantasies he had about other women or reenacting things he'd seen on porn sites?*

Her most concerning questions, though, are about how the book relates to Michael. *Was he reading the book in order to better understand how to help people with sex addictions or to better understand himself and his own sex addiction?* She finds it hard to believe that a man so devoted to leading people to Christ could also be harboring such a secret life of decadence.

She thinks about Michael's wife, Sarah. *Did she know he was a sex addict and that was the cause of her unhappiness?* The more she thinks about it, the more sense it makes. *But if she knew, why would she stay married to him? How could you live with someone like that?*

Her thoughts come to a hard stop. *Was she about to divorce him, and he killed her to prevent it?* She lays out the evidence: Michael's story about finding Sarah doesn't sound believable; the note she left behind; Jessie Pinkston's confrontation of Michael and Michael's reaction. *It all adds up.*

She considers sharing all this with Jed to get his opinion, but she knows he'll say she's overreacting and reading things into the situation. And there's no one else she can share her suppositions with without running the risk of starting a rumor—a rumor that could ruin a man of God, if she's wrong.

Next, she examines her feelings about Michael. *I enjoy being around him. I like that he's a good listener and is always interested in my opinion, not dismissive to me like Jed was at times. He's definitely good looking, 'easy on the eyes' my Grandma would say.* She pauses for a moment. *Yes, I'm attracted to him and have had impure thoughts about him. And I'm certain he's attracted to me.*

She looks back at Carnes's book and thinks about different times Michael has moved closer to her than necessary when discussing church music or he's touched her on the arm when making a point with her, all of which could be completely innocent, *but not if he's a sex addict. According to this book, he's grooming me, intent on a sexual conquest.* She shudders and feels nauseated at the thought.

Rising from her chair, she heads into the kitchen and pours herself a glass of wine. She lifts the glass to her lips and freezes. *Are there other women in the church he's grooming or even gone farther with?* Stunned, she sets the glass down.

Suddenly, the back door opens and she screams.

"Mom?" Mark calls out. "Are you okay?" He comes racing into the kitchen, a look of alarm on his face.

"I'm fine, I'm fine. You just scared me, that's all."

"Scared you? I opened and closed the door like I always do. Why would that scare you?"

"I was so deep in thought it caught me off guard." She gives him a kiss on the cheek. "How was play practice this evening?"

"Really good. I never thought I would enjoy anything like being in a play, but I've having a blast. Thanks for encouraging me to give it a try."

Liz smiles. "I'm glad you're enjoying it."

"So, what were you thinking about when I came in? Must have been pretty serious."

"To be honest, I think I was like Alice in Wonderland and had fallen down a rabbit hole, starting with a tiny suspicion and building it into full-length drama best suited for the Lifetime Channel." She adds a small laugh in hopes her explanation will satisfy him.

He looks at her for a second, then shrugs and moves to the refrigerator. "What is there to eat? I'm starving."

That night, sleep proves to be as elusive as a butterfly for Liz as she wrestles with her thoughts about Michael and what to do with them. A memory comes to her of seeing Hope Rodriguez coming into the church building just as she was leaving from a meeting with Michael. It was late afternoon and Helen was getting ready to go home, which would leave Michael and Hope alone in the building. Liz hadn't thought much about it but did notice Hope's face was a little flushed. *Maybe it was flushed with excitement in anticipation of what was about to happen between her and Michael.*

By the time 5:00 a.m. rolls around, Liz gives up on sleep. As she showers and washes her hair she makes up her mind she is going to confront Michael with her suspicions.

*****

Five hours later, she pulls into the church parking lot but stops short when she recognizes Jed's car as one of the handful of cars parked there.

I do not want to see him and get pulled into a verbal tug-of-war over the divorce.

So, she drives to the opposite side of the building and, using her key, enters through another door that leads to the choir practice room.

Sitting down at the piano, she begins playing, in hopes it will calm her. She's never known anyone who confronted their pastor like she's going to with Michael. *This is no small matter.*

She's tried to envision the different scenarios that could happen when she puts the evidence in front of him. *What if I'm completely wrong about it all? How will that affect our relationship? Will he ask to have me replaced as Music Minister? And what if he admits he is a sex addict but asks me to keep it private? What will I do then?*

She closes her eyes and shakes her head. *Whatever's going to happen is going to happen. I trust God to be in control.*

After thirty minutes, she makes her way through the building to the office complex. Through the glass doors of the small lobby she sees Jed's car is gone. Taking a deep breath, she approaches the offices.

"Hi, Helen," she says as she enters. She's struck by the sudden idea that perhaps Helen would have been a good person with whom to discuss her theories.

"Good morning, Elizabeth. Can I help you?"

It is so like Helen to bypass any pleasantries or small talk. Jed has told Liz harrowing tales of Helen's iron rule over the school he attended. "She should have been in the military," he said. "She could have easily replaced General Patton."

Liz asks, "Did you ever find out whose phone that was you and I found in Michael's office."

"As a matter of fact, I did," Helen replies.

Liz waits for her to divulge who the owner is, but when it becomes clear Helen will not volunteer the information, Liz asks, "Do you mind telling me whose it was?"

"It was Michael's."

If Liz needed any confirmation she was following the right track, this is it. "Is Michael busy?"

"I wouldn't know, as he doesn't keep me informed on such matters."

Liz shifts her weight impatiently. "Can I go in and see him?"

"I've not yet seen him turn anyone away who wanted to see him, even if they were interrupting his sermon preparation. I don't think that's wise of him, but that doesn't matter. He's his own person and can do things the way he wants to."

Liz senses frustration and irritation, but before she can comment on it, Helen says, "I think it's time for me to retire from this job. Let the church hire someone more accustomed to how things are nowadays. One drawback to being a church secretary is you are afforded the opportunity to see how things are done behind the scenes." She pauses, then adds, "And that can sometimes be disillusioning."

Liz frowns at this sudden turn in what was a light conversation between them. "What's happened?"

Helen waves her off. "It's nothing in particular. You, yourself, having been married to Jed, know things are not always what the public believes them to be."

Liz nods and sighs. "That is very true." Her mind tumbles back through various projects Jed had a hand in over the years and how differently the headlines read from what was the truth.

"Well, hi, Liz."

Michael's voice jerks her back to the present.

"You two ladies looked a little spaced out there. You must have been having a pretty serious conversation."

"Nothing that matters," Helen says.

"What brings you by here?" Michael asks Liz. "We didn't have anything scheduled, did we?"

"No, this is a spur of the moment thing. I wanted to talk to, if you have the time."

Michael beams. "Absolutely! Come right in."

As Liz walks toward his office, Helen says, "You're a smart woman, Liz. Trust your instincts."

Liz almost stops and turns around. *Why did she say that? Does she have a sense as to what I'm about to do?* Liz can find no other explanation and, so, is encouraged by Helen's words.

CHAPTER FORTY-ONE

As Liz passes through Michael's doorway, she feels she's entering a lion's den.

He shuts the door behind her, something she never gave much thought to before, but now it puts her on edge.

"Have a seat," Michael says as he sweeps his hand toward the loveseat.

Liz sits down and sets her handbag beside her. She takes in his smiling face but catches his eyes giving her a once over. *Has he always done that, but I never noticed?*

"It's good to see you," he says.

"Why do you say that?"

"I guess because I miss having conversations with a woman ever since Sarah died. Sure, I can talk to the guys, but I get tired of talking about sports and jobs and hobbies."

"So, you and Sarah used to spend lots of time talking? Because I got the impression from her that that was an area you all struggled with."

Frowning, Michael says, "I don't know why she would say that. Sure, we had problems, like most couples, but I thought communication was one of the strengths of our marriage."

Liz tries to read any signs he's lying but detects nothing, even though she knows he is. *I know what Sarah told me.*

"There's something I've never told you," he says. "I wish I could be in your choir for just one service so I could see what your face looks like. All I see is your back as you direct them. I bet your face glows like an angel's."

Liz blushes at the compliment and hates herself for it. One of her goals in this meeting is to keep her feelings in check. She tries to brush him aside by saying, "You might see me scowling over someone missing a note."

Michael laughs. "I find that hard to believe. I can't imagine a scowl on a face like yours."

His laugh is one of the first things she liked about him when he moved to Bardwell. The pitch and staccato rhythm of his laugh reminded her of her grandfather's. In spite of herself, she smiles, then second guesses her mission. *There's no way he is a sex addict.* But Helen's words echo in her mind and help steel her resolve.

"What brings you by?" Michael asks.

Here goes nothing. "I need your help in understanding some things that don't quite make sense to me."

He sits backs and crosses his legs. "I'll help, if I can."

"The first thing is, this book." She reaches in her bag and brings out her copy of Carnes's book. She watches his face closely and sees he recognizes it before she shows him the front of it. He licks his lips and takes a deep breath.

Turning the front of the book where he can plainly see it, she taps it with her finger. "A copy of this was lying open on top of your desk when Helen and I went in. I was curious about it, so I bought a copy and have read it. What I'm wondering is, why are you reading it?"

Michael fiddles with the collar of his shirt, uncrosses and re-crosses his legs. Rather than looking at her or the book, he looks toward the ceiling. "Even though we live in a small, rural town, I'm confident there are people here who have sex addictions, probably some people in our church." He looks at her, and says, "I thought I should try to educate myself on the problem in order that I might be better equipped to help someone should they come to me looking for help."

This is the answer Liz expected he would give, so her next question is already on the tip of her tongue. "Are you sure you're not reading it in order to better understand yourself?" She can hardly believe her own ears at the boldness of the question.

There's a look of uncertainty in Michael's eyes, and his cheeks turn pink. Then, like a cloud passing over the sun, the look is gone, and he says, "Is that what you think of me, Liz? You think I'm a sex addict? Because if it is, I am greatly wounded. I've devoted my life to encouraging people to life a Christ-like life. How could I do that if I lived the kind of life a sex addict lives?"

Some of Liz's resolve melts and is replaced by indecision. "Well...just because you're a Pastor doesn't mean you're perfect. Everyone has sin in their life."

"That is very true. I've never tried to hold myself up as perfect. But the sin you're accusing me of...that's...that's hard for me to swallow." Tears pool in his eyes.

Liz suddenly feels like he is playing her with fake tears. She sits a little straighter, and asks, "What possible reason do you have for owning two phones?"

Michael glances toward his desk, then leans forward with his elbows on his knees. His jaw muscles ripple underneath his cheeks as he looks at the floor. Silence fills the space between and in the silence, Liz feels a crescendo building, a crescendo so strong it scares her. She waits.

Finally, Michael takes a deep breath and sits back up. "Why do you think I have two phones?"

This time, his ploy to redirect the conversation makes her mad, and she's glad of it. "That's not what's important," she says firmly. "I want to hear your answer."

"You want the truth, don't you?"

"Yes."

"Even if it changes how you feel about me?"

"You don't know how I feel about you."

"That's true. But I would like to know."

"You keep trying to turn this conversation away from what I'm looking for, and that makes you look and sound guilty."

He sighs. "Okay, the truth is, I use the second phone to communicate with my father. And, of course, you'll want to know why that's the case. Well, Sarah was always jealous of my father and our relationship. She felt I was too dependent on him and spent too much time talking to him. I think she felt he and I had a closer relationship than she and I. She was always checking my phone to see if I'd called him or texted him, so I bought another phone and kept it hid. You probably saw the hiding place inside the book, didn't you?"

Of all the possible answers to her question that she'd imagined, this answer never occurred to her...*because it's completely unbelievable!* "You're really good, you know that don't you? You know exactly how to manipulate people's emotions and get them to believe whatever you want them to believe. Is that the way all successful evangelists are? Is that what makes them successful? Well, I don't believe anything you've said. I can't prove you're lying, so I'll not talk about this to any of the deacons. I'll continue to work with you in coordinating the worship music, but if you had any other designs on me or us, you can throw them out the window. I don't trust you."

Before he has a chance to reply, she stands up and leaves his office. As she passes by Helen's desk, the secretary raises her eyebrows in an unspoken question.

Liz nods her head in the direction of Michael's office and says, "There's something off in there."

Helen replies, "I agree."

CHAPTER FORTY-TWO

"Is it Sunday?" Gabriella asks.

"No," Hope chuckles, "it isn't Sunday."

"They why are we at church?"

Leaning in the back door of her car, Hope unbuckles her from her car seat. "We're just going to visit with Brother Michael."

"He's not going to preach, is he? Preaching is boring."

Hope takes her hand as they walk across the parking lot. "No, he's not going to preach. You'll learn to appreciate preaching more, when you get older. It helps you understand God and Jesus better."

As they approach the building, Hope sees Liz exiting the building. Her face is cloudy, and she appears distracted.

"Hi there, Liz," Hope says.

Liz looks up, sees them and a smile breaks out on her face. "Hope and Gabriella, how are you?" She kneels down and opens her arms.

Hope releases Gabriella's hand, and the child runs to Liz. It has taken Hope a bit to not be jealous of how much Gabriella enjoys Liz and to realize Liz's attention toward Gabriella doesn't have some sort of ulterior motive. *She really is a good person.*

"She really likes the clothes you bought her," Hope says to Liz.

Standing up while holding Gabriella in her arms, Liz answers, "Did they all fit?"

"Perfectly. Is everything okay with you? You looked upset when you came out of the building."

The clouds return to Liz's face. "What are you two up to here at the church?"

"We're going visit with Michael some. I want Gabriella to get to know him better and him to know her better, too. I'm hoping it'll make her more eager to attend church. She finds it pretty boring right now."

Liz looks over her shoulder toward the church building, then back at Hope. "Just...uh...be careful, Hope. Things aren't always what they appear to be."

Hope frowns. "I'm not sure what you mean. What 'things' are you talking about?"

Liz looks at Gabriella, then at Hope. "Maybe we can eat lunch together some time, and I'll explain."

"Sure, just give me a call."

Setting Gabriella down, Liz says, "I'll do that—and soon."

Hope watches Liz walk to her car and tries to figure out what she was trying to tell her and why she didn't want to talk about it in front of Gabriella, but Hope can't decipher it. Her interest is seeing Michael and letting him get better acquainted with Gabriella as the first step in her plan to Michael letting them move in with him. *Nothing could make me happier than the three of us living together as a family.*

The two of them enter the building and walk to the offices.

Usually when Hope sees Michael, Helen has already gone home, so she feels some anxiety about facing the woman. Every time she's encountered her at church, she's felt very intimidated, even though Helen has been sweet and conversive with Gabriella.

Helen gives Hope what appears to be a stony stare when she enters, but her face immediately brightens when she sees Gabriella.

"Ah, my sweet Gabriella," Helen says. "Seeing your beautiful face has been the best part of my day, so far."

Gabriella twirls her hair around her finger, and says, "Thank you."

Helen looks at Hope and says, "I don't usually see you around her during the daytime, except for church. What brings you by?"

Whether intended or not, Hope feels the sting from the barbed end of Helen's comment. *Does she know what's going on between me and Michael? Are there hidden cameras or microphones in his office?* The questions make her uneasy.

"We came by to see Michael—I mean Pastor Michael. Is he busy?"

Helen waves dismissively toward his office and says, "You might as well go in, everyone else in town has today."

Hope takes Gabriella by the hand and they proceed into Michael's office. She's immediately struck by how pale and distressed he looks sitting behind his desk.

Hope clears her throat, and he jumps up, looking panic stricken.

When he sees her, he closes his eyes and tilts his head back. Taking a deep breath, he looks back at her and sighs, "I'm glad to see you." He looks down at Gabriella, and says, "And you, too."

"Are you okay?" Hope asks. "When I first walked in here you didn't look well."

His color returns, and he flashes her a warm smile. "It's just been a challenging morning. Some days are easier than others." He walks around the desk and squats in front of Gabriella. "To what do I owe the pleasure of having two pretty girls come to see me?"

"You're not going to preach, are you?" Gabriella asks.

Michael laughs.

"Gabriella!" Hope snaps at her.

"No, I'm not going to bore you with my preaching," Michael says with a smile. "I only do that on Sundays."

"I'm sorry," Hope says. "I never know what's going to come out of her mouth."

"It's okay, I'm not offended at all. One of the things I like about young kids is how honest they are. It's ironic that as we get older it's easier to tell a lie than it is to tell the truth. Then, on the downhill side of life, say after sixty, that trait of honesty returns, sometimes brutally so."

Hope thinks about it for a moment. "You know, you're right. My grandmother, Mama T, was brutally honest and didn't care if it hurt your feelings or not."

He looks toward the loveseat. "Do you all want to sit down?"

"Yes, if you have time. Helen says you've been awfully busy today. I know I saw Liz leaving. I figure you all were discussing the music for Sunday. She does an amazing job, doesn't she?"

Michael's smile drops off his face for a second and there's a flicker of fear in his eyes, but that quickly vanishes as he puts his smile back on. "Yes, she does," he says. "She's a very talented lady."

"She seems to be holding up pretty well through the divorce from her husband. It's kind of weird to me that this church that has gone through so much drama, what with you coming as a new pastor, then what happened with Sarah, then the music person gets a divorce, but it hasn't seemed to affect the church. I mean, sure it's affected people, but everybody's still very loving and accepting. And new members are joining all the time. I've just never been a part of something like this. It's nice."

"I'm glad you made this your church home," Michael replies. "I agree with what you said. This is a unique group of people. I feel blessed to be a part of it."

Gabriella climbs off the couch and begins wandering around the office. Hope decides to let her go and see what happens, hoping that maybe Michael will see she's bored and he'll try to do something with her. She looks at Michael, whose focus is on her, rather than the meandering Gabriella.

He mouths the words, "It's good to see you."

While this pleases Hope, it's not what she wants from him. She looks deliberately at Gabriella, thinking he'll follow her lead. "Look but don't touch, Gabriella," she says. Out of the corner of her eye, she sees Michael still looking at her. "Don't break anything," she says.

She wants to tell Michael that Gabriella loves having stories read to her, but when she turns to look at him she finds him leaning toward her, eyes glued on her.

In a whisper only loud enough for her to hear, he says, "Would you like to come to my house this evening?"

His question nearly knocks her off her seat. She looks at him in disbelief, wondering if she heard him correctly. "What did you say?" she whispers.

"I want you to come to the house this evening. I want to finish what we started the other night in the sanctuary."

Hope's mind spins like a whirling dervish. His suggestion is definitely one of the steps she was calculating to take in her overall plan to convince him to let her and Gabriella move in with him, but she figured she would be the one who would instigate it. *I don't want him to just want me though, I want him to want Gabriella, too.*

About that time, Gabriella finishes her exploration of the office and approaches Hope. "Can we go now, Mama?"

Hope looks at her and then back at Michael. His eyebrows are raised and his eyes glow with desire. As Gabriella climbs back on the loveseat beside her, irritation flirts with Michael's features, but he sits back and gives them an easy smile.

"She's a precious girl," he says.

"I'm ready to go, Mama," Gabriella insists. "I'm bored."

Hope suddenly feels as if she's perched on a precipice and her next decision will either give her what she wants or it will lead to her destruction. "I guess we need to go," she says to Michael as she stands up.

"I understand," he replies. "But what about my suggestion?"

Mindful of Gabriella's presence, Hope chooses her words carefully. "I think it's a good one, but Justin is working tonight."

"I see. Then perhaps another time would be better."

"Yes, we can do that. I'll give you a call."

"I look forward to it."

Hope's heart races as she leads Gabriella out of the office and into the parking lot. An overwhelming and inexplicable feeling of needing to escape sweeps her toward her car. *What's the matter with me? What's going on?*

She straps Gabriella into her car seat.

"What's wrong, mama? Your hands are shaking."

How can I answer her when I can't figure it out for myself? "It's nothing," she says. "Everything's fine."

CHAPTER FORTY-THREE

After Hope leaves Michael's office, he collapses into the armchair. *What a day this has been!* Fatigue reaches into every part of his body, and he feels a headache coming on. From Jed coming by with deacon Lester Wade in tow to discuss Lester's idea about a mission trip to Honduras that members of the church can participate in, to Liz's appearance with a quiver full of ideas and accusations that hit uncomfortably close to the truth, to Hope's surprise visit with Gabriella, he feels as if he's been on an emotional roller coaster or thrown into a blender.

Lester's idea was a bold one: take enough people to construct two houses, distribute two thousand pounds of food to the people who live close by, find doctors who will accompany them and run a medical clinic. The idea originally came about when the previous pastor was at the church, and Lester had gone so far as to travel to Honduras and lay some groundwork. But nothing went any further after the pastor was let go. Jed seemed to think now is a good time because excitement is high in the church. Michael told the two of them that he was definitely on board with the idea and would love to go on the mission.

What he isn't sure about is how to deal with Liz. For certain, he has to put on hold any ideas about getting her into bed with him. In her hypervigilant state there will be no way to entice or manipulate her. In fact, he needs to swing the pendulum as far in the opposite direction as he can, making every effort to be mindful of her personal space and keeping all their conversations focused on music for the church.

He also makes a mental note to be more aware of Helen and what she can hear and see going on in his office. *She's held in high regard by the deacons, so much so, that one word from her could derail all my efforts in Bardwell and get me sent packing.*

Then, he brings up the image of Hope sitting across from him, close enough to touch but not to kiss. He's not sure if it's because she's been given a second chance at parenthood but something has lit a candle in her. Her face practically glows, and an energy radiates from her that makes her even more desirable. *If Gabriella hadn't been with her today, who knows what might have happened.* He gets aroused thinking about it.

Rising from the chair, he starts toward his bathroom, intent on spending some time fantasizing and pleasuring himself, but a knock on his door stops him.

Turning around, he almost falls backward.

"Good day to you, Pastor," Jessie Pinkston says.

In spite of all his effort, Michael can't force a smile. Terror holds him in its hand and squeezes him so tightly he can't think of anything to say.

"May I come in?" Pinkston asks.

Michael nods and waves him in, then takes a seat behind his desk before his knees buckle.

"I hope I'm not interrupting anything important," Jessie says.

Michael finally finds his voice, and says, "It has been a busy morning around here, which has prevented me from focusing on preparing my lesson for Sunday, but I've got a little time for you before I shut my office door and start studying."

Jessie works his mouth around as if he's chewing tobacco and getting ready to spit. "You know, I've often wondered where pastors get their ideas for their sermons. Is there a book you use for that, or do the ideas come from your own life experiences?"

Michael is certain this isn't the reason for Jessie's visit. *If he'd found out something about Sarah's suicide note, wouldn't get right to the point? Maybe he's just fishing.* "I would say, for me, both those things are true, plus the news, magazines, conversations with people. An idea can literally come from anywhere and can happen unexpectedly.

"Really? You mean you might get an idea from this conversation right here?"

Michael feels he's about to step in a trap, so he answers carefully. "I suppose it could."

Jessie takes out his pen and notebook and writes something. "That's very interesting."

Everything in Michael wants to pursue this line of thinking and ask him why it's interesting, but he wants to be rid of him as quickly as possible, so he holds his tongue.

"Have you ever done a series of lessons on The Ten Commandments?"

This catches Michael off guard and makes his footing feel less secure. "Actually, I have. I did a series of ten lessons one time, one on each of the commandments. I'll probably do that here sometime in the future."

"I think about The Ten Commandments a lot," Jessie says. "Those ten simple things formed the basis or foundation of all the other elements of the law that God gave Moses. I think my job would be much easier if everyone observed The Ten Commandments, don't you?"

Michael wants to tell him to shut up babbling and get to the point, but, instead, he nods in agreement.

Jessie taps his pen on his knee absent mindedly while he gazes at some unknown distant point. A few seconds pass, and he says, "Which of the commandments do you think gets broken more than the others?"

In spite of his reticence to talk to the man, Michael is intrigued by the question and so, thinks about for a moment. "I suppose in today's world it would be taking God's name in vain. Seems like more and more people can't talk without cussing."

"That's a good answer, and you're probably right. But I think about how many times in my line of work I've ended up working a case that began by someone breaking the 'thou shalt not covet' law. Somebody looks at another man or woman, wants what they see, which leads to breaking the 'thou shalt not commit adultery law,' and that often leads to breaking another law—'thou shalt not murder.'"

When he says the last phrase, his eyes bore in on Michael, pinning him to his chair. The headache that a bit ago was just getting started now explodes, making him feel like his head is going to split in two. He wants to close his eyes and rub his temples in an effort to ease the pain but doesn't trust how that might look to the officer. He can't help from squinting at the pain. Blinking, he manages to say, "I see what you're saying."

"You know," Jessie says, "most murders are spur of the moment, unplanned sorts of things, even unintended sometimes."

Michael finds the slow, halting pace of the conversation maddening, especially the long moments of silence, but he refuses to unbutton his lips for fear something incriminating will fall out.

Jessie sucks on his teeth and flips some pages in his notebook. "I suppose you're wondering why I came by. You remember that note you found beside your wife when she died. Do you remember there was a set of fingerprints on it that couldn't be identified?"

Michael's mind races ahead and predicts what is coming next. He feels like he's trapped in a car stranded on a railroad track and a train is speeding toward him. The inevitability of being broadsided is set in stone. He nods his head in answer to Jessie's question.

"It's the strangest thing," Jessie says. "A woman was found in a river not too far from here. She'd been murdered and dumped. There were no identifying papers on her, so the deputy who found her used her fingerprints to search. There were no matches with people who had a criminal past, so he thought he'd try seeing if it matched any prints in the system of Jane Does. Guess what?"

Michael refuses to answer.

"Okay, I'll tell you. That woman's prints match the prints on that note because I'd loaded them into the data base when I was trying to identify who they belonged to. What do you think about that?"

Michael answers honestly, "I hardly know what to think. How did the woman die?"

Jessie shakes his head. "Don't know, yet. The coroner will have to figure that out. But here's the thing. I think your wife knew this person. You know, no sign of forced entry, no sign of a struggle, so she had to have known her."

"I see," Michael says slowly.

Jessie continues, getting more animated, "And if Sarah knew her, there's a good chance you knew her, too. What we'd like you to do is take a look at the body and see if you can help identify her."

CHAPTER FORTY-FOUR

After leaving Michael's office, disturbing and conflicting thoughts fill Hope's head. *Why didn't I jump at Michael's invitation? Why did alarms ring in my head, warning me to stop? It looked like he was irritated at Gabriella. Does he not like kids and that's why he and Sarah didn't have any? Liz's warning to me—what was that about? Was it about Michael? Does she know something I don't? He's a man of God; why should I be afraid? He would never do anything to hurt me.*

In all her other relationships with men, she's never heard any warnings or seen any signs telling her to put on the brakes; she's just gone with her feelings. *And where has that always gotten me?*

Of course, in hindsight she could see the men's flaws and realize being with them wasn't the smart thing to do.

Is this how it is with normal people, they stop and think about whether or not being with someone is wise? Why is it that Michael, the one man who is perfect for me, is the person my mind decides to step in on and tell me I need to tap the brakes and slow down? She grits her teeth and looks in the rearview mirror at Gabriella playing on her tablet.

"I think I need some ice cream. What about you?"

Gabriella's face lights up as she drops the tablet onto the seat beside her. "Ice cream, ice cream, ice cream!"

Hope turns in to the Dairyette and pulls into the drive-in lane. "Two soft-serve ice cream cones," she says into the speaker, "with sugar cones."

Gabriella claps her hands and cheers.

When the attendant hands her the ice cream cones, Hope hands one to Gabriella. "Be careful and don't make a mess. Remember, you have to lick it around the edge of the cone, not just at the top."

Since Gabriella came to live with her, Hope has made more of an effort to eat "like normal people," including occasional treat like these ice cream cones. In the past, eating has always been difficult for her. Now though, she's noticed she's been gaining weight and it doesn't bother her. She looks back at Gabriella and the circle of ice cream around her mouth. *She's been good for me. She's changed me.*

Gabriella looks up, and says, "Why did we go see the preacher?"

"I thought it might make you more interested in church if you met him face-to-face and got to know him a little bit. You like him, don't you?"

"He doesn't like me."

"Gabriella, that's not true. What makes you say that?"

"I can just tell. He's not fun like Justin is. Justin gets in the floor and plays with me. I like Justin."

A tinge of guilt touches Hope's heart, knowing her intentions to leave Justin and move in with Michael.

"I like Justin, too," Hope says, "but Michael is a very nice man. You just don't know him as well as I do." *At least, I think I do.*

When they get home, Hope begins preparing supper in anticipation of Justin coming home for a couple of hours before having to return to pull a night shift. His willingness to work extra shifts so they can afford to buy things for Gabriella has meant a lot to Hope and opened her heart to him.

But as soon as Justin walks in, she can see he's not well.

"What's the matter?" she asks.

"I don't know," he groans. "I feel like I'm wearing shoes made out of concrete. I'm just exhausted."

"Justin!" Gabriella squeals as she comes running from her bedroom.

Hope steps in front of her and catches her. Picking her up, she says, "I think Justin is sick. I'm going to take his temperature. You need to stay away from him so you don't get sick. Okay?"

Gabriella frowns and looks at Justin. "You sick?"

"Maybe. But Hope is right. I don't want to make you sick." He takes a seat in his recliner.

Hope looks at Gabriella. "You know where the thermometer is?"

"Yeah."

"Will you go get it for me?"

"Sure."

Hope sets her down and turns her attention to Justin. "You got a headache or stomachache? Does your throat hurt?"

"It hurts to swallow, and my head hurts."

"Here it is," Gabriella yells as she runs into the room holding the thermometer aloft.

Hope takes it from her, turns it on and sticks it in Justin's mouth. She touches his face with the back of her hand. "I don't know how much you have, but you definitely have fever."

The thermometer beeps, and she removes it from his mouth. Looking at it, she says, "One hundred two, point nine."

"No wonder I feel bad," he moans.

"You need to call the casino and tell them you're not coming back tonight."

"But—"

"No 'buts.' You're going to bed."

Gabriella eases closer to them. "Is Justin going to die?"

The adults say no in unison.

"I'll be fine," Justin tells her.

"He's just got the flu or strep throat or something like that," Hope says. "He needs to rest. You and I can take care of him, can't we?"

"I want to give him a hug."

Tears spring up in Hope's eyes, and she notices Justin's eyes turn red. "That's the sweetest thing, sweetheart. But we don't want you to catch whatever he's got. Why don't you go pull back the covers on our bed so he can get in?"

Delighted to feel like she is helping, Gabriella skedaddles toward their bedroom.

In a husky voice, Justin says, "Ain't she just the sweetest thing? I never knew I could love a child so much."

Hope's emotions hold her voice captive, so all she can do is nod her head and reach for his hand to help him out of the chair.

*****

Hope awakens in the middle of the night, panting and sweating. She was dreaming of having sex with Michael and had an orgasm. She smiles at the memory and the feeling. *That's the kind of dream I could get used to.*

Turning her head, she looks at her clock: 1:37 a.m. She slips out of bed and pads into the kitchen, where she gets a drink of cold water.

An idea pops into her head that is so outrageous she laughs out loud. *That is crazy! But wouldn't it be amazing?*

She retreats to the bedroom and slips on a pair of jeans and her sneakers. In the bathroom, she combs her hair and brushes her teeth. Excitement and anticipation make her feel giddy. *I can't believe what I'm about to do.*

Without another thought, she exits the house and starts walking to Michael's.

CHAPTER FORTY-FIVE

Michael lies in the dark, staring at the ceiling. Sleep refuses to give him a place to escape to as every time he closes his eyes, all he can see is Brittany's face.

The last thing he wanted to do was agree to Jessie Pinkston's request to help identify the body of the drowned woman, because he had no doubt it was Brittany. But he could think of no way of refusing without casting suspicion in his direction.

On the drive to the morgue, he kept telling himself, "It'll be okay. They have nothing that can connect her to me."

What he wasn't prepared for was the ghoulish condition of her face with its empty eye sockets. In spite of his plan to appear cool and detached, he vomited on the floor as soon as he saw her.

"I'm sorry," he said, as he took the paper towels offered. "Why in the world would you want to torture me by making me look at such a thing?"

Jessie replied, "I'm just trying to get to the bottom of what happened to your wife. Do you recognize his woman?"

"No! I've never seen her before."

"Then how could her fingerprints have been on Sarah's note?"

"You're the investigator. You're going to have to figure it out because I have no idea."

Now, Michael can't escape from the image of Brittany's face. It's like it's been tattooed on his memory.

"What ifs?" creep into his thoughts: *What if they connect the abandoned car to Brittany? What if they trace her back to Topeka? What if someone in Topeka remembers seeing me with her? What if they show pictures of her to Helen? What if she tells them about Brittany coming to my office?*

Each "what if?" increases his heart rate until it feels like his heart is going to gallop out of his chest. Sitting up on the edge of his bed, he takes some deep breaths in an effort to slow his heart.

He switches on the bedside lamp, hoping it will clear his mind. But immediately, he hears the words from Scripture, *You may be sure that your sin will find you out.*

The warning chases him out of bed, and he hurries into the kitchen as if being chased by wild dogs. He runs his hand through his hair and turns on the light over the stove. *Is this what it feels like to go insane?*

He hears an odd sound and turns in that direction. Every nerve ending in his body is firing as he holds his breath to hear if the sound recurs.

There it is again! Something at the back door.

He inches that way, grabbing a screwdriver off the counter as he passes. Two feet from the door, he reaches for the doorknob but freezes when a loud whisper comes from the other side of the door.

"Michael, are you awake?"

He doesn't recognize the voice.

Whoever it is taps on the door, and says his name again. This time there's a ring of familiarity in it.

"Hope? Is that you?" he says through the door.

"Yes, Michael, it's me," she says excitedly.

What in the world is she doing here in the middle of the night?

He unlocks the door, opens it, and Hope slips inside. Her eyes are large, but not from panic like he expected she would be; they are large with desire.

"Hope, are you okay? Has something—"

Before he can finish his sentence, her mouth covers his, and she wraps her arms around his neck. He finally breaks away, but only to catch his breath, then he returns her passion, pushing her against the door. His mind is empty, and his movements are instinctual.

"Oh, Michael," Hope says, "I want you, I need you."

Her breath is hot on his face. He pulls her t-shirt off over her head and stares at her braless chest.

"Oh, Hope."

She slips her hand past the elastic band of his shorts, finds him and squeezes.

Two hours later, having made love in the kitchen, on the couch, and on the bed, they lie naked on the tangled covers of Michael's bed, his arm under her head and her face on his shoulder.

"Never in my wildest fantasies," Michael says, "have I dreamed of having sex like that. You are amazing. I guess it's true that big surprises come in small packages."

Rubbing her foot up and down his leg, Hope says, "You were pretty special yourself. Seems like we fit together pretty well." She laughs.

He, too, laughs at her double-entendre. "That is certainly an accurate statement."

She props up on one elbow and looks at him. "I've never known anybody like you, and no one has ever made me feel the way you do."

He looks at her and smiles. "Well, I could say the same thing about you. You're easy to be with, and that's important to me."

She sits up beside him on her knees.

He looks at her breasts swaying but doubts he has another erection left in him.

"I love you, Michael."

He reaches for her breast and caresses it. "You look amazing."

"Did you hear what I said?"

The edge in her tone jerks him away from where his mind was going, and he looks at her face. "What?"

"Did you hear what I said?"

"I don't know. Did I miss something?"

"I told you I love you."

"Well, I love you, too, Hope."

"No, Michael, not like that." She puts one hand on his chest and the other on her own. "I mean, I *love* you." Twin tears trickle down her cheeks. "I want you and me and Gabriella to be together forever."

This catches him off guard and brings him fully alert. Sitting up, he faces her. "But you're with Justin, Hope."

"Justin's a decent guy, and he tries hard, but I don't love him. Now that I've met you, I don't think I've ever loved anyone. You've shown me what true love is. When I'm with you, I feel safe and secure, like everything's going to be okay."

Michael feels panicky. "Look, Hope, you're not thinking this through. What would my church say about moving you in with me? I mean, you lived with Luther, then with Justin, and then you want to live with me. How would that look? What does that say about you?"

She scoots back away from him and pulls the sheet up to cover herself. "What do you mean? Are you saying I'm not good enough for you?"

"I'm not saying that, but that's what the church members will think. I know it's not right, but that's the truth. People can be very judgmental when it—"

Her voice rises as she cuts him off. "You don't love me, do you? Not like I love you. I thought what happened here tonight, the way we shared our bodies with each other, meant something to you." Tears race down her face and drip onto the sheet.

"Hope, I really care about you." He reaches for her, but she slaps his hand away.

"Don't!" she cries. Covering her face with her hands, she begins to sob.

CHAPTER FORTY-SIX

Blinded by her tears, Hope stumbles down the middle of the street towards the trailer park. If her body could look like she feels, her chest would be laid open, raw and ragged, with her heart cut out. It's a kind of hurt she's never experienced; the closest to it would be when her parents were killed. This, though, has an element of rejection born because she opened her heart to Michael and handed it to him.

It never crossed her mind he wouldn't be excited about her plan. *I was a fool for thinking that! I'm a useless piece of trash, and that's all I'll ever be. It's what everyone thinks. What I thought Michael and I had was nothing more than a fantasy I dreamed up in my head. So, what was I to him? What did all our intimate conversations mean?*

The faces of all the men she's been involved with through the years scroll through her memory, and she acknowledges the common denominator between them: wanting sex from her. *Is Michael no different than them? Is that all I'm good for? To be used like a tool to satisfy a man's pleasure?* Suddenly, she bends over and vomits on the street.

Moving to the side of the street, she sits on the curb with her feet in the gutter. The symbolism is not lost on her.

What's the point? What reason is there to keep going?

The street light overhead flickers off as dawn begins its job of sweeping away the vestiges of night. Looking up, she says, "If only I could flip a switch and remove the stains of last night."

Out of nowhere, a Carolina wren flies down, perches on the curb less than three feet away from her and bursts into song. The move shocks Hope. As she watches it, it hops closer to her, cocking its head from side to side.

"Did you have a bad night, too?" Hope asks. "Or are you trying to cheer me up?"

The bird stops singing and looks at her.

Hope notices a small beetle crawling in the gutter.

Without warning, the wren hops down, picks up the beetle and flies into the foliage of a nearby tree.

Hope squints in hopes of spying the nest, but the light is too dim and the foliage too thick. Suddenly, she stands up. *Of course! That's my reason for going on—Gabriella! God, forgive me for forgetting.*

Lifting up her shirt tail, she wipes her face dry and walks quickly toward the trailer park.

The closer she gets, the more resolve and certainty she feels. *I don't need Michael. I don't need any man. All I need is Gabriella, and all she needs is me. I'll teach her how to be independent, how to not trust men, how to make her way in life unencumbered.*

When she sees Justin's trailer, she breaks into a run. Inside, she goes to Gabriella's room and crawls in bed with her. She whispers, "Me and you, you and me, that's the way it'll always be."

*****

Hope feels someone shaking her and calling her name.

"Hope, wake up."

Coming fully awake, Hope unwraps her arms from around Gabriella, who stirs at being moved.

Hope sits up and rubs the sleep from her eyes. "What time is it?"

"Nine o'clock," Justin says. He hands his phone to her. "It's Beverly Cotton, the social worker. She said she's been trying to call you, so she called me instead."

Hope looks at the phone like it's a snake and draws back from it. "Tell her I'll call her later," she whispers.

He thrusts the phone at her. "She says it's important."

Reluctantly, Hope takes the phone and gets out of bed. "You stay with Gabriella," she tells Justin, as she walks into the living room.

She speaks into the phone, "Hi, this is Hope."

"Hi, Hope. This is Beverly Cotton, you remember me?"

Fear dances up Hope's spine, causing her to shiver. "Yes, I remember."

"I've got some great news, Hope," Beverly says. "Gabriella's parents have been found."

For Hope, it's as if Beverly's announcement unsuspends all the stars in the heavens, and they begin falling on her. She collapses onto her knees.

Beverly's voice continues, but Hope recognizes nothing she says.

After a few moments, she hears Beverly say, "Hope, are you still there?"

"You can't have her," Hope says.

"Now, Hope, you know you don't mean that. The plan all along was to reunite her with her parents."

"You can't have her. I can't let her go."

Beverly's voice softens. "I know this is hard for you, Hope, terribly hard. You saved this girl's life, and you two went through some very harrowing times, but now it's time to give her back to her parents. Like I said a moment ago, they were not involved in any way in Gabriella ending up where she was. She was kidnapped and they have been sick with worry ever since. Can you put yourself in their position and see how hard it's been for them?"

Inevitability presses on Hope until she lies in a fetal position on the floor. In a small voice she says, "Okay."

"Good for you, Hope. I'll be coming to pick up Gabriella around eleven o'clock.

CHAPTER FORTY-SEVEN

"But I like living with you and Justin." Gabriella sits on the edge of her bed and looks at Hope and Justin kneeling in front of her.

"I know you do, Sweetie," Justin says. "And we like you living with us, but you're mama and daddy have missed you."

Hope feels like she's in one of those houses at tourist destinations where all the floors are tilted and nothing is square. One wrong move and the balance she's trying to maintain in order to hold her emotions in check will disappear, and she will plunge into a sea of quicksand, never to be seen or heard from again.

She takes hold of Gabriella's hands. "I promise, I will never ever forget you. You will always hold a special place in—" Emotions rush up her throat and squeeze off her voice. She mouths the words, "my heart," and she touches her chest.

Gabriella jumps off the bed, throws her arms around Hope's neck and begins to cry. Hope hugs her, and Justin wraps his arms around both of them.

Hope hears footsteps approaching.

"Hope," Beverly says, "it's time to go."

Justin stands and lifts Hope and Gabriella off the floor at the same time.

Beverly kneels in front of Gabriella. "Your mama and daddy are going to be so excited to see you." She hands her a stuffed teddy bear. "I thought you might like to have some company on the drive."

Gabriella looks at its face for a second, then hugs it to her chest.

Beverly takes her hand and stands up. Looking at Hope and Justin, she says, "There are no words to express accurately what this time with you has meant to Gabriella and how it will influence her for the rest of your life. I'll call you and let you know how things go. And I'm going to keep a check on you, Hope. I promise." She squeezes Hopes arm, nods at Justin and leads Gabriella out of the room.

Hope listens for the front door closing and the car pulling away. Then she screeches at the top of her voice, turns and begins pummeling Justin's chest, saying over and over, "No, no, no."

CHAPTER FORTY-EIGHT

As the sun touches the horizon on its way to start the morning on the other side of the world, Hope walks across the cemetery, carrying a plastic shopping bag.

At Lisa's grave, she kneels down.

"You know, now I understand why you did what you did: you lost hope. When every door you try closes in your face, and you can see no other doors to try, it's time to give up. I wish I knew where you were right now. I wonder if heaven and hell are really the only options and even if they are real places."

She looks up. "Sorry, God, but I just don't get it anymore; I don't get You anymore, if You were ever there to begin with. I tried it Your way—went to church, believed in what was being said, even fell in love with someone who said he was Your servant. And how did that turn out? I believed You were the one who gave me a second chance at being a mother, and I embraced that opportunity. That was the cruelest trick of all. Well, I'm done with You."

She reaches in the shopping bag and takes out a bottle of water and a bottle of Tylenol and sets them on the ground.

"I knew we'd be united again someday, Lisa. I just wish I had done something sooner, it sure would have saved me a lot of pain and a world of heartache." She smiles. "But now, I'm coming to be with you. I can't wait to see you and hear all about what's been going on with you since you left. I'm curious what life's like after death."

Opening the bottle of water, she takes a sip. Then she takes the lid off the Tylenol and pulls off the inner seal.

She thinks for a moment about Whitney and Carol Anne and how upset they will be her. *I guess that's the only real regret I've got about doing this.* She had thought about calling Whitney but knew she'd try to talk her out of it. She smiles at the memory of the three of them eating lunch together, sharing drinks and laughs. *The only real friends I've ever had.*

Looking at Lisa's headstone, she picks up the Tylenol in one hand and the water in the other. "See you soon."

She puts the Tylenol bottle to her mouth, tips it up and pours in a mouthful, then she washes it down. Again, she repeats the process.

Then she lies down on Lisa's grave, turns on her side and closes her eyes.

~ THE END ~

FROM THE AUTHOR:

I want to personally thank you for purchasing and reading HOPE LOST. Every time I publish a book, I hold my breath to see if people will like it. It's a pretty scary thing to do. But readers who enjoy my books keep coming back for more and encouraging me to keep writing. For that, I thank you.

It would be very meaningful to me if you would take the time to post a review of HOPE LOST on Amazon (whether you like it or not).

Now, regarding Hope Rodriguez. She's complicated, isn't she? And she has the worst luck (sometimes because of her own bad choices). Readers have expressed to me how empathetic they feel toward her, but also how frustrated and upset they are with her at times.

If you've read any of my books, you know I like things to work out in a positive way for my characters, a "happy ending," if you would. In the third and final book in this series, Hope will finally find what she's been looking for her whole life, but not without some difficulty. HOPE RETURNS will release in the spring of 2021. I hope you'll be looking forward to it.

Made in the USA
Middletown, DE
08 January 2022

58078873R00205